28-11-20
19/12/20
27.9.22

as

Get **more** out of libraries

Please return or renew this item by the last date shown.

ou can renew online at www.hants.gov.uk/library

by phoning   0300 555 1387

Hampshire
County Council

'If you enjoy a well-written mystery with a well-constructed and
thought-out plot line then this is the book for you… it is my BOOK OF
THE MONTH' – *Crime Book Club*

'the story unfolds at a great pace and grips until the end'
– *Fiction Is Stranger Than Fact*

'Well written and chock full of surprises, this hard-hitting, edge-of-the seat instalment is yet another treat... Geraldine Steel looks set to become a household name. Highly recommended' – *Euro Crime*

'Good, old-fashioned, heart-hammering police thriller... a no-frills delivery of pure excitement' – *SAGA Magazine*

'the critical acclaim heaped on Russell thus far in her literary career is well deserved' – *Bookgeeks*

'a macabre read, full of enthralling characters and gruesome details which kept me glued from first page to last' – *Crimesquad*

'*Dead End* was selected as a Best Fiction Book of 2012'
– *Miami Examiner*

CRITICAL ACCLAIM FOR *ROAD CLOSED*

'A well-written, soundly plotted, psychologically acute story'
– **Marcel Berlins,** *The Times*

'Well-written and absorbing right from the get-go... with an exhilarating climax that you don't see coming' – *Euro Crime*

'Leigh Russell does a good job of keeping her readers guessing. She also uses a deft hand developing her characters, especially the low-lifes... a good read' – *San Francisco Book Review*

'perfect character building... cleverly written... can't wait for the next one' – *Best Books to Read*

'*Road Closed* is a gripping, fast-paced read, pulling you in from the very first tense page and keeping you captivated right to the end with its refreshingly compelling and original narrative'
– *New York Journal of Books*

CRITICAL ACCLAIM FOR *CUT SHORT*

'*Cut Short* is a stylish, top-of-the-line crime tale, a seamless blending of psychological sophistication and gritty police procedure. And you're just plain going to love DI Geraldine Steel' – **Jeffery Deaver**

'Russell paints a careful and intriguing portrait of a small British community while developing a compassionate and complex heroine who's sure to win fans' – *Publishers Weekly*

'an excellent debut' – *Crime Time*

'It's an easy read with the strength of the story at its core... If you want to be swept along with the story above all else, *Cut Short* is certainly a novel for you' – **Crimeficreader**

'Simply awesome! This debut novel by Leigh Russell will take your breath away' – ***Euro Crime***

'an excellent book...Truly a great start for new mystery author Leigh Russell' – ***New York Journal of Books***

Cut Short is a book I had to read in one sitting... excellent new series' – ***Murder by Type***

'a sure-fire hit – a taut, slick, easy-to-read thriller' – ***Watford Observer***

'fine police procedural, with a convincing if disconcerting feel of contemporary Britain' – ***The Compulsive Reader***

'*Cut Short* featured in one of Euro Crime's reviewers' Top Reads for 2009' – ***Euro Crime***

'*Cut Short* is not a comfortable read, but it is a compelling and important one. Highly recommended' – ***Mystery Women***

'gritty and totally addictive debut novel' – ***New York Journal of Books***

Also by Leigh Russell

Geraldine Steel Mysteries
Cut Short
Road Closed
Dead End
Death Bed
Stop Dead
Fatal Act
Killer Plan
Murder Ring

Ian Peterson Murder Investigations
Cold Sacrifice
Race to Death
Blood Axe

LEIGH RUSSELL

DEADLY ALIBI

A DI GERALDINE STEEL MYSTERY

NO EXIT PRESS

First published in 2017 by No Exit Press,
an imprint of Oldcastle Books Ltd,
PO Box 394, Harpenden,
Herts, AL5 1XJ, UK

noexit.co.uk
@noexitpress

ISBN
978-1-84344-850-1 (Print)
978-1-84344-851-8 (Epub)
978-1-84344-852-5 (Kindle)
978-1-84344-853-2 (Pdf)

2 4 6 8 10 9 7 5 3 1

Typeset in 11.25pt Times New Roman
by Avocet Typeset, Somerton, Somerset TA11 6RT
Printed in Great Britain by Clays Ltd, St Ives plc

To Michael, Joanna, Phillipa and Phil

Acknowledgements

I would like to thank Dr Leonard Russell for his expert medical advice, and all contacts in the Metropolitan Police for their invaluable assistance.

I would also like to thank the inimitable Annette Crossland for her loyal support.

Producing a book is a team effort. I am fortunate to have the guidance of a brilliant editor, Keshini Naidoo, and I am very grateful to Ion Mills and Claire Watts, along with all the dedicated team at No Exit Press, who transform my words into books.

My final thanks go to Michael, who is always with me.

Glossary of acronyms

DCI   – Detective Chief Inspector (senior officer on case)
DI   – Detective Inspector
DS   – Detective Sergeant
SOCO – scene of crime officer (collects forensic evidence at scene)
PM   – Post Mortem or Autopsy (examination of dead body to establish case of death)
CCTV – Closed Circuit Television (security cameras)
VIIDO– Visual Images, Identification and Detections Office

Prologue

The chain was on the door. This wasn't the first time she had locked him out. Cursing under his breath, he rang the bell. Summer had arrived but it was growing dark and had just begun to rain. He shivered, waiting impatiently for her to let him in.

He rang the bell again. His anger mounted until he thought his head would burst from the pressure. He banged on the door. It quivered beneath his furious onslaught, but remained shut.

'Open up, will you? I can't get in. You know bloody well the chain's on the door!'

A few moments passed before he heard her voice. 'Who is it? What do you want?'

'Who the hell do you think it is at this time of night? It's me, of course!'

His hair was dripping and his shoulders were damp by the time he heard the faint scraping of the chain sliding across. He would probably end up with a cold, thanks to her crazy paranoia.

Slowly the door swung open. She stood motionless, staring at his chest, refusing to meet his gaze. Her face was pale and she looked scared. He tried to swallow his annoyance, reminding himself that she couldn't help it.

'I didn't know who it was,' she muttered.

'Who else would it be at this time of night?' he repeated.

Seeing the fear in her eyes, his anger dissolved into pity. She was pathetic.

'I wasn't sure if it was you.'

'Who else would it be?' he replied, speaking more gently.

As he leaned down to kiss her, she turned and moved away. Closing his eyes to savour the scent of her shampoo, he wasn't sure if she even noticed the touch of his lips on her hair. He wanted to stroke the soft glossy curls, but she was already out of reach. Watching her narrow hunched shoulders as she walked away, he wanted to yell at her to stand up straight and stop being so feeble.

Struggling to swallow his returning rage, he felt himself shaking. Almost against his will, he felt his hands tighten into fists. He took a deep breath, holding the air in his lungs for as long as he could. He had to calm down so he could deal with the situation rationally.

In spite of his good intentions, it wasn't long before the row began. Recognising the signs, he was powerless to stop it developing.

'What the fuck do you think you were doing? Just who do you think you are, treating me like that?'

Boxed in, there was no escape from the blows that rained down in a sudden frenzy.

'Don't you ever do that again! Ever! You do that again and I'll kill you!'

They had played out this scene so many times before. Recovering from the violent outburst, and the subsequent fit of self-reproach, they would revert to a kind of normality.

Until the next time.

One day it would go too far.

1

WAKING WITH A START, she was just in time to see they were leaving Oakwood station. She swore under her breath because she had missed her stop. Feeling sweaty and slightly sick, she glanced around. In an old-style Piccadilly line underground train, there was no easy way to move away from the only other passenger in her carriage. With one more stop before they reached the end of the line, it wasn't worth the effort of yanking open the external doors between carriages. Instead, she sat perfectly still, trying to ignore him.

Every time her eyes flicked over to him, he was staring at her. She was drunk enough to want to leap to her feet and shout at him, 'What the fuck are you staring at, you fucking weirdo?', sober enough to resist the temptation. For all she knew, he might react violently. He had a mop of greasy dreadlocks, and his mouth hung slack beneath his wildly staring eyes. It was impossible to tell if his pupils were dilated, but there was definitely something demented about his expression.

Unnerved, she pulled her hood up and kept her eyes on the filthy floor of the carriage. Without looking at him, she was aware of his presence, every muscle tensed to resist if he approached her. She wanted to close her eyes and drift off to sleep again, but she didn't dare relax her vigilance. In a few minutes they would reach the end of the line. She willed the train to move quickly, hoping there would be other people around when they arrived.

To her dismay, the train juddered to a halt before they reached the station. Every second she sat opposite the stranger seemed to stretch out as though time had become elastic. The air in the carriage felt so stuffy, she thought she would throw up. Sick and frightened, she struggled not to burst into tears. She was too old for this. It wasn't as if she had even enjoyed the evening. After ten years of London clubbing, she was disillusioned with her pursuit of meaningless fun. There must be more to life than frenetic dancing, shagging strangers, and throwing up in gutters.

And now this.

The stranger stirred. 'We're not moving,' he said.

She froze. Out of the corner of her eye she could see him leering at her.

'Don't be upset,' he went on, his words slurring into each other. 'There's nothing to be upset about. Now we get to spend more time together.'

A thrill of terror ran down her spine. This was it. He was going to attack her. She wondered if her rape alarm would deter him. It was deafening, but with no one else around to hear it, the shrill sound would be pointless. As she glanced around for the emergency cord, the train jolted and moved again.

She fished in her bag for her Oyster card and clutched it, so she would be able to leave the station as quickly as possible. If she was fast enough, she would be out in the street before he could follow her. She checked her hood was up and sat on the edge of her seat. As the train drew into the station, she leapt up and dashed to the door.

Without looking back, she could sense the other passenger was close behind her as the train left. She smelt his stale breath when he spoke.

'You in a hurry?' he asked softly.

She didn't turn round. It was best not to answer. He might think she hadn't heard him.

'I asked you a question, bitch.'

A hand gripped her upper arm so suddenly it made her yelp. Biting her lower lip, she spun round, lashing out in terror. As she yanked her arm out of his grasp, her elbow hit the side of his chest. Struggling to cling on to her, he lost his footing. She staggered back and reached out, leaning one hand on the cold wall of the tunnel. Before she had recovered her balance he fell, arms flailing, eyes glaring wildly as he disappeared over the edge of the platform onto the rails below. There was a sharp crack followed by a dull thud and a faint wheezing.

With a shudder, she craned her neck and peered over onto the rails where the man lay, twitching and moaning. He appeared to be having a seizure of some sort. Drawing back, she hurried towards the exit, forcing herself not to break into a run.

At that time of night the station was deserted. For a terrifying instant she thought her Oyster card hadn't registered. But the barrier slid open and she was through.

Outside, the street was empty. In desperation she looked around for a taxi. There was nothing else for it. She had to get away from there. Pulling out her phone, she called her father.

'What are you doing, calling me in the middle of the night? Do you know what time it is?'

'Dad, I need your help.' She hated herself for saying it.

'What?'

'I fell asleep on the train. Can you pick me up? Only...' she hesitated to mention the weirdo.

'Is everything all right?' her father asked.

'Yes, everything's fine,' she lied. 'I can take care of myself. But I can't see any taxis here and I need a lift home.'

Taking a deep breath, she tried to calm down. As her panic subsided, she realised that she could be in serious trouble. Her father wouldn't turn up for about half an hour, maybe more. In that time, the weirdo might recover or, if he was dead, his body could be discovered. Either way, she wasn't keen to risk being raped or else dragged into a police enquiry. As she vacillated, she checked on her phone and found a night bus that ran from Cockfosters. The next one was due in just over five minutes.

She was on the point of calling her father. Thinking better

of her impulse, she stuffed her phone back in her bag. Let him worry about her. It would serve him right. Smiling to herself, she set off for the bus stop.

2

GERALDINE WANTED TO BE alone on her birthday. It wasn't her age that was making her miserable, although she was hardly pleased to be turning forty. The reason she was preoccupied was that her mother was going to be cremated that week. So although she had reached a significant birthday, she didn't feel like celebrating. She hadn't discussed her feelings with anyone.

'You can't change decade without getting hammered!' Sam insisted, her short spiky blonde hair sticking up on top of her head as though to emphasise her indignation. 'Just because you're a detective inspector, and getting on a bit, doesn't mean you have to be all stuffy and boring.'

Geraldine couldn't help laughing at her young detective sergeant. 'Well, thanks for reminding me that I'm so much older than you, and getting older by the minute. I'm not in my twenties any more.' She didn't add that partying was the last thing on her mind. 'But seriously, Sam, don't tell everyone. I don't want any fuss.'

'Aren't we even going out for a drink? We don't have to make a huge deal out of it. We can go out just the two of us.'

Geraldine smiled. She wasn't close to many of her colleagues. Although she knew that Sam socialised with a lot of their fellow officers, nevertheless she was gratified by her sergeant's friendship.

'I can't,' she said. 'I'm going to see my sister.'

That was not an out and out lie. Geraldine *had* arranged to visit her adopted sister, but not until the weekend.

'Not even one drink?'

Geraldine shook her head. 'Not even one. I'm not as young as you.'

With a guilty twinge she remembered the bottle of wine she was planning to open at home that evening after work.

'Are you trying to tell me the fun ends once you quit your twenties?'

Geraldine smiled at her friend's daft grimace. 'I can't remember back that far.'

'If that's the case, I need to pack in as much fun as I can, while I still can. Time's running out for me. I'll be thirty in a couple of years so I need to party now, even if I won't remember it when I'm old. Older,' she added quickly.

Geraldine laughed. 'Imagine how I feel.'

'Look, fair enough you've arranged to spend this evening with your family, but we must go out at the weekend and celebrate. You can't deprive me of this chance to go out on the town. I don't have much longer to go before I'm thirty and then what? Will I really have to grow up and be sensible all the time? Bloody hell. You had to blurt it out, didn't you? And there I was, thinking the fun would never end. Another ten years, and I'll be sipping cocoa at home in the evening, and in bed by nine. You had to tell me, didn't you?' She heaved an exaggerated sigh and Geraldine grinned.

When Sam left, Geraldine turned to her screen, but she was too dejected about her mother to feel aggrieved by her latest budget cut. What would once have started her ranting no longer seemed important. She was growing older. One day she would end her life among strangers, as her mother had done. Pulling herself up short for allowing such negative thoughts to cloud her mind, she turned her attention back to her screen. Whatever else might be happening in her life, her job mattered. As a detective inspector working in serious crime, investigating murder cases, she couldn't allow her personal problems to affect her focus, even for a moment.

Sam called by Geraldine's office at the end of the day.

'Still here?' she asked, looking slightly put out. 'I thought you were off to see your sister this evening?'

Geraldine did her best to conceal her irritation. It felt as though Sam was checking up on her. At the same time, she didn't want to be caught out in a fib.

'Oh, is that the time?' she said, instead of answering directly. 'I'd better be off. Thanks, Sam.'

Quickly closing down her screen, she grabbed her bag, and left the building with Sam at her side.

'Have a good evening,' Sam called out as they parted in the car park. 'And don't forget I owe you a drink.'

'Only one?'

'Now, now, remember you have to be careful at your age.'

At home, Geraldine poured herself a generous glass of wine before taking her iPad out of her bag. She hadn't yet finished checking her budget. Juggling the figures, she tried not to imagine what Sam would say if she could see her now.

When her phone rang, she almost didn't answer, assuming Sam was calling to find out if she had changed her mind. There was still time to go out drinking. Glancing at the call screening, she was pleased to see the name. She had worked with Ian Peterson in Kent before her relocation to London. They had remained friends, and kept in touch even after he had moved away to York. Surprised and pleased that he had remembered her birthday, she picked up her phone.

'Hi. How are you?'

Ian was one of Geraldine's few good friends, but he wasn't calling to wish her a happy birthday. He had called to talk about his marital problems. When he finally got round to asking how she was, she muttered that she was fine. After she hung up, she was overcome by regret that she hadn't been honest with him. He was her closest friend, apart from Sam. Working together led to a kind of bond she had not experienced with anyone else. She had always been able to talk freely with him, but he was preoccupied by his own problems and it wasn't fair to burden him with hers. Besides, his situation could be put right. His wife was alive. Nothing could be done to alleviate Geraldine's misery. With her mother dead, she felt isolated in her grief. On her fortieth birthday, an occasion most people would celebrate with friends or family, she had never felt more alone.

She stared at one glass on the table beside an open bottle of red wine. She was used to being on her own. It didn't normally bother her. In fact, as a rule, it suited her. Occasional bouts of loneliness were a price she was willing to pay for her independence. But this evening her thoughts were darting around in confusion. The following morning she was going to her mother's funeral. Working with the deaths of strangers every day had not prepared her to deal with her own grief.

3

THERE HAD BEEN NO chance of him falling asleep until he heard the front door close, telling him that his daughter was home. The last train left from town at around midnight, so she should have been back by now. He had tried to relax, listening out for any sound from downstairs. Five minutes had passed. And another five minutes. In the darkness, time had moved slowly.

It had been gone half past twelve when his phone had rung.

'Dad, thank goodness you're still up. I fell asleep on the train.

'Where are you?'

Beth was at Cockfosters station, about ten miles away. It was the end of the line. He glanced at his watch. At that time of night it might only take him twenty minutes to drive there.

'The station's deserted, and I don't know what to do.'

She had known exactly what to do. She had called him.

'She's twenty-seven,' his ex-wife would say if she knew what had happened. 'She's an adult. Stop running after her. Let her find her own way home. What would she do if you weren't there? She managed all right by herself when we used to go away. It's not healthy to be so obsessed with her. You have to let her live her own life.'

His ex-wife accused him of wanting to keep Beth dependent on him, but it was easy for her to be harsh. Beth wasn't her daughter. He wondered if Veronica was right, and his overprotectiveness was to blame for Beth turning into such a wild teenager. Only six when her mother had died, she had become withdrawn. When Daniel remarried, he had hoped her stepmother would encourage her to feel more settled. Hitting puberty, Beth had flipped to the opposite extreme. Veronica and he had spent years arguing about his daughter's unruly behaviour, but she had grown out of it in the end. She had finally landed herself a job with prospects of a kind.

'It's only a job, dad. There's no need to go overboard.'

'Stick with it and you could end up managing the shop.'

He climbed out of bed, feeling his way in the dark.

Beth sounded slightly hysterical. 'Can you come and get me? I wouldn't ask, only it's late, and I'm outside and there aren't any taxis. There's a man in a van, watching me. Please come, dad.'

Pulling on pants and jeans under his pyjama top, he hurried downstairs. He should have told Beth to go back inside the station and call the police if she felt threatened, although they were unlikely to turn up before him. Fumbling with the phone as he drove off, he called her back to reassure her he was on his way, but there was no answer. He put his foot down. If he was pulled over for speeding, so much the better. The patrol car could drive to Cockfosters station with him.

Although the streets were not exactly busy at that time of night, there were still a surprising number of cars on the road. As he drove, he calmed down. He realised Beth had exaggerated the potential danger of her situation to make sure he went to pick her up. He should have known better than to worry. She could manipulate him so easily. There was no reason why she couldn't stay sober and leave her own car at the station when she went out. He had given her a nice motor he had done up himself at the garage. But she insisted on going out late, drinking and goodness knows what else besides, and then expected him to be on tap to pick her up whenever she needed a lift. Irritated, he rehearsed what he was going to say. Her stepmother was right. Beth was old enough to know better, too old to be causing him this kind of stress in the middle of the night.

'How could you fall asleep on the train at this time of night? You knew how late it was.'

Yet he was pleased she had chosen the safest option, and knew he would say nothing that might discourage her from calling him if she was stranded again. All that mattered was that she was safe. He could easily catch up on a few hours' missed sleep.

A battered black Ford Transit van was driving away from the station as Daniel pulled up. As it passed, he caught sight of a dark-haired man driving, with a blond woman at his side. Too late he remembered Beth had mentioned a van parked at the station. He looked round just in time to catch the registration number. Apart from the van, the road was empty. Annoyed, he climbed out of the car. Beth could at least have run over, grateful to him for turning out at that time of night. Instead she expected him to leave his warm seat to go and look for her. He strode into the station but couldn't see her. He looked around but the station was deserted. He went over to the ticket office and knocked on the window but no one came to his assistance. He hadn't expected to find anyone there.

'Beth?' he called out.

Recovering from his momentary panic, he tried to think logically where she might be. Either she had gone to the toilet, or a late train had arrived, or else she had decided to make her own way home. Perhaps a taxi had turned up. It would be incredibly selfish of her to have summoned him, only to make her way home independently, but he wouldn't put that past her. She might have thought she could get home before he left. It would have been a nice surprise if she had.

He checked his phone. There was no message. The only call he had received that night had been at twelve thirty-seven, when he had been lying comfortably in bed. He tapped redial and got through to her voicemail.

'Beth, it's me. Where are you? Call me as soon as you get this, please. I'm at the station, waiting for you.'

He waited ten minutes in case she was in the toilet, before he went home. As he opened the front door, he was sure she would be there, in the hall, crying about her phone having run out of charge.

'I'm really sorry. When a taxi turned up I took it,' she would explain. 'I thought I could get here before you left. It was so cold, hanging around at the station, and I didn't feel very safe with no one else there, so I thought it was a good idea to get home.'

The hall was empty. He ran up to Beth's room. She wasn't there. He checked the kitchen, and the living room, the toilets and bathrooms, everywhere in the house, even his own bedroom. There was still no answer from her phone. In desperation he called her stepmother.

'Is Beth with you?'

'Jesus, Daniel, is that you? Do you know what time it is?'

'Have you heard from Beth tonight?'

'What?'

'Beth's disappeared.'

'Let's talk about it tomorrow. It's nearly two o'clock in the morning for Christ's sake!'

In the background he could hear her husband's voice growling.

'I know it's late, and I'm sorry to call you, but I wanted to check she wasn't with you before I called the police.'

'Look, Daniel, you've got to stop getting so het up about her. It's no good for you. Carry on like that and you'll give yourself a heart attack. She's twenty-seven. She's entitled to spend the night wherever she wants…'

'No, you don't understand. It's not like that.'

'She'll be home in her own time. Stop worrying. She's probably spending the night with a friend. Good of her to let us know, but that's Beth. If you hadn't spoiled her…'

'No. She called me after midnight to ask me to go and pick her up…'

'There you are then. It's outrageous.'

'No, you don't understand.'

He explained what had happened.

Veronica sounded irritated. 'Are you sure she wanted a lift?'

'Yes. She called me from the station to say there weren't any taxis and she needed to be picked up.'

Veronica mumbled crossly about mini cabs and Uber before she hung up.

Thinking about the deserted station Daniel remembered the black van that had been pulling away as he drove in. He was no longer sure that the blond woman had not been Beth, after all. He should have followed it. But at least he had made a note of the registration number. Whoever had taken Beth was not going to get away with it. Shaking, he called the police.

4

EVERY THURSDAY TOM WENT out with his mates from work. To begin with he had appreciated his wife's ready acceptance of this arrangement.

'Why should I mind?' had been her response when he asked if he minded his going out without her. 'I'm pleased you're seeing your mates. It's not like you're out on the booze every night, not like some.'

Tom had suspected Louise had been planning to run off with her fancy man for a long time. Although he had only seen her in a café with a stranger once, he had been convinced they were seeing each other. There had been an unmistakable air of intimacy between them, and he had glimpsed a tenderness in her expression that he had never seen before. She had never looked at him in that way, as though she wanted to store every detail of his face in her memory to treasure when she was alone.

She had laughed at him when he mentioned it, and told him he was reading far too much into it. But her earnest denials hadn't been enough to quell his suspicions.

'Why did you lie about it?' he had fumed, after he had seen them together.

'I wasn't lying,' she had protested, flicking her head so that her shoulder length blonde hair swung with the movement. 'I just forgot, that's all.'

'You forgot you'd gone out with another man?'

'Oh Jesus, Tom, do you have any idea how ridiculous you sound? I wasn't "going out with another man". I happened to bump into him when I was out shopping and we went for a coffee together, that's all. There was nothing more to it than that. We used to work together. I hadn't seen him for years, and I haven't seen him again since then. It's hardly something I'm likely to remember.'

At first annoyed with him, she had become tearful, until he had felt compelled to pretend to believe her. He loved his wife. With her blue eyes and wide smile, she was the most beautiful woman he had ever met. He knew he was lucky to have her. The last thing he wanted to do was upset her. After a pointless argument, they had a chilly reconciliation. Somehow Louise had made him feel as though the argument had been his fault. He had done his best to forget all about the incident, but the memory rankled.

It was a while before he had begun to suspect her motive for tolerating his Thursday outings might not be as generous as he had supposed. While he was out, playing cards over a few beers, she was at home. He had always taken it on trust that she was alone. But once it had occurred to him that she might have a regular visitor while he was out, he couldn't get the idea out of his head. He pictured her fury if she discovered his suspicions. Every Thursday evening he had to force himself not to rush home early to check, telling himself he was overreacting. In reality, he was afraid of what he might find there.

So he had continued to go out on Thursdays as usual, and might have continued doing so indefinitely, if one evening he and his mates hadn't packed it in early. It was bound to happen sooner or later. He felt as though he'd been sitting on a time bomb, waiting for a terrible truth to blow his world apart. He almost wanted to drive around for an hour, so he wouldn't arrive back earlier than usual, but something compelled him to go straight home.

As he drove, he told himself he was being an idiot. But when he reached his front door, he thought he heard voices in the hall. His heart racing, he ran back to the car and kept watch. After about half an hour the front door opened, and he caught sight of a man stealing away from the house. At ten to midnight, this was not a casual social call. A stranger had been in his house, with his wife, while he was out. Given the way Louise had lied about it, there could be no doubt about what was going on. Sitting motionless in the car for a few moments, he was uncertain what to do.

He was still home slightly earlier than usual, so there was no rush for him to go inside just yet. Meanwhile, his wife's visitor was hurrying off down the road. Tom was tempted to catch up with him and smash his face in. But after a moment's reflection, he decided to follow him and find out where he lived. It felt strange, cruising along, trying to avoid drawing attention to himself. He often drove as fast as he could. He'd never before tried to drive as slowly as possible. Aware that he should feel relieved, he was almost disappointed that the man never once looked round. He was oblivious to the fact that he was being stalked by a man who wanted to kill him.

Eventually, Tom lost him when he cut across a park. He considered abandoning the car and following him on foot. His hesitation probably saved him from doing something stupid. Too angry to think straight, he spun the wheel and returned home, arriving at around his usual time. Louise was already in bed. With a shiver, he wondered if she had been there before her visitor had left the house.

5

'BLOODY HELL, WILL YOU look at that?' Moira called out as she approached. Stevie was already in the doorway, sheltering from the rain. Although he had been working as a volunteer in the Oxfam shop for over a year, he hadn't yet been given a key. As manager, Moira was supposed to arrive first, but Stevie was usually early. She felt slightly guilty, but the young lad never complained.

'I hope you haven't been waiting long,' she added, glancing at her watch.

'So not only have they given us their old junk, we've got the whole damn bin as well.' She manoeuvred her way past the green wheelie bin. 'Still, I suppose we can use it for rubbish.'

'What's in it?' Stevie asked.

'I don't know. Let's get inside out of this rain before we start poking around. You never know, there might be something nice in it.'

Stevie grinned. Tilting the bin, he pushed it into the shop behind Moira.

'It's really heavy.'

'Why don't you take it through to the back and have a look?' Moira suggested. 'Then you can come and tell me what treasures you've found.'

It was a long time since Moira had felt curious about the things people deposited on the doorstep. Most of it was garbage. People tended not to leave valuables outside overnight. Even the things that were donated over the counter were virtually worthless. It was sad, really, watching people give up their old junk with as much fuss as if it had been worth a fortune. Of course it often had sentimental value to the owner, but that didn't make it worth anything to the shop. She had barely started to key the code into the till when Stevie came running out of the back room, flapping his arms.

'There's a woman inside the bin!' His voice was shrill with excitement. 'I can't wake her up!'

Moira smiled kindly at him. Poor lad. He was a good-looking boy. She sometimes forgot he was a bit simple. There must be a mannequin in the wheelie bin, or perhaps a child's doll.

'That's nice,' she said. 'What else is in there?'

Stevie looked surprised. 'There's nothing else. She's all crumpled up. I called her, and shook the bin, and she never moved. Do you think she's dead? I didn't touch her,' he added earnestly. 'I seen the murder shows on the telly. I know you mustn't touch anything at a crime scene because it could contaminate the evidence.' He paused, watching her tapping at the till. 'Shouldn't we call the police?'

Moira nodded, frowning. It was time to start the day's business but she supposed she ought to go and see what Stevie was fussing about before she opened the door. Customers rarely came in first thing in the morning.

'Come on then,' she said, 'let's go and see what you've found. And then we'll get the door open.'

Following Stevie across the store to the back room, she noticed the hats needed tidying and made a mental note to put Stevie on to it as soon as they had dealt with the wheelie bin.

'Well, what have we got here?'

Stepping forward, she peered over the top of the bin and drew back with a faint yelp.

'Sweet Jesus, I see what you mean,' she said. 'It does look like a body.'

She leaned forward and stared inside the bin. Below the mannequin's head, its arms and legs appeared to have been folded up and crammed down. Its face was almost hidden by a wig that resembled real hair. Tentatively she reached inside and touched one of the ears. It felt hard and cold. She turned her attention to the face. Pushing the head backwards against the side of the bin, she squinted down at battered features. That was odd. She had never seen a mannequin with a bruised face before. It must be dirt from the interior of the bin, which would have been filled with rubbish at one time.

'Who is she?' Stevie asked.

'No one,' Moira replied. 'It's just a model. Now come on, let's open up the shop. We're already late.'

'But what about her?'

'We'll deal with that later. Just leave it here for now.'

They went back into the shop.

'You're dirty. You need to wash,' Stevie said.

'What?'

Looking down, Moira saw a dark stain on one of her hands, where she had touched the mannequin's head. Involuntarily, she wiped it on her skirt, leaving a bright red smear on the fabric.

'It looks like blood,' she whispered.

All at once she felt sick. Running back to the store room, she took another look inside the wheelie bin. Whoever had abandoned the bin the previous night had not been donating their unwanted belongings to charity. They had been getting rid of a dead body.

'I do believe you're right,' she muttered to Stevie, who was also staring down inside the bin.

'Is she dead?' he whispered.

Moira nodded.

'Who is she?'

'We don't know that. Hopefully the police will be able to find out.'

'I know. They can tell who you are from your teeth.'

'We'll leave her exactly as she is,' Moira said, 'while we go and phone the police. And then we're going to have a nice cup of tea with plenty of sugar.'

'You don't take sugar in your tea.'

'That's true, but I think I will today. This is not a normal day.'

'No,' he agreed solemnly. 'This is not a normal day.'

Stevie trotted obediently behind her back into the shop. Moira closed the door to the back room firmly.

'Go and check we shut the street door when we came in,' she said as she picked up the phone.

'We have to open the door. We can't shut it. Not when it's opening time.'

Stevie seemed more disturbed at the prospect of staying closed during opening hours than at finding a dead body.

'Go on, now,' Moira insisted. 'We can't let anyone in. This is a crime scene.'

As Stevie scurried over to the door, she picked up the phone. 'I need the police please. Yes, the police. Someone left a dead body at the Oxfam shop in Highgate High Street. Yes, a dead body. We've found a woman inside a wheelie bin, and she's dead.'

Hanging up, she told Stevie the police were on their way. Then she burst into tears.

'It's all right,' he reassured her. 'They won't think you did it. No one's going to put you in prison. It wasn't your fault. Anyway, I found her, so if anyone's in trouble, it's going to be me. You don't need to worry. It's going to be fine. You'll be fine. I'm the one who's going to be in trouble. They'll find my fingerprints on the bin, not yours. That's how they do it. They look for fingerprints.' He looked around, a worried expression on his face. 'I shouldn't have touched the bin. Now they're going to think it was me, aren't they?'

'Don't worry, the police aren't going to suspect either of us.' She could not help smiling at him through her tears. 'You're a good lad, Stevie.'

'I'll tell them you didn't have that blood on your hands when you got here,' he said seriously. 'Otherwise they'll lock you up.'

6

WITHOUT TELLING ANYONE AT the police station the reason for her absence, Geraldine had booked the morning off. She hadn't mentioned her mother's cremation to anyone apart from her adopted sister Celia, who had offered to accompany her. It was a long way for her to travel and, in any case, Celia was four months pregnant.

'There's no need. You didn't know her,' Geraldine had answered. 'You never met her, and she wasn't your mother.'

'I want to support you.'

'That's good of you, but you don't need to come for my sake. I know she was my mother, but she was a stranger to me too. I only met her once, very briefly. It's not like when our mum died.'

'Well, if you're sure. You would say if you wanted me to come with you, wouldn't you?'

'Yes, and thank you. It's really nice of you to offer.'

Uncertain of her own feelings, Geraldine preferred to go to the funeral by herself. After waiting for years to meet her birth mother, death had cheated her of any hope of ever developing a relationship, or even having a conversation, with her. There was so much Geraldine wanted to know, but her adoptive mother was dead by the time Geraldine had learned the circumstances of her birth. Now her questions might never be answered. She would probably never discover her biological father's identity. He might not even be aware of her existence. The finality of that thought was like a physical pain in her guts.

What was particularly upsetting was that it could have been

very different. Geraldine had repeatedly requested to meet her birth mother when she had discovered, as an adult, that she had been adopted at birth. For years her mother had steadfastly refused to see her. Only after a coronary had she relented and they had met once, briefly. Shortly after that, Milly Blake had suffered another heart attack, and this one had proved fatal.

While her mother had been struggling to make ends meet, Geraldine had been brought up in a stable family, alongside her adopted sister, Celia. She understood that, as a sixteen-year-old single parent, her birth mother had felt it was best for both of them if she was adopted. If she hadn't given her daughter that chance for a better life, perhaps Geraldine would never have become a successful detective inspector, working in North London. Geraldine understood that. What was harder to forgive was her mother's refusal to meet her years later.

Before she died, Milly Blake had written a letter informing Geraldine that she had a twin. Shocked, Geraldine had managed to trace Helena Blake, and confirm they shared a mother and a date of birth. Their father was not named on the records of their birth. She knew nothing about her twin sister except the little their mother had divulged, and the limited information she had been able to ascertain from the borough intelligence unit. It was enough.

Everything she had learned about her twin dismayed her. With no permanent address, Helena had moved around a lot, in and out of London, returning at intervals to South London where Milly Blake had lived. A heroin addict, she had been arrested several times for petty theft and prostitution, no doubt committed to support her drug habit.

It was distressing but, having discovered she had a twin, Geraldine was wary of meeting her. She had joined the police force driven by a desire to help protect civilised society. Doing what little she could to make the world a better place, she had always considered herself a morally upright citizen. She had no intention of rejecting her own sister because she was a user, the kind of person Geraldine only encountered across an interview table. Nevertheless, it was a potentially difficult situation.

Geraldine had worked hard for many years to build the life she wanted. Her successful career and her independence were largely a result of her own efforts, with a little help from her inheritance from her adoptive mother. She didn't want anything to undermine her carefully constructed life. But despite her reservations, she couldn't suppress her excitement at the thought that she might meet her twin sister that morning. She wondered if Helena felt the same.

Dressed in black trousers and jacket, with a new white shirt, she sat down on her bed and took her mother's photograph out of the drawer in her bedside cabinet. It was the only picture she had of her mother, and must have been taken when she was about sixteen. The faded image could have been a photograph of Geraldine herself as a teenager. Milly Blake might even have been pregnant with Geraldine and Helena when it was taken.

The girl in the picture bore little resemblance to the sick stranger Geraldine had met in the hospital. They would never have a conversation, never exchange a smile. Geraldine would never feel her mother's arms around her. She supposed she had been whipped away from her mother quite quickly after the birth. The decision to give her up for adoption had probably been made before Geraldine was born. A penniless single mother of sixteen couldn't have brought up twins by herself in those days. Milly had only kept Helena because she hadn't been expected to survive for long.

She took her mother's letter out of the drawer, where she kept it with the photograph.

'When you were born,' her mother had written, 'they told me Helena was going to die. But she didn't. And then time went by and I couldn't give her away. It sounds bad, but nothing I ever did went right. Now I'm gone, you need to find Helena, and help her. God knows, I tried. I wish I'd kept you as well but what happened was better for you. The social worker said the family you went to were good people. It would have been better for Helena if she'd gone with you but she was sick and they said she wouldn't live. I can't help Helena but you can, if she's still alive.'

With a sigh, Geraldine replaced the photograph and the letter in her drawer. They were all she had from her mother. She had recovered from her anger at the way her mother had prioritised Helena's welfare over her own. Her reservations about meeting her twin had nothing to do with sibling rivalry. She was simply worried about seeing her hard-won life disrupted by a stranger. She had seen too many prostitutes and drug addicts on the other side of an interview table to choose to welcome one into her life with open arms. Her situation was challenging enough without this unlooked-for complication.

But Helena was her sister.

It began to rain as she set off for the crematorium. She felt nervous, knowing she might see her twin for the first time. She didn't know if they were identical, but was sure she would recognise Helena if she saw her. By the time she arrived at the crematorium, the rain had passed over. The car park was almost deserted. A couple of men greeted her when she went in.

'I'm here for Milly Blake. I'm her daughter.'

One of her daughters, she ought to have said.

The younger of the two men glanced towards a solitary coffin. It looked very small in the empty room. The place was well maintained, with carpeted floor, polished wooden seats and clean white paint on the walls. Compared to a graveside it was very sanitised, with no sign of the furnace concealed behind red velvet curtains. Geraldine sat down near the front and waited. It was very quiet. After a few minutes an elderly priest arrived, a reminder that Geraldine's mother had been brought up as a Catholic. Her parents had probably not reacted kindly to their daughter's teenage pregnancy. Milly's condition was likely to have been considered scandalous to a Catholic family forty years ago. Geraldine wondered how it had come about. She would have liked to have known how her parents had met and whether they had been in love, and if her father had known about the pregnancy. There were so many unanswered questions.

The priest approached her and seemed relieved when she reassured him that she was happy for him to choose the text for the ceremony. A few moments later he began, mumbling in a dreary monotone about life everlasting. It seemed an odd phrase to use in connection with someone who had just died. After intoning some prayers, the priest announced a hymn and began to sing in a reedy voice. One of the men who had greeted Geraldine on her arrival joined in, his baritone drowning out the sound of the priest's thin warbling.

As they finished a hymn, Geraldine glanced around and noticed a woman had slipped in and taken a seat on the far side of the room. Straggly dark hair stuck out from under her head scarf, framing a gaunt face. Despite her skinny build she looked oddly familiar, like a figure glimpsed in a nightmare. With a thrill like an electric shock, Geraldine recognised the large dark eyes that she had inherited from her mother. Helena had arrived.

Seemingly oblivious to what was going on around her, Helena sat staring straight ahead throughout the remainder of the service. She didn't react, even when the curtains opened and the coffin disappeared. Geraldine studied her covertly, surprised that Helena didn't seem curious about the stranger who resembled her so closely, yet looked so different to her. From what Geraldine could see of it, Helena's hair was streaked with grey. Her skin had an unhealthy pallor, and from across the room her lips looked cracked and dry. She showed so little interest in the woman who was obviously her sister that Geraldine wondered if their mother had even told Helena about her. Despite her curiosity, she thought it might be best to simply leave at the end of the funeral, without speaking to anyone. She had managed for forty years without a twin in her life. She wasn't sure she was ready to meet Helena yet.

7

AS THE CEREMONY DREW to a close, Geraldine rose to her feet and slipped out of the room. She hoped it wasn't disrespectful to the priest to leave without thanking him, but he was looking the other way. She would have had to cross the room to talk to him. Telling herself that he must be used to people failing to behave with customary good manners on such occasions, she hurried off. It wasn't the priest she was avoiding, but the haggard woman who had ignored her throughout the service. Their mother's funeral might not be the ideal venue for their first meeting.

Outside, she glanced at her phone and swore. A call had come in while she had been at the crematorium. One death interfering with another, she thought miserably, as she called the station and noted the details.

'An Oxfam shop?' she repeated, slightly surprised.

As she reached the car park, she looked up. Helena was a few feet away, hurrying towards her. It was too late for Geraldine to pretend she hadn't seen her. She turned to face her unknown sister.

'You're Erin.'

About to tell Helena her adopted name, Geraldine hesitated. Erin Blake was the name on her original birth certificate. She wasn't sure whether she wanted to invite this stranger into Geraldine Steel's life. First it might be wise to establish a relationship with her using her birth name. Helena had taken the first step and approached her. There was nothing to indicate she would be unfriendly. All the same, Geraldine was apprehensive. She was afraid her experience with the worst aspects of human nature had made her cynical.

'It's hard to believe we're twins, innit?' Helena said, squinting in the bright sunlight. 'Ain't you always wondered what it would be like, having a sister?'

'I have got a sister. I've always had a sister. She's...'

On the point of revealing that she had a sister called Celia, Geraldine hesitated. She wanted to get to know Helena before introducing her to Celia and her daughter, Chloe.

She wondered if Helena had lost a tooth, her lopsided grin looked so unnatural. Realising Helena thought Geraldine had been referring to her when she had mentioned her sister, she added, perhaps more sharply than she had intended, 'I didn't know you existed until I was given a letter from Milly Blake, our mother, after she died.'

'I know who Milly Blake is,' Helena snapped, her smile twisting into a sour expression.

If anything, this brief exchange strengthened Geraldine's determination to proceed cautiously with her newly discovered twin. The knowledge that they were so intimately related was unnerving. As far as Geraldine knew, Helena was not only her closest relative, she might be her only living blood relation. Even if there was a host of other family members, she could never be as biologically close to anyone else as she was to her twin. Apart from Helena's unhealthy complexion and bloodshot eyes, they looked almost identical. Part of her yearned to take Helena home with her and take care of her. Torn by indecision, she stood gazing at her twin.

If Helena had been penniless, or incapacitated in some way, Geraldine wouldn't have hesitated to offer to help her. She felt guilty for not rushing to embrace her, but even in the fresh air of the car park Helena smelt of stale cigarette smoke and sweat, and her eyes had an unhealthy yellow tinge.

'You seen mum before she died?' Helena asked. 'The nurse at the hospital said you was there.'

'Yes, I barely met her a couple of times.'

'What she say then?'

'Nothing really. She was asleep most of the time. We barely spoke.'

Geraldine did her best to hide her bitterness. The disappointment of her mother's death was still raw.

'She give you a letter?'

Geraldine nodded, wondering where this was heading.

'Show me then.'

'I'm sorry, I haven't got it here.'

'I want to see it.'

On Helena's cracked lips the words sounded oddly threatening.

Experienced in questioning dodgy and aggressive characters, Geraldine was surprised to feel a flutter of panic, but she kept her voice level as she answered. 'You can't. I just told you, I haven't got it any more.'

'What you mean? What you done with it?'

'It got thrown away.'

'You threw mum's letter away?'

'Not deliberately. It was thrown away by mistake.'

Geraldine could see her sister wasn't taken in by her duplicity. She hadn't intended to lie, but the contents of the letter were none of her sister's business. It was addressed to Geraldine alone, and private. Helena had been able to enjoy their mother's company for forty years. All Geraldine had from her was that one letter. She didn't want to share it.

'So you telling me she never said nothing about me when she was in the hospital?' Helena sounded incredulous.

Geraldine nodded. 'I only spoke to her once, after she suffered her first coronary. Didn't you go and see her in hospital?'

'No one told me, did they? I had to leave for a while, and I never knew.' She took a step closer to Geraldine who edged away. 'You knew she was in the hospital. You never told me, did you?'

'I didn't know about you until after she died. And even then I had no way of contacting you.'

Geraldine started to walk away, muttering about needing to get to work. Helena followed her into the car park.

'I wanted to meet her but she always refused,' Geraldine added, not wanting Helena to think she had turned her back on their mother.

She didn't go on to explain how Milly Blake had thought Geraldine would be ashamed of her biological family, or that she had written the letter to ask Geraldine to help Helena. Standing close beside her, Helena was shaking, evidently suffering from some kind of withdrawal. Whether it was drugs, alcohol, or smoking, was impossible to tell. It might have been a combination of all three.

'Oh well, happy birthday for yesterday,' Helena said. 'You got a fag?'

'I don't smoke.'

Helena shrugged and fished a packet out of her bag. She lit up with a red plastic lighter and inhaled deeply. 'Where we going then?'

Geraldine didn't pause in her stride. She had a crime scene to investigate. Their mother wouldn't have been pleased, she thought miserably, but she wasn't about to submit to moral blackmail from a dead woman she had only met once.

'We need to meet up, but not right now. I have to get somewhere,' she answered. 'It's work.'

'Work?' Helena scowled. 'Can't you even take the day off to bury your mother? Oh well, you can drop me at the station. You got a car, ain't you?' she added, catching sight of Geraldine's expression.

Geraldine hesitated. 'It's not my car. It's a work car. And now I really have to get going. But we should keep in touch,' she added vaguely as she turned away, irrationally glad that she had driven there in an unmarked vehicle, not her own car. She strode towards it, hoping Helena wouldn't follow her, yet sure that she would.

Helena trotted to keep up with her. 'Where you off to in such a hurry then? Must be a good job if you got a car with it. No one ever give me a car. It don't look like you want for much,' she added, 'nice set of wheels you got there.' She whistled appreciatively, her eyes alight with sudden interest. 'A very nice set of wheels.'

Geraldine didn't answer. She wondered if Helena would be so friendly if she knew what Geraldine did for a living, but she didn't feel inclined to share any of her life with this stranger yet.

'Goodbye then,' she said firmly.

Helena glanced around nervously. 'What about giving us a lift then?'

'Sorry, I'm not going past the station.'

'Any station'll do...'

Geraldine was already in the car, checking the doors were locked. Feeling guilty, she drove off. But her sister had survived for forty years without Geraldine chauffeuring her around. Doing her best to stifle her guilt, she put her foot down. All her instincts warned her that any favour she did for Helena would backfire. But she knew she had to see her again.

She braked suddenly. The least she could do was drop her sister off at a station. She wouldn't have refused a lift to a stranger. Besides, Helena had been brought up by their mother. She must be feeling bereft at the death of her only known parent. Looking up she saw Helena walking quickly towards the street, puffing on a cigarette. Patiently she waited for Helena to catch up with her. Opening the window, she called out.

'Put out your cigarette and I'll give you a lift, if you like. I'm going past Highgate station.'

Without answering, Helena opened the passenger door.

'Could you get rid of your cigarette, please?'

'Oh fuck off. Just because you're giving me a lift don't mean you got the right to tell me what I can and can't do. I just lost my mother.'

Helena climbed in, and inhaled deeply.

'She was my mother too.'

Helena exhaled. Smoke swirled around in front of her face. 'You never even knew her.'

It sounded like an accusation. Geraldine decided to let it go. With the windows open, the stench from one cigarette wouldn't linger long.

'What was she like?' she asked.

'What do you care? You never went to see her.'

'I wanted to but she refused to meet me.'

'Yeah, right.'

'Look, Helena, I appreciate you must be upset, but I'm telling you the truth. I asked repeatedly if I could see her, but she always refused. You can check with the social worker involved if you don't believe me. If I'd known I had a twin sister I'd have wanted to meet you too, but I didn't even know I had a sister, let alone a twin. How was I supposed to know? No one told me anything. And anyway, you never made any attempt to get in touch with me either, so there's no need to be aggressive.'

'Big words don't impress me. So you had an education. Well ain't you the lucky one?'

'Helena, I know you're feeling angry right now...'

'You don't know nothing.'

Geraldine swallowed her disappointment. She hadn't lived Helena's life. It wasn't fair to judge her. They drove on in silence as far as Highgate station. When at last they pulled up, Helena leaned back in her seat and closed her eyes.

'You need to get out here. I have to get to work.'

Helena opened her eyes and looked sideways at Geraldine. 'I don't want to get out of this nice car just yet. What you going to do about it, then? You got to move off soon. You can't stay on a double yellow line. They'll do you. So let's get going. You can start by showing me where you live.'

Geraldine hesitated. She felt uncomfortable making

demands on the sister she barely knew, but there was nothing else she could do.

'I'm sorry, Helena, but you haven't given me any choice. I need to get going, and the nature of my work means I can't allow anyone to hold me up. So please get out of the car right now. I'm sorry to rush you, but I really do have to go.'

Helena shook her head. 'You can't push me around, and you can't tell me what to do. I may not be as clever as what you are, but I'm not an idiot. So come on, let's go before the pigs do you for stopping here.'

'The traffic police aren't going to prosecute me.'

'Who are *you* then? The bloody queen? Listen, Erin, you don't know nothing about the police. They'll do anybody for anything, or for nothing if they feel like it.' Helena snorted. 'I should know. They got their targets, see. They don't care what reason you got for being here. You could tell them you stopped because you was having a heart attack, they won't give a stuff. If they can get you, they will. I'm giving you some sisterly advice, you got to move. You ought to be more worried about the police, or you're going to end up in trouble.'

With a sigh, Geraldine pulled out her warrant card. 'I'm guessing you know what this is.'

Helena's jaw dropped. 'Oh fucking hell, just my luck!'

'I'm a detective inspector, and right now I'm expected at a murder scene, so you need to get out of my car.'

Without warning Helena made a grab for the identity card but Geraldine's reflexes were fast. She raised her hand and held the card out of her sister's reach. Swearing, Helena wrenched the door open and jumped out of the car.

'Let's not part on bad terms,' Geraldine called out before she drove off.

She didn't know if Helena had heard her.

8

HE GLANCED AT HIS watch and nodded to himself. By now someone was bound to have discovered the corpse. He hadn't exactly hidden it well, but that was of no consequence to him, and it certainly didn't matter to her.

He'd done a good job, disposing of the body like that. Admittedly it had been a stroke of luck finding the wheelie bin empty. Even so, he'd been nothing short of inspired to think of using it. He was fairly confident he hadn't been spotted. No one had been around outside so late at night. If a neighbour *had* seen him, they would have assumed he was putting out rubbish, and were unlikely to remember anything about it. There was no way anyone could have suspected what was inside the bin. Until now.

Someone would have noticed the bin outside the charity shop. Whoever it was had probably wheeled it inside. It was macabre, but he couldn't help laughing to think how surprised some poor sod must have been on lifting the lid. He wished he could have been there to watch. Maybe they had looked inside it straight away, before moving it, surprised by how heavy it was. But wherever the contents had been discovered made no difference to him. Or to her, come to that.

He was fairly sure people who worked in charity shops were volunteers. It must be boring, standing behind a counter day after day, working for nothing. Well, he had given the staff there something to liven up their day. Not that he had left her there just to give the staff a bit of excitement, but it had been an inspired way of disposing of the body. He wondered if the people who found her would appreciate how clever he'd been.

Probably they'd be too disgusted by the sight of her bloody head to admire his brilliance. But it wasn't his problem if she'd been discovered by someone squeamish.

He hadn't planned to kill her, only somehow he had lost control of himself. All he'd wanted to do was punish her for trying to trick him. It was as though a red filter had fallen in front of his eyes. It was purely by chance that the chisel had been in his pocket. With a surge of adrenaline he had become aware of his hand, raised in the air. Before he'd realised what he was doing, the chisel had struck. It had all happened so quickly. The craziness hadn't lasted long. Once her skull had split open, that had been the end of it.

Since that one burst of rage, he had felt completely cold. All that mattered now was to avoid being caught. Finding the bin had saved him a lot of trouble. He'd been able to leave the scene of her death within minutes of arriving at the house. No one would ever know he had been there. He smiled to himself, pleased at how neatly everything had worked out, in the end. Admittedly, he'd killed a woman, but there was no real harm done because he had walked away unscathed.

All that could incriminate him now was the murder weapon. He hadn't yet decided what to do with the bloody chisel, but once he'd disposed of it, he would be in the clear. So far he had been very careful. With his victim safely concealed in the bin on top of the bloody rug, he had gone into the kitchen to find something with which to clean up. Finding a pair of yellow plastic gloves, he'd rummaged in the cupboards and found a sealable plastic bag. Without stopping to wipe the blood from the chisel, he had dropped it straight into the bag and closed it. With the sealed bag safely stowed in his pocket, he'd decided to ignore the carpet. He couldn't see any splashes of blood, which seemed to have all been absorbed by the rug. If the police searched, they were bound to find traces of blood however thoroughly he scrubbed it. Plus, the longer he hung about, the greater was the risk of discovery.

There were a few steps outside the back door, and the bin was heavy. He didn't want to risk it tipping over and spilling its load in full view of any neighbours who happened to glance out of their window, perhaps disturbed by the noise. Realising he was no more likely to be seen going out of the front door than if he pushed her along the side of the house, he'd pushed the bin straight out of the front door. The only real struggle had been lifting it into the back of the van waiting there.

Closing the back door of the van as quietly as he could, he had glanced around. There was no one about, as far as he could see. No lights had come on, no curtains had twitched as he'd driven off.

He had been heading towards Hampstead Heath, with a vague plan to leave her there, when he had spotted the Oxfam shop up ahead.

Elated by his own resourcefulness, he had scrambled across the seats and climbed out of the passenger door so the van stood between him and the security camera across the road. The camera probably didn't work, but there was no harm in being careful. Keeping his back to the camera until he was shielded by the open door of the van, he had dragged the bin out, grunting with the effort of hoisting it up the kerb and on to the pavement.

A few moments later he had driven away, free from the wretched body in the bin. And he was going to remain free. The police wouldn't be able to trace him. He risked being locked up for the rest of his life if he blundered. But he was going to be careful. In any case, the difficult part was over. There was just the chisel to dispose of, and he would be safe.

They would never catch him.

9

LOOKING IN HER REAR view mirror, Geraldine watched Helena stalk off and vanish in the grey drizzle. Any relief she might have felt at seeing her go was swallowed up by sour regret. She wondered whether she would ever see her sister again. Despite her disappointment, she remained wary. The risk of allowing Helena into her life could be considerable. Meanwhile, she had work to do. There was a crime scene waiting for her. She wondered if it was unnatural for her to feel more comfortable viewing a corpse than attempting to interact with her sister. As she drove away she realised that, to her shame, she hadn't thought about her mother once since the funeral. Fixated on the twin she had just met for the first time, she had thought about nothing else. Admittedly she had only met her birth mother once, very briefly, but she felt guilty all the same.

She found the Oxfam shop in Highgate High Street without any problem. It was easy to spot from a distance, with several police cars parked outside. A uniformed constable at the door gave Geraldine a respectful nod and stood aside for her to enter. Inside the shop, a grey-haired woman in a pink cardigan was hovering by the counter, an anxious expression on her powdered face. Her eyes looked slightly moist and she dabbed at them with a pink handkerchief as Geraldine introduced herself.

'It was Stevie who found it,' the woman said. 'You can't imagine how horrible it is. It's still there, out the back.' The woman shook her head. 'I didn't think it was real, not at first. I thought it was a shop mannequin. I mean, it's not something you expect to see left in a rubbish bin outside an Oxfam shop, is it?'

'Take a seat, and a constable will take your statement when you're ready,' Geraldine said.

Clearly the woman had nothing to do with the murder. Geraldine turned away and a uniformed constable pointed her towards the back of the shop.

'The young lad over there found the body,' he muttered. 'His name's Steven, and to be honest, I don't think he's the sharpest tool in the box.'

Geraldine turned her attention to a lanky youth who was leaning against the wall. She wondered if he was usually so pale.

'Steven?' she said.

'Stevie. I'm called Stevie,' he corrected her, blinking nervously.

His dark hair was short, and sprinkled with dandruff.

'Stevie, I'm Detective Inspector Geraldine Steel. Let's sit down and then you can tell me everything that happened.'

Stevie shrugged and told her he didn't know what happened, only that he had pushed the wheelie bin into the store room at the back of the shop.

'Moira asked me to take it to the store room. That's where we sort out all the things people leave. I didn't mind taking it there. It would've been too heavy for Moira to push. It was heavy even for me, and I'm strong. I'm very strong.'

'Yes, I can see that. What happened when you pushed the bin into the store room?'

Opening the large green bin, he had seen the dead woman.

'Moira didn't know it was a real body,' he added. 'She thought it was a doll, but I knew straight away, soon as I saw it. I told her it was a dead woman in there. But what I want to know,' he went on earnestly, 'is why she was put in a wheelie bin. Those bins are for rubbish, aren't they? Why was she put in there? She was dead, wasn't she? But she wasn't rubbish.

That's not right, is it? It shows no respect for the dead. And why was she brought here?' He screwed up his eyes. 'I think it was a mistake. I don't think anyone knew she was in there!' He looked earnestly at Geraldine. 'Do you think anyone knew she was in there?'

Once she had gathered as much as she could about how the body had been discovered, Geraldine went to the store room where the body was still crammed inside the bin. The mortuary van was waiting to take it away. Not much of the dead woman was visible apart from the top of her head, but Geraldine wanted to have a look at the body exactly as it had been left there. She shone a torch inside the bin but could see little past the dead woman's head, her fair hair stained with blood. She could not even be sure she was looking at a dead woman. It could just as easily have been the body of a man with long shaggy hair inside the bin.

Geraldine straightened up and nodded. 'There's nothing to be gained from keeping the body inside that bin. You might as well take it away, and get going establishing an identity.'

As a rule, Geraldine liked to observe dead bodies before they were removed from the scene of the crime. More often than not, such an examination revealed vital information about the killer. But in this case, there was nothing much to see, other than the bin. The sooner the dead body was taken away and examined, the better. Geraldine watched as the bin was wheeled out of the back of the shop. The body would be extracted and scrutinised, samples would be sent away for a toxicology report, and the bin would be examined for fingerprints and DNA. With any luck it would yield evidence that would reveal the killer's identity straight away. She glanced around. There was an empty space in the cluttered store room where a few moments before the bin had been standing.

It was puzzling that the body had been deposited outside a shop in a busy high street. It must have been left there during the night, when the area was deserted. Even so, there were

CCTV cameras along the road, and outside the shops. She would set a team to work straight away, collecting whatever evidence was available. At least one camera must have a record of a vehicle stopping outside the shop. With luck they would have no problem tracing its owner.

In the meantime, Geraldine needed to establish the identity of the woman who had been abandoned in a rubbish bin, like so much garbage. She felt a flicker of revulsion towards the killer. Of course it made no difference to his victim that her killer showed so little respect for the dead. But Geraldine was afraid such a murderer would show no respect for the living either. And such an attitude could make him very dangerous indeed.

10

FRIDAY EVENING WASN'T THE best time to request a post mortem, but the pathologist agreed to set to work first thing on Saturday morning, even though he hadn't been expecting to work that weekend.

'Not what you want to be doing with a hangover,' he said when Geraldine phoned to see how he was getting on.

'It's not what I'd want to be doing at any time.'

'I meant having to get up so early after a late night,' he grumbled. 'I wasn't talking about conducting the post mortem per se. Examining bodies is the job I choose to do. It might not be your cup of tea, but I happen to find it interesting.'

Geraldine extricated herself from the conversation as quickly as possible. Miles was clearly in a foul mood. By the time she visited the mortuary a couple of hours later, the pathologist had recovered his normal good humour. The skin around his hazel eyes crinkled in a smile above his mask as she entered the room. Returning his smile, Geraldine wondered where his enthusiasm for carving up cadavers might have led him, had he not found his niche as a Home Office pathologist. It was sobering to think the same question could be levelled at her, given her interest in the victims of violent murder. She dismissed such dark thoughts. Her mother's funeral, and meeting her sister, had disturbed her.

'So what can you tell me?'

'Well,' he hesitated. 'What do we know about her?'

'That's what I've come here to find out. So far all I can tell you is that she's dead, and she was found in a wheelie bin left outside the Oxfam shop along Highgate High Street. We're trying to find out who left her there, and when, and who she is, but it's going to take time. We've got a team studying CCTV footage from across the road.'

'So you've no idea yet who she was? What her circumstances were?'

'Other than that she's dead, you mean?'

'Well, yes, I gathered she's dead. My training does count for something, you know.'

Geraldine laughed. 'What else? Can you tell me anything about her life before she was killed?'

'I thought that was your job. Are you telling me you really have no idea who she was?'

'Not yet. We haven't identified her, but we're working on it. No reports of missing women that match her description have been logged, but we should know who she is by Monday from her dental records, if we haven't found out before then. So, in the meantime, what can you tell me?'

Miles turned back to the body. 'We're looking at a woman of about forty.'

'She looks younger.'

'I know. At first glance she could be an adolescent, with her youthful face and her slim build. But she was around forty when she died.'

Geraldine nodded. Small, flat-chested and quite skinny, the dead woman looked about sixteen.

'So this is a woman in early middle age,' Miles went on.

Geraldine frowned. She didn't think of herself as middle-aged, but at forty she could no longer get away with kidding herself she was still a young woman.

'There's an indentation from a ring on the third finger of her left hand, but she wasn't wearing a wedding ring when she was brought in. She was not well-nourished, although there's nothing to suggest she was sickly. My guess – and it is only an educated guess – is that she suffered from a subclinical eating disorder. In other words, she was borderline anorexic. Other than that, she seems to have been in reasonable health before she was killed, physically at least. I can't comment on her mental state. There was a blood-drenched rug in the bin, crammed in beneath the body, that's gone off for forensic examination. It looks as though she was standing on the rug when she was attacked. The rug was one of those shaggy ones, and it absorbed most of the blood that hadn't soaked into her clothes before she was deposited in the bin, probably very soon after she was killed.'

He fell silent and Geraldine stood gazing down at the corpse for a moment. It was hard to believe this lump of greyish flesh had once been a living breathing woman. She waited for the sense of urgency that consumed her whenever she saw a murder victim, the feeling that she had to see the killer punished. That was what gave her life a sense of purpose. For the first time, she felt only a cold indifference. It was a shock to realise she didn't really care who had committed the murder. She took a step back, wondering what to do. If she had lost the passion for justice that had so far driven her on, she would never cope with the demands of her job. She stared at the body, willing herself to care, but felt only a debilitating tiredness. Everybody died. Did it really matter if the end came prematurely?

'Penny for your thoughts,' Miles interrupted her gloomy reverie.

'What was the time of death?' she asked automatically.

It was easier to follow procedure than come up with relevant questions. At least that way, there was no need to think.

'Between eleven pm and midnight on Thursday. She was shoved into the bin fairly soon after, at least a couple of hours before rigor began to set in.'

'If only you could talk,' she muttered at the dead woman. 'How was she killed?'

Miles nodded, oblivious to the fact that she was just going

through the motions. She didn't care how or when the woman had died. She would have died one day anyway.

'It's just conceivable she fell and hit her head, but the nature of the impact makes it almost certain she was deliberately hit from above.'

'With?'

'A large sharp object, a blunt knife, the edge of a brick, it's not easy to be precise as her skull caved in. She bled, so it's possible any traces of the murder weapon, if there were any, could have been washed away, but my guess…' He hesitated.

'Go on,' Geraldine urged him. 'This is off the record. I understand it's speculation, but it's going to be based on your expertise and extensive experience.'

'Oh, how can I resist such flattery? All right, but this *is* just a hypothesis. Guesswork, really. Just between us.'

'Understood. This goes no further. My lips are sealed, and I don't think she's going to be breaking your confidence.' She glanced down at the pale face on the slab.

Geraldine had worked with Miles Fellowes on a number of cases, and she appreciated his willingness to share his conjectures with her. They both knew his unverified supposition bordered on unprofessional. As a pathologist, his job was restricted to reporting the facts he uncovered. Her discretion had earned his trust, and he was prepared to speculate off the record. While she was aware that he might be wrong, he had frequently come up with useful ideas for her to consider. More often than not, his theories proved correct. Wary of giving undue weight to his initial inference, she nodded her head to indicate she was listening.

'My guess is that she was hit with considerable force from above so I'm guessing she was killed by a strong person who was taller than her – maybe six foot. Assuming I'm on the right lines, I'd say you're looking for a man. He was wielding an object that was probably metal as it left no chips or dust behind that I've been able to find. I could be wrong on all counts.

Forensic examination of the bone fragments and tissue will be able to tell us more.'

'But you're fairly confident she was hit by someone taller than her?'

'Possibly. She could have been sitting down, or her attacker could have been standing over her, maybe on a step or something, but she's barely five foot, so I'd say her killer could easily have been tall enough to swing the murder weapon from above her head. And it was just the one blow.'

'Perhaps her attacker hit out in anger,' Geraldine said. 'In your expert guess, what would you say the murder weapon was?'

'Bearing in mind that I am just guessing...'

Geraldine gave an impatient nod.

'It looks very much as though she was hit with a large knife, perhaps some sort of kitchen knife or cleaver. A bread knife could have done it. The blade was sharp enough to penetrate the skull before it shattered under the impact. There's one clear incision here, that runs across the smaller fractures. But the blade that struck her was quite narrow.'

'So that's what killed her, the blow to the head?'

'Without a doubt. I'm sure of that, at least. And she'd been in a fight before the fatal blow was struck.' He raised the dead woman's right hand and pointed out slight grazing on her knuckles.

'A fight?'

'Yes. You can ignore some of this weird pattern of bruising. That happened post mortem, when she was crammed into the wheelie bin. One of her arms was broken in the struggle to fit her inside, but like I said she was already dead by then. It's just as well she was so slight or there might have been more damage.'

'Just as well?'

'For whoever was trying to dispose of her, I mean.'

Geraldine nodded. 'Well, it made no difference to her,

anyway. If she *was* killed in the heat of the moment, I wonder if the bin was there, at the house, or did her killer take her away somewhere before putting her in it?'

'If he brought the bin with him, that would be a bit weird, but it would be proof of premeditation.'

'Once we know where she lived, we'll know whether the killer used a bin that was already there, at the house.'

'There was some household waste at the bottom of the bin – a bag of vegetable scraps in a bag.'

Geraldine pulled a face. Somehow it seemed more disgusting that the dead woman had been shoved into a used bin. It was annoying that the bin had no identification on it.

'Do you think she knew her attacker?' she asked.

'I can't say. But I can tell you it appears she tried to fight him off. There are a number of defence wounds, and traces of skin on her knuckles where she tried to hit whoever was assaulting her.'

'And that's not her own skin?'

'I can't say definitely until it's gone off for analysis, but it's probably not her own skin. It looks different under close examination, even just with the human eye.'

Their eyes met in mutual understanding. That was a stroke of luck.

'Not so lucky for her killer,' Miles said, as though he could read her mind. 'If it *was* her killer she was fighting with.'

'Had she been drinking?'

'I don't think so, but we'll get the full tox report on Monday. I'll know more then.'

Geraldine gazed down at the victim. The dead woman had large blue eyes and childlike features. With her white face and bloody hair, she looked like a ghost from a horror film.

Geraldine sighed. 'What happened to you?' she whispered. 'Who did this to you?'

Overhearing her, Miles laughed. 'If she could tell us that, we'd both be out of a job!'

That evening Geraldine phoned her friend Ian, to check that he was all right.

'I don't know,' he replied. 'I mean, I'm OK, but I don't know what to do. I went to see Bev like you suggested, but there was no point. It's over. Maybe I should just go ahead with a divorce.'

'Don't rush into anything. You need to talk to her properly. What if it turns out you're the father, and she wants you back?'

'To be honest, even if a paternity test showed the baby's mine, I don't think I'd want her back, not after the way she's behaved. She left me to go and live with him. She said that was what she wanted. Even if the baby's mine, it's over between me and Bev. God knows how long their affair's been going on. She told me the baby's not mine. Even if it is, what difference does that make? I'll never be able to trust her again, and if I can't trust her, why would I want her back?'

A line from a poem slipped into Geraldine's mind, something about it being better to have loved and lost than never to have loved at all. But listening to Ian talking about his failed marriage, she wondered if she was better off being single.

11

THE MAN FACING GERALDINE was tall and thin. Although the room was cool, his hand trembled slightly as he rubbed his sweaty forehead with the sleeve of his shirt. Geraldine noticed the cuff was grubby, in keeping with his generally dishevelled appearance. When she invited him to take a seat, he flopped down on the chair in one ungainly movement, a man uncomfortable in his own skin. As he lowered his arm, she noticed a small bruise beneath his right eye. Another was discernible through the stubble on his chin. He stared solemnly at her and she returned his gaze steadily. She couldn't be sure, but she thought he looked scared.

Quietly she introduced herself, and he told her his name. Having read the statement he had given the duty sergeant, she knew why he had come to the police station that morning.

'When did you last see your wife?'

He hesitated. 'She went out on Thursday, and I haven't seen her since.'

'Thursday?' Geraldine repeated. 'Today's Sunday.'

'Yes.'

'You waited three days to report her missing?'

It was a statement of fact, not an accusation, but he looked uneasy. It could have been embarrassment.

'I didn't think anyone would be interested. I didn't think anyone would listen.'

'*I'm* listening, and I'm interested to hear what you have to say.'

Geraldine didn't tell him the reason for her interest. The

woman in question had gone missing the same day the victim in her latest case had been killed.

'Tell me about your wife.'

He shrugged. 'I already told all this out there, to the officer on the desk.'

'Tell me again.'

'What's going on? I don't have to tell you anything. I'm not on trial here.'

It struck Geraldine as a strange response in the circumstances.

'Mr Cordwell, Chris, I'm trying to help you find your wife.' She suspected he knew very well what had happened to her. 'Now, please, answer my questions.'

He frowned at her without answering.

Geraldine spoke gently. 'I'd like you to tell me where you think your wife went on Thursday, and why she didn't come home again. Tell me everything you can about her. But first, I don't suppose you've got a picture of her on your phone?'

Taking his phone from his pocket, he flicked through a few screens before holding it out her. The woman looked very different to the corpse at the mortuary, but Geraldine recognised the large blue eyes and youthful face. She had discovered the identity of the woman in the wheelie bin.

'It's not like she's flighty or anything. I mean, she's never gone off like this before. She's forty. She's not a kid.'

Geraldine stared at him, wondering how much he knew about his wife's death.

'How did you get those bruises?'

He looked startled.

'Those bruises on your face. Where did you get them?'

He made an involuntary movement with his right hand to touch the bruise beneath his eye with the tips of his fingers.

'It's nothing,' he muttered, dropping his gaze and staring down at the grey floor as though it suddenly interested him. 'I slipped and fell over, that's all.'

'You weren't involved in a fight?'

'A fight? No!' His head flicked up, eyes wide, and he sounded genuinely shocked.

Geraldine suspected that he was lying. His pale face flushed, and he couldn't meet her eye.

'I'm not one for fighting.' His fake laughter was pitiful. 'You can ask anyone.'

Geraldine didn't tell him that she intended to do just that. She spoke sternly. 'Mr Cordwell, if you lie or are in any way economical with the truth, it could have very serious consequences. So I'm going to ask you again. Were you involved in a fight recently?'

Chris didn't strike her as an aggressive man. On the contrary, there was something craven about him. His spindly arms and legs looked too long for his puny body, and he cringed when she raised her voice. But she was too experienced to be influenced by his feeble response to her questions. She had encountered far weaker men who had turned out to have violent tempers. It was hard not to reach any conclusions.

'Look, this isn't about my trivial injuries,' he burst out. 'My wife's gone missing and something has to be done about it. I need your help.'

Geraldine took a deep breath. 'Mr Cordwell, Chris, I'm afraid I have some bad news for you.'

'Bad news? What do you mean? What's she been saying?'

'What's who been saying?'

'Jamie. My wife. Where is she? I want to see her. If you know where she is, please...'

'Chris, it appears your wife met with an accident.'

'An accident? What do you mean? Where is she?' His concern was genuine, at least. No longer uneasy, he leaned forward in his chair, his questioning suddenly urgent. 'She's OK, isn't she?'

'I'm afraid your wife is dead.'

'Dead? Jamie? No, she can't be. That's not possible. There was nothing wrong with her. Nothing at all. I would have known if she was ill. Healthy people don't just die, for no reason. You're making a mistake. She's missing, that's all. She'll be back soon. I'm not listening to any more of this.' He stood up.

'Please, sit down. A woman's body was found on Friday morning, in the High Street.' Geraldine didn't add that the body had been discovered in a rubbish bin, as though the reality of death could be any starker. 'I'd like you to come to the mortuary and make a formal identification.'

'What makes you think it's Jamie? I don't understand. Just because I reported her missing, doesn't mean you have to start jumping to conclusions. This dead body has nothing to do with me or my wife. It's not – it can't be – you don't even know Jamie.'

'Chris, you just showed me photos of your wife.'

He hung his head suddenly, allowing his shoulders to droop. When he looked up, his face was ashen. He nodded mutely when Geraldine repeated her request for him to identify the body. All at once he seemed to rally.

'You don't know it's her,' he mumbled. 'You wouldn't be asking me to confirm it's her if you were sure. You don't know it's her.'

They both knew he was clutching at straws. Geraldine decided to take Chris to view the body herself. She wanted to observe his reaction. His face, already pale, seemed to turn even whiter when he saw the dead woman's face. A sob burst from his lips. He pressed his lips together and nodded before turning away.

'That's her,' he muttered. 'That's Jamie.'

Geraldine watched as his shoulders shook slightly while he wiped his eyes. His distress was genuine. But it was not necessarily an indication of innocence.

That afternoon Geraldine had arranged to go and see her sister in Kent. There was no reason to cancel the visit. After typing up her decision log, she set off. It was a pleasant trip, despite the traffic which seemed to be almost as heavy on a Sunday as it was on a weekday. Geraldine's niece was out, which gave her and her sister time to chat. Celia seemed fed up.

'What's wrong? Not long to go now,' Geraldine said, looking at Celia's bump.

'Just over five months.'

'Is everything OK?'

'Yes.'

'What's up then? You don't sound very happy about it. You can't change your mind now,' Geraldine said, attempting to sound lighthearted.

'Oh, I want the baby, of course I do. Apart from anything else, I don't want Chloe to be an only child.'

Geraldine nodded. She remembered that was the reason their mother had given for adopting her when, after giving birth to Celia, she had been unable to have any more children.

Celia paused. 'But – oh, it's all right for you,' she burst out suddenly. 'You've got an interesting career. I'm forty-one, nearly forty-two, and what have I done with my life? Yes, I know, I'm married and I've got Chloe, and I wouldn't change that for the world, but I've never really done anything. I look at the other women in my antenatal classes, and all they ever talk about is maternity leave, and how soon they're going back to work. They all grumble about not being able to afford to give up their jobs, but I know they can't wait to get back to work. They say things like how they couldn't imagine being stuck at home all the time, and then they look at me and I feel so old and useless and boring. You can't imagine what it's like for me. I was telling them about you last week, how you work on murder investigations. I think it was the first time some of them had listened to a word I'd said. Your life's so exciting.'

Geraldine laughed. 'Not really. I think having a family must be far more exciting than anything I do. Life must be more interesting than death.'

For all her efforts to be encouraging, Geraldine wasn't sure that she had said much to comfort her sister.

'Family's important,' she added, trying not to think about Helena.

Celia's biological mother had cared for her, and she had a family of her own. Nothing Geraldine did could compensate for the fact that she was, ultimately, alone.

12

ON MONDAY, THE FORENSIC team conducted their examination of Chris's living room and confirmed traces of blood on the carpet. Geraldine went along to speak to them.

'There's surprisingly little blood,' a scene of crime officer told her. 'Only a few traces.'

'But enough to confirm she was killed here?'

'Yes. It looks as though the rug absorbed most of the blood. She was probably wrapped in it as she was lifted into the bin which had been wheeled in here. There's no sign of her being carried out of the house, but we have found faint traces of wheel tracks on the carpet which match the wheels on the bin. We'll have all the details in the report, but that's basically what happened.'

It was possible someone had been seen pushing a wheelie bin in or out of the house on the night of the murder. Before returning to the police station, Geraldine questioned the residents on either side of the Cordwells. The first couple said they had only recently moved in, and had barely spoken to their next door neighbours. Geraldine wasn't sure if they were unable or unwilling to speak to her.

The middle-aged woman living on the other side of them was more helpful. The woman's eyes brightened with anticipation when Geraldine introduced herself and went in.

'I was shocked, but,' she lowered her voice although there was no one else there, 'I can't say I was surprised.'

'What do you mean?'

Geraldine shook her head to refuse the offer of a cup of tea.

She was cautiously pleased that the Cordwells' neighbour was willing to talk. Such sources could be invaluable, but they were just as frequently time wasters, lonely people straying into fantasy in their excitement at finding an audience.

'There was a lot of shouting,' the neighbour confided, her enjoyment of the drama detracting from her account.

'Shouting?'

'Yes. I never heard her voice raised in anger, poor thing, but he was another matter.'

'Go on.'

'I could only hear him when they were in the hall, so it wasn't often, but I've no doubt he carried on like that when they were inside, where I couldn't hear.'

'What did you hear, exactly?'

'Well, I can't be sure,' the woman answered, suddenly coy. 'I mean, I can't repeat what he said word for word. I didn't write it down or anything. I wouldn't want you to think I was nosy.'

'Can you give me the gist of it? You said you overheard Mr Cordwell shouting? How can you be sure it was him?'

'Well, he kept shouting at her.'

'What did he say?'

The woman shrugged. 'I don't know. I couldn't see them, and I couldn't hear what he was saying. I just heard him through the wall, shouting.'

'How do you know he was shouting at her?'

'Because I heard him,' she replied. 'He sounded angry, and there's no telling what a man might do if he's angry enough. And well, it must have been her, mustn't it? I never saw anyone else go in that house.'

Geraldine wasn't sure how trustworthy the neighbour's account was, but she thanked the woman for her help.

Back at the station, she arranged for a team to question the other neighbours in the street. While that was being set up, she decided to go and see Miles in case he had any more information for her. She preferred to speak to him in person. Understandably, he spoke less freely on the phone. Listening to what he had to tell her, she frowned. A likely scenario was beginning to emerge.

'We've sent samples of skin from under her nails and on her knuckles off for analysis. Here's hoping we find a match on the database. And we might have the same DNA on the bin as well.'

Geraldine nodded. 'Although of course if it's the husband's, that would be on the bin anyway. I mean, it was his bin.'

Geraldine stared down at the white-faced corpse. With luck the net was beginning to close around her killer. She looked up and nodded briskly at Miles.

'Well, this is going to be very useful. Anyway, we've found out her identity, so I'll get back to the husband again straight away, and we'll get a sample of his DNA. I'll find out about the bin as well.'

It was not difficult to come up with a theory that fitted all the evidence. If Chris's DNA matched the fragments of skin found under his wife's nails, the case was as good as sewn up. The investigation was making rapid progress.

'Thanks, Miles, you've been invaluable as always.'

He inclined his head with a smile. 'So full of praise and yet so distant,' he replied, with a mock sigh. 'I keep waiting and waiting for you to invite me over for dinner. Are you going to leave me hanging on forever?'

Geraldine laughed. 'Doesn't your wife feed you?'

Back at the station, Geraldine wrote up the latest information before summoning her sergeant. Over a coffee they discussed the latest findings. Tucking into a slab of chocolate cake, Sam nodded cheerfully.

'So it's the husband,' she concluded when Geraldine had finished speaking.

'Honestly, Sam, I don't know where you put it all.'

The sergeant was well built, but by no means overweight.

She looked fit, and Geraldine knew her colleague was a martial arts expert.

Sam shrugged. 'I didn't have much breakfast and anyway, we could be called away anywhere, at any time, and it's not a good idea to work on an empty stomach. You never know when you might have to miss a meal in this job.'

Geraldine laughed. 'That doesn't mean you should take every opportunity to eat as much as you possibly can, whenever you can. You only have to see food and you're eating it. I don't understand why you never put on weight.'

'That's because I eat all the time,' Sam explained earnestly. 'My body's used to it. Eating is my normal state. If I stopped, even for a day, I'd put on weight as soon as I started eating again. I have to keep up the momentum.'

'That's bollocks, even for you.'

Sam laughed. 'There's nothing wrong with a healthy appetite. So, are we going to arrest this wife killer?'

Not for the first time, Geraldine was aware she needed to put a brake on her young sergeant's eagerness for action. She was reminded of her own enthusiasm when she had been Sam's age. 'We need to check his DNA first,' she reminded her. 'He might not be the one his wife was fighting with.'

'But he probably was.'

Geraldine wanted to discuss the implications of the wheelie bin having been brought into the house.

'Miles thought she was moved into the bin pretty quickly, and the scene of crime officers seemed to agree with that. If the bin was brought into the house before she was killed, in readiness...'

'Proof of premeditation,' Sam responded promptly. 'So this was someone who knew where the bin was, and knew it was empty, or had emptied it in preparation, and was able to wheel it inside without his victim challenging him.' She finished her coffee. 'The husband is always the most likely suspect, so let's not overcomplicate things. Just this once, can't we find the culprit straight away, arrest him and be done with it, without going all round the houses?'

'I know it can be tedious, but we have to go through the process. There's no point in rushing and getting the wrong end of the stick. You know very well it's not enough to make an arrest. We've got to have all the evidence to make a watertight case. I've got to say, you're being very impatient, even for you.'

'Yes, well, it's Emma's birthday this weekend and we're supposed to be going away.'

'I daresay the investigation will survive without you for a couple of days.'

'I'm not going away in the middle of a case!'

'You mean you don't want to miss out on any action.'

Sam looked uncharacteristically dejected. 'It's all right for you, Geraldine. You're single and you can drop everything and concentrate on work whenever you want. It's not easy when you're in a relationship.'

'I thought Emma was fine with what you do, and the demands of the job?'

Sam's dilemma reminded Geraldine of her former sergeant. Ian's wife had blamed the break up of their marriage on the time he spent working. It happened a lot to Geraldine's fellow officers. Long hours and extreme stress were not conducive to a settled home life. She felt sorry for Sam who had seemed so happy with her girlfriend. She gave a sympathetic smile, but resisted trotting out platitudes. This was a situation Sam was going to have to resolve for herself.

'Emma's fine. It's not that. She'll be nice about it, and understanding. She always is. But it's not fair on her. She's always there for me.' She sighed. 'It's just hard, sometimes, trying to juggle two lives.'

Needing a sample of Chris's DNA, they set off. He was staying in a hostel not far from the council estate where he lived, not far from Highgate High Street, near Waterlow Park.

'It was him,' Sam said. 'It had to be.'

Geraldine suspected her sergeant was right.

'No wheelie bin outside,' Sam muttered as they drove past.

Geraldine nodded. Not everyone kept their bins on display at the front of their house, and many households had more than one bin, but it could be significant.

Unkempt and unshaven, Chris looked and smelled as though he had slept in his clothes.

'Do you know who did it?' he asked anxiously. 'Have you got him?'

'We think so,' Sam replied.

Chris inhaled deeply and his expression relaxed slightly. 'You'd better lock him up or I'll – I'll smash his face in,' he said, clenching his fists.

His threat sounded pathetic. He looked as though he could no more attack his wife's killer than he could fly. Geraldine wondered if he really had killed his wife. If he had, he was a good actor.

'We're working on several leads,' Geraldine said, when they were inside and sitting down. 'But we came here to ask for a sample of your DNA.'

'What for?'

Geraldine answered quietly. 'Just for the process of elimination.'

'I don't understand.' His eyes widened in alarm. 'You can't think I killed her! She was my wife!'

'Everyone who was in contact with your wife before she was killed has to be ruled out of the investigation. That's the way we work, Chris, narrowing it down and excluding people until we find our suspect. You do want us to find out who killed Jamie, don't you? So come on, it's standard procedure, and nothing to be worried about.'

'Assuming you're innocent,' Sam muttered.

Geraldine gave her sergeant a warning glare.

He acquiesced with a surly growl. 'Oh well, go on then, if you must you must, I suppose.'

He opened his mouth and submitted to Sam collecting a sample. As the sergeant finished, Geraldine casually mentioned there was no bin outside the house.

'What?'

'You don't have a bin outside.'

'Oh yes, we had one, of course we did, but it was stolen.'

'Stolen? When was that?'

He frowned. 'As it happens, I noticed it had gone on Friday, the same day Jamie went missing.'

'You didn't report it,' Sam said.

'What? No, of course I didn't.'

'Why not?'

'Are you people for real? My wife had gone missing. Why would I be thinking about a bin? Wife. Bin. Which would you worry about? You really think I could think about anything other than Jamie at a time like that? Really?'

The two women left soon after. Sam thought it was significant that Chris's bin had disappeared, but Geraldine pointed out that the missing bin proved nothing. With a van, or a hatchback, anyone could have driven the bin to the High Street after dark. A team had been studying CCTV film from cameras closest to the charity shop. So far no one had been spotted pushing a wheelie bin along the street on Thursday night. A camera nearly opposite the charity shop had recorded a van stopping outside the shop at half past two, but in the darkness the vehicle had blocked the view of the shop doorway. It was possible someone had trundled a bin out of the back of the van and into the shop doorway. The Visual Images, Identification and Detections Officers were trying to enhance the image of the number plate, but so far without success. The street was empty at night. It had been easy for the van to pull into the kerb without turning far enough for the registration plate at the front or back to face the camera.

'We have to be patient,' Geraldine told Sam.

'It won't be long now,' Sam answered cheerfully as she

drove them back to the police station. 'We just need to know if the DNA is a match, or find the driver of that van, or both, and it will all be sewn up.'

Geraldine hoped her sergeant was right. It was tantalising to have so much potential evidence, none of it yet conclusive.

13

'THERE ARE READY MEALS in the freezer, and I've filled the fridge,' Louise called out. 'And I'm up to date with the washing.'

'Stop fussing, will you?' Tom replied. 'You won't be gone for long. I think I can survive a couple of days without you.'

'OK, I'm off to bed,' she said. 'I've got an early start tomorrow.'

Tom didn't answer. As soon as she set off in the morning, he intended to follow her. She had told him she was going on a training course in Birmingham, catching a train from Euston in the morning, but he suspected her trip had nothing to do with her training as a hair stylist. If she was off to catch an early train to Birmingham, he would be very surprised. When he went upstairs to the bedroom, she was repacking. He watched out of the corner of his eye as she folded her new jeans, and laid them carefully in the case, with several of her favourite shirts. He wanted to take a look in her case while she was in the bathroom, to see what else she had packed, but decided against it. If she caught him ferreting around in her case, it would be difficult to explain what he was doing.

He slept uneasily, constantly checking the time on his phone and listening out for any movement. It was a relief when she clambered out of bed. He could tell she was taking care not to disturb him. Convinced she wanted to creep out silently because she was hiding something from him, his unspoken accusation was making him suspect her of being similarly furtive. He hated himself for being so distrustful, but he couldn't bring himself to confront her. He didn't want to listen to more of her lies. In the meantime, not knowing if her affair was still going on was driving him nuts.

If he could catch her meeting her lover, at least he would know the truth. He was positive she was going away to spend the night with another man. The thought that she might not come back terrified him. He had told her glibly that he could manage without her for a couple of days. That was true. But the prospect of spending the rest of his life without her was too painful to contemplate. All the same, he had to know what was going on before he lost his mind.

The station was fairly busy as he followed her on to the platform at Holloway Road. Wearing a hat he had bought especially to help him pursue her unrecognised, he peered out from beneath the brim. She didn't even look round. She had no idea he was there. Her innocence gave him a slight pang, but he remembered seeing a man creep out of his house at midnight and his resolve hardened. She changed trains at Kings Cross. Here there was no problem keeping out of sight, the station was so crowded. At Euston Square she left the station and hurried along the street to the mainline station. Watching her studying the departures board, he realised she really was going to Birmingham, and she appeared to be travelling alone.

He had been a fool to follow her to Euston. Short of stalking her all the way to Birmingham, he still had no way of knowing whether she was travelling there for a hairdressing course, or to meet someone. But he was going to find out.

14

THE NEXT MORNING GERALDINE arrived at work early, determined to carry out an extensive search on Jamie Cordwell. There was no mention of any injuries in her medical records, and no evidence of any hospital visits. Geraldine studied all the documentation, but couldn't find anything useful.

Before she had time to do anything else, results came in from the forensic team, seeming to confirm Chris's guilt. The Detective Chief Inspector summoned the team together as soon as the news came in. There was a buzz of excitement in the major incident room as they gathered. Geraldine saw Sam hurrying along the corridor and stopped to wait for her. They went in together.

'What's happened?' Sam asked. 'What's going on?'

'Didn't you see the latest report?'

'I'd just popped down to the canteen for a quick breakfast. Honestly, you can't even take a five-minute break in this place without something happening.'

'Sam, your talents are wasted here. You should be working in a restaurant. Or you could be a food critic, judging pub grub.'

'So? What's the latest?' Sam asked, ignoring Geraldine's teasing.

Before Geraldine could reply, Adam Eastwood marched into the room. In his mid-forties, dark-haired and dapper, the detective chief inspector's eyes shone with suppressed excitement, although his expression remained stern. His voice rang out clearly across the room as he made his announcement.

'We've had a bit of a breakthrough. The results of the DNA

tests are back. Those of you who've seen the latest report will know that the scraps of skin found beneath the victim's fingernails belonged to her husband. They were fighting shortly before her death. His DNA and fingerprints were found on the bin in which her body was dumped.'

Whatever had sparked the row, something had thrown him into a violent rage, resulting in a fatal attack. There seemed little doubt that they had found the killer. The Visual Images, Identification and Detections Officers were still hunting for the van in which Chris had transported the wheelie bin to the High Street during the night.

'That will be the final piece of the jigsaw,' Adam said.

'If we've got the right man,' Geraldine added, more loudly than she had intended.

Everyone in the room turned to stare at her.

'You met our suspect,' Adam said. 'What was your impression of him? You seem to be implying that you don't think he's our man.'

Geraldine hesitated. 'I don't see that finding his DNA on the victim means anything. She was his wife. Of course his prints and his DNA are going to be all over her.'

'And his skin beneath her fingernails?' someone pointed out. There was a murmur of consent around the room.

'She could have been scratching his back,' a constable suggested.

The mood in the room dampened slightly. It was true, they had been very quick to reach a conclusion on limited evidence.

'You haven't answered my question, Geraldine,' Adam said. 'What's your impression of him?'

'He seemed a bit feeble,' she replied cautiously.

'Feeble-minded?' someone called out.

'He beat his wife up before he killed her,' Sam pointed out, glancing up from her phone where she had been checking the data.

Geraldine nodded. 'Yes, it certainly looks that way.' She

paused, struggling to explain herself. 'There was something sneaky about him, but he didn't strike me as violent.'

'A surreptitious wife beater,' Sam said.

There was no denying the findings looked conclusive. Before Geraldine set off to bring the suspect in for questioning, she went to see Adam.

'Geraldine, there's something I'd like you to be aware of, but this isn't to be spread around.' His eyes narrowed. 'It hasn't got any bearing on our present case, but two months ago, Chris Cordwell was falsely accused of abducting a young woman from outside Cockfosters station.'

'Bloody hell.'

'It came to nothing at the time, so we'll have to discount it for now. There isn't an official record of it as such, because the accusation turned out to be completely groundless. I wouldn't have mentioned it, only it might help you to put pressure on him. Bear it in mind.'

'Do you think we should look into it?'

Adam shrugged. 'It was investigated at the time and the accusation was dismissed.'

Nevertheless, Adam had thought it worth mentioning.

'Are you suggesting I let him know we're aware of it, when I question him?'

Adam nodded. 'It won't do any harm for him to understand he can't hide anything from us. Let him think we know everything there is to know about him. You know the drill. But we're not ready to make a formal arrest just yet.'

Geraldine understood the detective chief inspector wanted to wait until they had compelling evidence against Chris. It wouldn't require a particularly skilled lawyer to argue that the suspect's DNA and fingerprints at the scene of the crime proved nothing. Even if they knew he was guilty, they still had to prove it.

'Let's bring him in for questioning, see if we can get him to talk,' he said.

'Don't worry, I'll get him here and work on him.'

'Are you in any doubt he's our man?'

'No,' Geraldine replied, but the uncertainty in her voice was apparent to them both. 'Not exactly,' she added. Adam raised his eyebrows in an unspoken question. 'That is, I do think he's guilty, but until we can prove it definitely, there's always a chance we could be wrong. I'm trying to keep an open mind.'

'OK, well bring him in, and I daresay we'll get a confession which will clear things up nicely.'

Before she went to see Chris, Geraldine checked the database, looking for a report of a missing woman, last seen at Cockfosters station. There was no mention of Chris's name, but she found the report Adam had mentioned. A young woman had allegedly been abducted from the train station two months ago. The missing woman's father had levelled the accusation based on the fact that he had seen a man driving a van away from the station on the night in question. As the area was otherwise deserted, the worried father had noted down the registration number of the van. His missing daughter was blond. So was the suspect's wife, who had confirmed that she had been in the van with her husband that night. The story had checked out in every respect. All due procedures had been followed in what had turned out to be a case of mistaken identity.

Geraldine took Sam with her to see Jamie's husband. They drove slowly through the London traffic without saying much.

'It looks like you might get away for the weekend after all,' Geraldine said at last. 'Emma'll be pleased.'

'I can't tell you how much I'm hoping we've got this right.'

'I take it that remark was prompted by your passionate desire to see justice done, not by your passionate desire for Emma,' Geraldine replied, a trifle sharply.

'Oh come on, Geraldine, you know what it's like. You must have...' Sam broke off, clearly afraid she had spoken out of turn.

'Yes,' Geraldine hurried to reassure her she was not insulted by Sam's comment. 'I do know what it's like to be in love. Being single doesn't mean I'm a nun.'

Her words sounded peevish. For a long time she had resisted the advances of one of her colleagues, aware that he was married. Eventually he had convinced her that he and his wife were estranged. Their affair had only just begun when he had been brutally murdered. To her dismay Geraldine felt tears in her eyes. Her mother's death had followed soon after the loss of her colleague with whom she had fallen in love. It had been hard to cope with so much loss, not least because she had kept her love affair a secret. She was accustomed to dealing with death in her professional life, but it might have been a mistake to think she could cope unaided with so much personal grief.

'Geraldine? Are you all right? Geraldine?'

'I'm fine,' she lied, staring out of her window. 'I'm just thinking about Chris Cordwell. If he's innocent, what's about to happen is going to be horrible for him.'

'It must be horrible for anyone to be a suspect, if they're innocent. And if he's not, he deserves what's coming to him. But I don't know why you feel sorry for a wife beater.'

'He's just lost his wife, and now we're going to accuse him of murdering her. All I'm saying is, if he loved his wife, and if he didn't kill her, all this would be pretty horrible.'

'If he really loved his wife, even if he didn't kill her, I don't suppose he's going to care much what happens to him. And anyway,' Sam went on brightly, 'the chances are it was him, and if he's as pathetic as he appears, he's bound to break down and confess, and...'

'And you'll be able to go away for the weekend without missing anything.'

'That's not what I was going to say.'

'It's what you were thinking though.'

'Absolutely not! What an outrageous accusation! Nothing was further from my thoughts.'

'Nothing?' Geraldine teased her sergeant, who protested, red-faced.

Geraldine laughed, her good humour restored. It was difficult to remain miserable for long in Sam's company.

'Let's see what he has to say when we take him back with us for questioning,' Sam said. 'I can't wait.'

15

CHRIS GLARED SULLENLY ACROSS the table at Geraldine. 'Before you start with your questions, I want a lawyer. I'm not saying another word until I have a lawyer. I know what you people are like.'

Sam looked interested. Before she could question the suspect, Geraldine gave her a warning frown.

'Then you must be aware that we know everything about you, Chris.'

He gave a dismissive grunt. 'You don't know anything about me.'

'We know that you were recently accused of abducting a woman.'

Chris scowled. 'That nonsense again? Yes, some young girl ran away from home, but it had nothing to do with me.'

Realising that Geraldine knew something about Chris to which she wasn't privy, Sam sat back in her chair.

'The girl's father came along and took down the number of my van, for no reason except that I was there. He was a nut job. Well, you didn't manage to pin that trumped-up charge on me, and you won't pin this on me either.'

'When did you last see your wife?'

'Alive, you mean?'

'Yes.' Geraldine answered quietly. He knew very well what she meant.

'I've already told you, I saw her on Thursday morning, before I left for work. I saw her every morning. She was my wife, for Christ's sake. She wasn't in when I got home that evening, and

I never saw her again. Not while she was alive anyway. I didn't kill her. And that's all I'm going to say.' He crossed his arms and pressed his lips together as though to illustrate his point.

'No one accused you of killing her,' Geraldine pointed out softly. She turned to Sam. 'Did you hear anyone suggest he killed his wife?'

'No.'

'So I wonder what put that idea in your head, Chris?'

'You think you're clever, trying to trip people up. You should show a bit more respect. I just lost my wife.'

'That's why we're here.' Geraldine paused before leaning forward and speaking very gently. 'It's understandable you're feeling upset, Chris. You loved your wife, didn't you?'

He glared at her without answering. His previous experience of being questioned had made him wary.

'It must be hard, knowing you had a row the last time you saw her alive. What were you arguing about?'

He sat up abruptly, his eyebrows raised. 'What?'

'There's no need to try and keep up this pretence. We know what happened. Something she said made you angry, and in the heat of the moment you lashed out. It wasn't the first time, was it? She tried to fight back. That much is clear from the evidence. The jury will be told that you lost your temper, but they'll find it easier to believe if you tell us right from the start what you were arguing about. Come on, Chris. No more lies.'

'I don't know what you're talking about! We never fought. We were married. We loved each other. Stop trying to trick me with your lies. It won't work. You can make up whatever crap you like, it won't change the fact that Jamie is dead. Someone killed her, and it wasn't me. I'm telling you, it wasn't me. And now, I demand to have a lawyer.'

Although Geraldine had stopped short of accusing Chris of murder, they all knew it had been implied. While they were waiting for the lawyer to arrive and talk to his client, Geraldine and Sam took a break to discuss how the interview was going so far.

'He'd hit her before,' Sam said as they took a seat in the canteen. 'The post mortem found evidence of them fighting. Only this time he went too far. Then he panicked and tried to get rid of the body.'

'Just because there's a history of violence, it doesn't necessarily mean he killed her.'

Sam took a large bite out of a doughnut and shrugged.

'But it's likely,' Geraldine went on, thinking aloud as Sam munched. 'Did you see how white he went when I told him we knew he'd beaten his wife in the past? He was certainly shocked. Was he angry at being reminded of it, or shocked that we knew about it?' She sighed. 'There's something he's not telling us.'

'Like how he hit his wife over the head with a sharp instrument,' Sam said as she took a swig of her tea.

At last the duty lawyer was ready for them.

'Chris, we're not accusing you of anything,' Geraldine reassured him. Not yet, she thought. 'You haven't been arrested yet.'

'So I could get up and leave?'

'If you want to refuse to co-operate with us when we're trying to find out who killed your wife.'

Chris glanced at his brief who gave an almost imperceptible shake of his head, and leaned over to whisper to his client. Portly and white-haired, the lawyer was well into his sixties. Gazing complacently across the table, he looked as though he was preparing to take a nap. Weighing his experience against his probable approaching retirement, Geraldine was not sure she would feel very confident about being represented by him if she was suspected of murder. For the sake of the suspect, she hoped the lawyer was more alert than he appeared.

'We just want to know what happened between you and your wife on the evening she was killed. There could have been extenuating circumstances to make a judge incline to be lenient. Perhaps she confessed to being unfaithful? Or did you get home and find her there with someone else? Was she unfaithful, Chris?'

His face flushed red and he squirmed uncomfortably in his chair. 'I told you, I never saw her that evening.'

'Would you like to reconsider your response? Only for some reason you don't seem very sure.'

'My client has already answered that question, more than once. If you persist in hectoring him, I will advise him to leave.'

Having heaved himself forward in his chair to make his declaration, the lawyer sank back and closed his eyes as though his work was completed.

Geraldine revised her opinion of him. Despite his apparent nonchalance, he was listening closely.

'You've told us, several times, that you weren't at home with your wife on Thursday evening. Can you tell us where you were?'

Chris shifted uneasily in his chair again. Wiping his forehead on his sleeve, he glared at Geraldine.

'No I can't. But I know I wasn't at home.'

'So where were you?'

'I can't remember.'

'You didn't report your wife missing straight away. Why not?'

'I thought she'd gone out.'

'For three days? Weren't you concerned? Or did you know very well what had happened to her?'

Chris stared at her, his eyes wide with fear.

'My client's under no obligation to answer that question,' the lawyer answered for him. 'He's told you he wasn't at home on Thursday evening. Where he went is no concern of yours.'

'Everything is of concern in a murder investigation,' Sam said.

'Indeed,' the lawyer agreed, 'however, I don't need to remind you that my client is not a suspect, and therefore not obliged to answer any of your questions. Unless you wish to arrest him?'

'I didn't...' Chris interrupted

The lawyer held a plump hand up to silence him before continuing. 'But I don't think you want to do that, with no evidence to suggest he's guilty.'

Stifling a sigh, Geraldine changed tack. 'You don't deny you own a black Ford Transit van.' She read out the registration number.

'Why would I deny it? You know it's mine.'

'And can you confirm that you were driving your van along Highgate High Street last Thursday evening?'

Chris glanced at his brief who was sitting, eyes closed, his hands folded over his rounded stomach. In the silence that followed, he opened his eyes and looked at his client, waiting. Geraldine held her breath.

'Look, I don't deny I own that van, but it wasn't being driven anywhere in Highgate last Thursday because it was in the garage having some work done.'

'What work?' Sam asked.

Chris frowned at her. 'It went in for a service. The brake pads needed replacing, and two tyres.'

Geraldine and Sam exchanged a glance which was not lost on the lawyer.

'Will that be all then?' he enquired, suddenly brisk.

'One more question. Which garage did you take the van to?'

'Bloody hell, you don't believe a word anyone says, do you?' Chris burst out irritably.

'It's my job to question everything,' Geraldine replied, noticing how readily he lost his temper.

'It was in the workshop, in Hillmarton Road. Go on. Ask them. They'll tell you I wasn't driving the van on Thursday. It was off the road nearly all week.'

The lawyer sat up. 'I think that answers your question,

Inspector. And now, unless you have any further questions for my client, I'm going to suggest he goes home.'

'No further questions,' Geraldine replied.

'Until we've checked out your story,' Sam added.

16

THE GARAGE CHRIS HAD mentioned was down a side street west of the Holloway Road, towards Tufnell Park. Geraldine drove there and found it without any difficulty. Leaving her car on the forecourt, she walked over to the workshop. Two men were working on cars at the back, while a third was looking under the bonnet of a van near the open doors. He straightened up as Geraldine approached. Quite tall and muscular, he would have been attractive were it not for his churlish expression.

He took a step towards her, blocking her way. 'Can I help you?'

'I'd like to speak to whoever's in charge.'

The mechanic glanced over his shoulder at the other two men who were busy working.

'You can speak to me. I'm the manager.'

Briefly Geraldine introduced herself and explained the purpose of her visit.

'So you see,' she concluded, 'this is a really important question. A man's liberty may depend on what you can tell me.'

The mechanic nodded to show he understood. Although he spent a long time wiping his oily hands on a rag, they did not look much cleaner when he had finished.

'Come on,' he said at last, 'we need to go and check in the office.'

With a quick glance at his colleagues, who had taken no notice of the newcomer, he led her across the open yard. The bright sunshine gave Geraldine a fleeting sensation of regret.

This was the weather for barbecues and sun loungers, not for pursuing murder investigations. She followed the mechanic into a small office where a girl seated at a desk looked up to welcome them. Her warm smile seemed to make the room glow, it formed such a marked contrast with the mechanic's dour expression.

'Take a break, Tracy,' the mechanic said curtly.

As the girl stood up her long hair swung, silky as a model's in a television advertisement. Before Geraldine had a chance to say she would deal with the receptionist and allow the mechanic to return to his work, the girl picked up her bag and slipped out through a door in the back wall.

'She was due for a break,' the man said by way of explanation.

He took the seat vacated by the receptionist and gestured at Geraldine to sit down on the other side of the desk.

'Now, what was it you wanted to know?'

Geraldine gave him the registration number of Chris's van. 'I need to know exactly when it was brought here for a service, and when he collected it.'

'The dates it was off the road?'

'Exactly.'

While they were talking, he fiddled about on the keyboard, frowning and screwing up his eyes to stare at the screen.

'Yes, here it is.'

As he read out the information, Geraldine felt like smiling. The van had been in the workshop from Monday to Wednesday during the week of the murder. Chris's wife had been killed that Thursday.

'Thank you very much,' she said. 'Can you let me have a copy of the details?'

'Of course. I don't know where Tracy files the paperwork. I mean, I could search through all the drawers but it would probably be quicker to wait till she gets back. I can email it to you now, if that helps. Where do I send it? Oh shit. Sorry, but the system's just crashed. It does that all the time. Do you want to jot down your email address for me, and I'll send you the booking form as soon as it's rebooted. I can send you the report and the invoice too if you like. It sometimes takes a few tries but I'll definitely get it all over to you by this afternoon. Tracy will be back soon. Or you can come back in an hour or so when she's here and she'll give you copies of the paperwork.' He shrugged. 'Put me under the bonnet of a car and I know what I'm doing...'

Geraldine hesitated, but there was no point in sitting around waiting. The flustered mechanic had as good as admitted he didn't know how to sort out the temporary glitch with his internet access. It would have to wait until the receptionist returned. In the meantime, Geraldine had her answer. All she needed was the written confirmation which would be delivered that afternoon.

'You're sure you can get that over to me today?' she asked as she gave him her email address.

'No problem. As soon as we get this sorted, I'll deal with it.'

'Thank you, and thank you for your time.'

For the first time, the mechanic smiled. He was clearly relieved to be getting back to work. Geraldine was even more pleased to return to the police station and record her findings. Within an hour, the promised email came through. Attached were copies of the invoice issued to Chris, and the report on the work carried out on his van. The dates confirmed that the work had been completed the day before Jamie was killed.

As soon as Geraldine logged the confirmation, instead of summoning her, the detective chief inspector came to see her in her office. He was beaming.

'We've got him then,' he announced, sitting down at the unoccupied desk in her office where their colleague, Neil, worked.

While Neil was away, Geraldine had the room to herself. The privacy that she had enjoyed in her previous post no longer felt so agreeable. At first merely tolerating her new working conditions, she had quickly grown accustomed to Neil's presence in the room. Both equally overworked, increasingly so with the latest cutbacks, Neil focused on his own tasks and rarely disturbed her concentration. Although the subject had never come up in conversation, she was sure he felt the same way about sharing an office with her. From time to time they went out for a quick lunch together. On such occasions Neil proved good company, and it could be very helpful to discuss a case with a colleague who was not working on it.

'Got him bang to rights,' Adam went on. 'I'm going to call the team together as soon as you've brought him in, but I wanted to have a word with you first, just to say that was a job well done. You and Sam can go and pick him up straight away.'

'Another box ticked,' Geraldine muttered. 'Thank goodness he was stupid enough to think he could lie his way out of it,' she added quickly to make it clear that she was pleased too.

'It's as good as a confession.' Adam grinned. 'If we could just find the murder weapon we'll be done, with no loose ends. No sign of it yet?'

'No.'

'Oh well, he's had time to get rid of it. But we've got enough without it.'

17

GERALDINE STRODE ALONG THE corridor to an interview room. As before, the portly lawyer was present. Only this time, the interrogation was going to be very different. Adam, not Sam, was at her side to question Chris about his wife's murder because this time, they knew he had lied about his van being in the garage on the night of the murder.

In the interview room, Chris sat slumped beside his brief who sat with his eyes closed.

'Can we get on with it?' He opened his eyes and glanced at his client. 'Don't worry, we'll soon have you out of here.' He turned back to Geraldine. 'This is the second time you've questioned my client today. You also questioned him yesterday and the day before.'

'He came here voluntarily on Sunday to report that his wife was missing,' Geraldine pointed out.

Adam interrupted. 'We can question your client as often as we consider necessary, until he tells us the truth. You seem to have forgotten that he's a suspect in a murder enquiry.'

The lawyer's eyes narrowed. 'Is he being charged?'

Chris let out a faint whimper and shook his head. 'No, no, it wasn't me,' he bleated. 'I could never hurt her. I – I just couldn't.'

'We know you beat her,' Adam replied. 'She had the defence wounds to prove it.'

'Defence wounds incurred while fighting off her killer,' the lawyer said.

'You need to study the post mortem report more carefully,'

Geraldine told him. 'Your client's skin was found under the victim's fingernails, and there are scratches as well as bruises on his face. There's no question they were fighting recently.'

'Were there any such injuries on *her* body to confirm that she had been assaulted?' the lawyer asked.

'She was hit on the head,' Adam answered.

'So,' the lawyer leaned forward in his chair, 'the evidence suggests that the victim was putting up a fight without anyone attempting to attack her?'

Geraldine hesitated, but Adam was quick to respond.

'We must presume that she was attempting to fight him off because he was wielding a weapon of some kind, poised to kill her with a blow to the head.'

'Presume?' the lawyer repeated quietly, sitting back in his chair.

Geraldine turned her attention to Chris. Pasty-faced and sweating, he looked terrified. She spoke gently.

'Chris, we're not yet clear about the exact circumstances leading up to your wife's death, but what we can prove beyond any doubt is that you killed her. You'll only harm your defence if you keep on trying to deny it. We know you did it. We have enough evidence to prove it. We understand how traumatic this must be for you. You never meant to kill her, did you? Things just got out of hand. You loved your wife, didn't you? So what happened that night, Chris? Did you discover she'd been having an affair? Did she refuse to have sex with you? Is that why she was fighting you off?' Chris looked as though he might burst into tears. He turned to his lawyer who shrugged as though he had nothing to say.

'No, no, you've got it all wrong. I would never have hurt her. Never. It's not – I'm not like that – I couldn't...' He stammered and broke off in confusion. Staring straight at Geraldine, he said slowly and clearly, 'I did not kill my wife.'

With a shrug, the lawyer sat up again. 'Your whole case is built on supposition and fabrication. There are so many holes in it, what you're trying to do is derisory. In the absence of any alternative suspect, instead of getting on with the job of finding the guilty party, you're wasting everyone's time here batting away on a losing wicket. I will ask you just one question. How do you imagine my client transported a dead body, in a wheelie bin, from his house to Highgate High Street, while his van was off the road?'

Geraldine shook her head. 'But your van wasn't off the road, was it, Chris? You took it in for repairs earlier that week, didn't you?'

'What? No, no,' Chris stuttered. 'I mean, yes I did take it in earlier that week, but I didn't pick it up until Friday. You can ask at the garage. Tell them,' he turned to his lawyer who was listening silently, 'tell them.'

'We've checked. Did you really think we wouldn't? You're panicking, aren't you?' Feeling almost sorry for him, she reminded herself firmly that she was talking to a man who, pathetic though he might appear, had killed his wife. 'I went to the garage to establish exactly when your van was off the road. We have copies of the documentation. I *suppose*,' she glanced at the lawyer, 'you thought it was a clever idea to take your van to the garage a few days before you killed your wife, hoping we'd believe it was still in for repairs on the night she was killed. If so, your scheme backfired. It suggests premeditation, you see. Although a clever barrister will no doubt find a way to raise doubts about that. Still, the fact remains you picked your van up just before you killed your wife.'

'No, no, I didn't.'

'The garage says you did.'

'They've made a mistake.'

'We have the evidence.'

'It's a mistake, it must be. They got the dates wrong.'

'I'd like to speak to my client,' the lawyer said heavily.

They took a break. When they reconvened, the lawyer

appeared unduly relaxed. Chris seemed more anxious than before.

'My client would like to tell you where he was on Thursday evening.' His broad face creased into a smile, although his voice remained solemn. 'He has an alibi, you see.'

'Oh please,' Adam interjected. 'And you want us to believe he's only just remembered this? Come on. What kind of idiots do you take us for? Really. First the nonsense with the van...'

'It wasn't a lie,' Chris muttered.

'And now this. Out of the blue, he has an alibi.' Adam shook his head.

'Look, I didn't want to mention it because she's married,' Chris told them. With a show of reluctance he confessed that he had been having an affair. 'Her husband's a vicious bastard. She's scared of him. I mean, really genuinely scared. She's always worried what he might do to her if he ever finds out we're seeing each other. The thing is, he saw us together one time. Stupidly we met in a café not far from her house, and he drove past and saw us. We might have got away with it only she was scared and lied about where she'd been, so of course he knew something was going on. Since then we've had to be careful. I promised her I'd never tell anyone.' He dropped his head in his hands.

'So it was convenient for you to get your wife out of the way?' Adam remarked.

Chris looked up in surprise. 'If I'd wanted to get her out of the way, as you put it, I'd have asked her for a divorce. I wouldn't have killed her! But Louise is married and...' he sighed. 'We talked about being together but it was all just too complicated. Her husband's threatened to kill himself if she ever leaves him, and she doesn't think he's kidding. So we settle for what we've got: one evening a week at her place, while her husband's out with his mates. It's not ideal. We have to listen out in case he comes back early, but it's the best we can manage, and it's better than nothing. We stay downstairs and keep the back door unlocked, so I can run out if I have to. We figured it would be more risky to meet anywhere else, because she might be seen. Louise is a very special woman, Inspector, but I still love my wife. I know you won't believe me...'

'A man can have an affair without wanting to murder his wife,' the lawyer drawled with a faint smile. 'Think how depleted the population would be if every adulterer did away with his wife. There'd be hardly anyone left! I advised my client to tell you about his alibi right from the start, but he had some naive notion that the truth would speak for itself. Well, now it has come out. My client was with his mistress that night.'

Now that he had confessed to his affair, Chris seemed eager to share the details of his alibi.

'I didn't get home till about half past twelve that night, maybe one o'clock. To be honest, I crept into the bedroom in the dark and just got into bed without even looking to see if Jamie was there.'

'You were in the same bed?'

Chris nodded. 'I'm telling you the truth,' he insisted. 'I got undressed in the dark, with my back to the bed, and then I just slipped under the covers on my side and shut my eyes. The last thing I wanted to do was disturb her and be subjected to all sorts of questions about where I'd been and why I was home so late. When I woke up in the morning, she wasn't there. I thought she'd gone out early. So I went to pick up the van – that was on the Friday afternoon. Louise gave me a lift home on Thursday. You can ask her. I'd got the bus to her place on Thursday night. She'll tell you, it's all true what I'm saying.'

Geraldine took Louise's details and stood up.

'I take it my client can go home now?' the lawyer asked.

Adam shook his head. 'I don't think so. The case against him is compelling.'

'Circumstantial. And he has an alibi.'

'For which we only have his word, and we know he's already lied to us about everything else. He's staying put for now.'

'I'm not lying!' Chris protested. He turned to Geraldine. 'Whatever you do, you have to promise me you won't let anyone else know about me and Louise.'

'Once your alibi's confirmed, you'll walk out of here and no one will ever need to know why,' the lawyer reassured him. 'Be patient, Chris. You'll be out of here soon enough. And the police will be discreet.' He turned and stared pointedly at Geraldine.

'Chris, we're not in the business of causing trouble. We're just trying to get to the truth of what happened to Jamie.'

'Well, it wasn't me,' he muttered crossly. 'I didn't kill her.'

If he was telling the truth, then it was possible he had just provided them with another suspect.

18

As soon as she was back at her desk, Geraldine searched for the woman Chris claimed would provide him with an alibi. He had given her Louise's name and contact details. Geraldine tried the mobile number first, but there was no reply. Next she called the home number without success, before trying the hairdresser's where Louise worked, to discover she was not working that day.

'Of course she's not there today,' Geraldine grumbled to herself as she hung up. 'Nothing's ever that easy.'

Confirming Chris's alibi would have to wait until later. In the meantime, Geraldine faced another job, one she could put off no longer. It would have been perfectly appropriate to delegate the task of speaking to the victim's parents to a local constable, but Geraldine always preferred to pass on such heartbreaking news herself, whenever possible. Her motivation was not solely compassionate. Although she felt she owed it to the victim to see this through, there was always a chance the family might pass on some significant information.

This was the part of her job she hated the most. While many aspects of her work had become easier with experience, this had become more of a challenge. Since the death of the colleague she had fallen in love with, observing other people's grief had become almost unbearably painful. Feeling wretched, she prepared herself to remain outwardly impassive while bearing witness to the human suffering that lay behind the murders she investigated. If each victim's murder ended with the death of that one individual, it would be terrible enough. As it was, every murder wrecked the happiness of so many other people whose lives the victim had touched. One prison sentence wasn't enough to punish most of the killers Geraldine saw put away.

'How do you tell someone a member of their family's dead, in a way that makes it easier for them to hear?' a new constable had asked her recently.

'You can't,' Geraldine had replied.

The victim's parents lived in a three-bedroomed terraced house in East London, off the Romford Road. It wasn't far from Stratford underground station on the Central line, so Geraldine took the train. The sun was shining, and there was a fresh breeze. Under almost any other circumstances she would have enjoyed the walk, but the nearer she drew to her destination, the more dejected she felt. Involuntarily, she slowed down. She felt like some mythical harbinger of death; there should have been a cloud of vultures hovering above her head. Instead, the sun shone as she reached the brick house where Jamie's parents lived. The property was well maintained, with clean white paintwork around the windows and arched porch, and a wooden picket fence bordering the small paved front yard. Two pots of geraniums stood on either side of the porch, their scarlet flowers startling against the wall.

A neat little woman opened the door. Her hair was tied back in a bun on the nape of her neck, and she was wearing an apron. It was probably the effect of the crisp white apron which made her look domesticated, but there was something homely and reassuring about her, as though she ought to be cradling a grandchild in her arms, while a cat wound itself lazily around her ankles. A faintly worried expression crossed her face when Geraldine introduced herself.

'Yes, I'm Phyllis Stockwell. You'd better come in.' She stood back to let Geraldine enter.

'Fred, it's the police,' she called out.

She led her visitor into a small living room. Geraldine was not surprised to find it was clean and tidy. Jamie's father rose to his feet with old fashioned courtesy and waited for her and his wife to take their seats before resuming his. Geraldine wished she had sent someone else to pass on the terrible news. It felt obscene to disturb this pleasant couple with the news that their daughter had been murdered.

Taking a deep breath, she began. 'I'm sorry to be bringing you some very bad news. It's about your daughter, Jamie.'

Mrs Stockwell's eyes widened and her hand flew to her mouth. 'Oh my God, what's she done?'

'She hasn't done anything. I'm afraid she's dead.'

'Dead? What do you mean? How did it happen?' Jamie's father asked.

'I'm so sorry to tell you she was murdered. A suspect is currently helping us with our enquiries.'

The couple looked at each other in consternation.

'So, he finally cracked,' Mrs Stockwell said at last.

Geraldine hid her surprise. 'Who are you talking about?'

'Now, Phyllis, there's no call to go speaking out of turn,' Mr Stockwell warned his wife.

Geraldine repeated her question.

'She just meant that our daughter wasn't an easy woman,' Mr Stockwell answered for his wife.

It was an odd response to the news that their daughter had been murdered, as though they blamed her for what had happened.

'What did you mean, Mrs Stockwell?' Geraldine insisted.

'Chris had a lot to cope with,' Jamie's mother said dully.

'Phyllis, that's enough,' her husband interrupted her.

Geraldine spoke cautiously. 'You don't seem very surprised, if you don't mind my saying.'

'It's the shock,' Mr Stockwell explained. 'It's going to take a while to sink in. And we're not demonstrative people, Inspector. Not everyone likes to make a show of their feelings in front of strangers. But she was our daughter. We'll be grieving for the rest of our lives.'

There was something desperately poignant about his restraint. Geraldine turned to the bereaved mother, hating herself for intruding further on their sorrow.

'Mrs Stockwell, is there anything else you'd like to say? Anything you'd like to tell me?'

'No. She's gone now and there's an end to it, but...'

'But nothing,' her husband interrupted firmly.

His wife hid her face in her hands. 'I can't believe it. I can't believe she's dead,' she mumbled.

'Now, now, Phyllis, try to stay calm.' He looked at Geraldine. 'Thank you for letting us know,' he said, curiously formal. 'Is that what people say? I don't know...'

Geraldine felt uncomfortable having to press them, but she had to ask whether they were suggesting they believed Chris had murdered their daughter. They both shook their heads.

'No,' Mr Stockwell replied. 'No, we don't think he would have done it, do we Phyllis?'

Mrs Stockwell shook her head.

Geraldine asked them to contact her if they thought of anything that might help the police establish the circumstances leading up to their daughter's murder. Assuring them they would be notified of any developments, she left. The Stockwells' reaction on hearing about their daughter's death had been curious. They had shown little grief, and even less surprise. It was almost as though they had been expecting it to happen. And then there was Mrs Stockwell's enigmatic comment about Chris having 'cracked', which made it sound as though Chris had been violent towards his wife. Yet they had been quick to defend him, when Geraldine had asked them outright if they thought he could be guilty of murdering Jamie. She wasn't sure what to make of it all.

19

GERALDINE TRAVELLED BACK TO the police station in the rush hour. After the emotional strain of speaking to Jamie's parents, she stood for half an hour on a crowded train. By the time she finally picked up her car and drove home, she felt drained. Grabbing a dinner out of the freezer, and pouring herself a generous glass of red wine, she collapsed on her sofa and looked on iPlayer to see what was available. She was about to go and put her dinner in the oven when her phone rang.

'Geraldine! I haven't spoken to you for ages!' Celia gushed.

'Listen, I'd love to chat but I've really got to go. I've only just got home and I'm starving. Can we speak tomorrow?'

Celia was accommodating, although Geraldine sensed that she was slightly put out. With a promise that she would call back the next day, Geraldine hung up. She had just put her dinner in the oven when her phone rang again. Muttering irritably under her breath, Geraldine answered.

'Hello. I had a message to call this number.'

'Who is that?'

'Who are you?'

A trifle irritated, Geraldine answered, stressing her job title.

'Oh, that's all right. I wasn't sure if I had the right number. My name's Louise Marshall. You left a message on my phone earlier. What's this about? Only well, I don't know who you are and...'

'Thank you for calling me back,' Geraldine interrupted her. 'You're quite right to be cautious, and you're welcome to go to your nearest police station and ask them to put you through to me, if you're at all concerned. Ask them to contact DI Geraldine Steel of the Metropolitan Police, working on the Cordwell case. That's all you need to say.'

'Cordwell?' Louise sounded frightened. 'I think you've made a mistake. I don't know anyone called Cordwell.'

'A friend of yours, Chris Cordwell, gave us your name. I need to confirm the details of his alibi with you. This has nothing to do with anyone else. Shall I continue?'

'Alibi? I don't understand.'

As briefly as she could, Geraldine explained that Chris had been accused of involvement in a criminal act on Thursday evening.

'He told us he was with you at the time the incident took place. Are you able to confirm that?'

The hesitation on the line was almost palpable.

'He was extremely reluctant to give us your name,' Geraldine added. 'His lawyer had quite a struggle to convince him it was necessary, but he's facing a very serious charge. I don't believe he would have given us your name if it hadn't been necessary.'

'What do you mean, necessary? How could it be necessary?'

'If you aren't able to confirm his alibi, he could be in trouble.'

'Alibi? I don't know what you mean. What alibi?'

'If you can't confirm that Chris was with you on Thursday evening, he could be in serious trouble,' Geraldine repeated patiently.

'How serious?'

'If a jury were to find him guilty, it would mean a mandatory custodial sentence...'

'You mean prison?'

'Yes.'

'Oh, poor Chris. What's happened?.'

'I can't say any more right now, other than to reassure you that we'll be as discreet as possible about your relations with Chris. But for his sake you do need to tell us the truth. Are you prepared to confirm that Chris visited you on Thursday? If he didn't, you only have to say so.'

'Did his wife put you up to this?'

'Louise, I give you my word Chris's wife knows nothing about this telephone call.'

What was more, she never would. That was a cast-iron guarantee.

'If you want to double check who I am, you can go to any police station and ask them to put you through to me. Geraldine Steel of the Metropolitan Police. Or we can meet, if you prefer. But I do need an answer from you.'

'The thing is, I'm not in London right now. I'm in Birmingham. But I'm coming back to London tomorrow evening. My train gets in to Euston at seven fifteen. I could come to see you when I'm back. Only I'd prefer to meet you at a police station, if that's all right with you.'

'Call me when you're back. I'll be waiting for you at the police office in Euston station.'

'OK. But listen,' there was a pause. 'If I tell you, you have to promise me you won't tell anyone.'

'I have to share anything you say with my colleagues on the case. But you have my word we'll be discreet.'

'Yes, of course, I don't mean that. But my husband mustn't find out.'

Geraldine reassured Louise that no one would pass any information on to him. It was self-evident that if Chris went to court, Louise might be summoned to give evidence, but if his alibi checked out, Louise's husband might never need to know.

'Chris *was* with me on Thursday evening.'

'Are you sure?'

'Positive. We see each other every Thursday. He comes to my house. I'd remember if he'd missed a week. Only his wife doesn't know, and nor does my husband. It won't all come out now, will it?'

'If you're telling the truth, there's no reason why this should go any further. Can you confirm his full name and address?'

'Chris Cordwell. I don't know if he has any other names.' She reeled off his address.

'What time was he at your house on Thursday?'

'He always leaves just before midnight. My husband never comes home before one on a Thursday, but Chris leaves earlier, just in case. He gets the bus over and then I sometimes drop him home.'

'Thank you. Can you contact me as soon as you're back in London and we'll arrange for you to make a formal written statement. It can wait until tomorrow. But it is important.'

'OK. And tell Chris I'll be there for him, whatever happens.'

Geraldine logged the details of the conversation. As she was finishing off, her phone rang again. Although she was tired, she was pleased to hear Ian's voice. It was often helpful to mull over cases with him. After turning the oven low, she launched into an account of the suspect in her investigation, and his alibi.

'A case of husbands wanting to murder their wives,' he remarked when she had finished.

'Only two husbands, and we don't know either of them genuinely wanted to kill anyone. It's probably just so much hot air.'

'Like most marriages.'

'Ian, I'm sorry. Are you and Bev still estranged?'

'It's kind of hard not to be when she's run off with another man and is about to have his baby.'

'You could have a paternity test when the baby's born. You don't know for sure it's not yours.'

They discussed Ian's situation briefly, but it was not long before the conversation drifted back to Geraldine's problem.

'The other woman could be lying to protect him,' Ian said.

'That's what Adam thought. The thing is, her story matched his and she volunteered the details without any prompting. Her times matched his before I mentioned anything specific.'

'That doesn't prove anything. They could have got together and concocted a story beforehand.'

'He didn't want to give us her name.'

'And yet he did. All very convincingly done, I daresay, and quite possibly carefully rehearsed in advance. I'm not saying they're lying. It's probably all genuine. I'm just pointing out the possibility that the alibi is fake.'

Geraldine knew he was right but she wasn't going to take Chris's word, or Louise's, without further investigation. First thing in the morning she planned to set a team to work checking whether Chris had travelled by bus that evening, and whether Louise's car had been picked up on camera driving towards Chris's house at around midnight.

'The trouble is,' she told Ian, 'if his alibi stands up to scrutiny, we're back to square one. We have no other suspect.'

Ian could only sympathise with her frustration, but there was nothing else to say. At last, she rang off and fetched her overcooked dinner from the oven. It was dry. She was too tired to eat anyway, but she forced some down before going to bed. It had been a stressful day, and looking into an alibi for their only suspect wasn't going to make the next day any easier.

20

THE ATMOSPHERE AT THE station was subdued on Wednesday morning. They were not quite a week into the investigation so it was early days. Normally no one would have had cause to feel disheartened at this stage of the case, but having thought they had it all sewn up, it was disappointing to face the prospect of having to start out all over again.

'It was him, it was obviously him,' Geraldine overheard Sam insisting to another constable. 'It's always the husband. His alibi's going to come crashing down around his ears soon enough. He might sound plausible – although that's a matter of opinion – but he's lying. He's got to be.'

'Let's not jump to conclusions,' Geraldine interrupted her.

A constable checking the suspect's movements had established that Chris's Oyster card had been used by someone boarding a bus at seven forty on Thursday evening, travelling in the direction of Louise's house. Careful scrutiny of surveillance film from the bus showed a figure who looked like Chris travelling on the bus. While that bore out his story, it didn't prove he had still been out at eleven o'clock that evening. There was plenty of time for him to have returned home to kill his wife.

Louise's car had been spotted by a team studying CCTV footage from cameras along the route. They reported that she had driven at least part of the way along the Holloway Road, away from her own home towards Chris's house, just before midnight. But that didn't prove he had been in the car with her. It was feasible that all their travelling had been a preplanned smokescreen to provide false evidence that Chris had not been home that evening. He and Louise could both be lying. The case against Chris was beginning to look flimsy.

'You mean I'm under house arrest?'

'No. We just need to know where you are.'

Grumbling about police harassment of an innocent man, he had gone home.

'At the moment, the only physical proof of his guilt is the defence wounds found on the victim. There's no question she was fighting her husband off. The evidence of that is incontrovertible. Shreds of his skin under her nails. Fresh scratches on his neck. But we need to find the murder weapon,' Adam said. 'Where the hell is it?'

'He could have buried it in the garden,' a constable suggested.

'His garden or Louise's garden?' someone else asked.

'It might be at the bottom of the lake near Kenwood House,' a sergeant chimed in.

Adam held up his hand. 'Enough. It could be anywhere by now, but wherever it is, we need to find it. There was a gap of two and a half days between her death and his reporting her missing on the Sunday, enough time for him to dispose of it before we knew who she was.'

'He could have given it to Louise to get rid of,' a young constable piped up.

'I said enough speculation about where the murder weapon has gone,' Adam said.

'I was only saying it's possible,' she muttered sullenly.

Geraldine sniffed. As a new constable, she would never have dared answer back to her detective chief inspector like that. Whether it was the contrast between the Met and the Home Counties, or the behaviour of a different generation, young officers seemed to have lost the deference that had been expected of her when she was in her early twenties. On balance, she thought that was detrimental to the disciplined teamwork on which their success depended. She glared at the young constable, who looked away with a careless shrug. That, too, was disrespectful. Geraldine felt uncomfortable. The world of policing seemed to be changing. She wasn't sure she fitted into this new culture.

'If his alibi holds up, we're back to the drawing board,' Sam said.

'We want to find out what happened,' Geraldine told her sharply. 'We're looking for the truth, not for easy answers.'

'The husband's our prime suspect, but we have to be sure he's the right suspect,' Adam agreed. 'And that means finding evidence.'

While the Visual Images, Identification and Detections team continued studying local film from the night of the murder, hoping to establish whether Chris had been in Louise's car after midnight, Geraldine and Sam returned to the garage to double check when the van had been off the road. Tracy was at her desk. She confirmed what the mechanic had told them. Leaving the office, Geraldine was startled to see that the bonnet of her car was open. A figure was sitting in the driving seat.

'What do you think you're doing?' she called out as she ran over, with Sam at her heels.

The mechanic who had helped her on her previous visit climbed out of the car. He looked surprised to see her.

'You?' he said. 'I thought this was here for a service.'

'How did you get in? I left it locked.'

The mechanic jangled a bunch of keys. 'I hope you're not going to charge me with breaking and entering,' he said with an anxious grin. 'It was a mistake. I didn't know you were here.'

Geraldine shrugged. 'I hope you didn't find anything wrong with it.'

'I'd only just got the bonnet open,' he replied, removing the protective sheet of plastic he had spread over the seat.

Geraldine and Sam climbed into the car. Their visit had been a waste of time.

'Let's see what Louise Marshall has to say when she gets back to London,' Geraldine said grimly, 'and if she really can give Chris an alibi.'

'Where's she coming from?'

'Birmingham. Her train gets in to Euston at seven fifteen so I've arranged to meet her at the police station there when she arrives. Why don't you come along?' As Sam hesitated, Geraldine remembered she had a partner waiting for her when she finished for the day. 'Not to worry if you need to get home,' she added as they left the garage forecourt.

'No, of course I'll come. One way or the other, we need to get to the bottom of this.'

Geraldine nodded. For all her occasional loneliness, she couldn't imagine curtailing her commitment to her work for a personal relationship. She wondered if that made her callous, but she dismissed her qualms. For a long time she had felt somehow adrift in her own life. Her confused feelings on meeting her biological sister seemed like a manifestation of that malaise. But before she could spend time trying to forge a relationship with Helena, she had a murder to investigate.

21

ALTHOUGH THE TRAIN JOURNEY back to London was an ideal opportunity to take a nap, Louise didn't doze off, despite her exhaustion. Normally the regular rhythm of the train engine would have lulled her to sleep without any trouble. She had been up very early the day before. Already tired, she had received a disturbing message concerning Chris which had kept her awake nearly all night, worrying. She had no idea what had happened, but being contacted out of the blue like that to discuss an alibi sounded serious. The police inspector had mentioned prison.

She wanted to speak to Chris, but he hadn't answered his mobile. She had been afraid to try his number a second time, in case his wife noticed the calls and became suspicious. She and Chris had a rule that neither of them would try to contact the other more than once a day, at most. It worked both ways. She didn't want her husband to find out about their affair any more than he wanted his wife to know about it. Repeated calls from an unknown number might be enough to provoke suspicion.

By the time Louise had spoken to the police inspector the previous evening, it had been too late to call Chris at work. In the morning she had borrowed a phone from another girl on the course to call his mobile. He hadn't answered. She had tried his work number and was told he wasn't there. That had worried her as much as her conversation with the police. As far as she knew, he had no plans to take any time off work while she was away. Something must have happened, and she wasn't around to help him.

She had been tempted to catch an earlier train back to London, but the cost of buying a train ticket on the day she was travelling was prohibitive. It would have been daft, when she would be back in London that evening anyway. Arriving a few hours earlier hardly warranted the additional expense. Besides, she told herself, Chris would have called if he needed her. She would just have to be patient. While she had been dithering, she had received a message from the conference organisers. They had been asked to inform her that a police driver would meet her at Euston station on her return to London. That clinched it. She stuck to her original travel plans.

At last her train arrived at Euston station. As she passed through the ticket barrier, a man approached her. He was wearing an official-looking peaked cap that hid the top of his face, and his mouth was hidden beneath a beard and moustache.

'Louise Marshall?' he enquired in a gruff voice.

'Yes. They told me you'd be here.'

'This way.'

Without waiting for a response, the driver seized the handle of her case and began walking away with it. Louise trotted after him. Tired and anxious, she was relieved that she didn't have to find her own way to the police station.

'I'm a bit surprised they sent you to get me. It must be important,' she said. 'What's it all about?'

She wasn't sure if the driver heard what she said to him. He was walking so fast, she had to hurry to keep up. Out of breath, and weary from travelling and the stress of worrying about Chris, she decided to wait until they were in the car to speak to him again. He strode round the corner from the station, pulling her case for her. Reaching a car park, he walked quickly past the entrance and led her to a dark car. It looked quite old, but she supposed the police were having to economise on everything, including their transport. Public spending cutbacks were constantly in the news. Given the current situation, it was amazing that they could afford to send a car for her at all. At the same time, it increased her anxiety. The inspector must be very keen to speak to her as soon as possible, to justify the expense. It was not just the car, but the driver's time that would be costing money as well.

Tossing her case in the boot, the driver opened the passenger door for her. When they were both seated, and she had thanked him again for picking her up, the driver told her to turn off her phone.

'Can I just call my husband and let him know I'm on my way home? I mean, this won't take long, will it? Only I don't want him to worry.'

What she really meant was that she didn't want him to become suspicious about her movements.

'There's no need, we'll soon be at the police station. You can call him from there.'

'I'd like to just give him a ring…'

The driver frowned. 'Best not to,' he said quietly.

There was something vaguely familiar about his voice. It reminded her of someone, but she couldn't think who it was.

'This is an unmarked police vehicle,' he added. 'If you switch your mobile phone on, it can interfere with communications from the command centre.'

'Oh, I'm sorry.'

She took her phone out of her bag. Before she could turn it off, the driver leaned over and took it out of her hand. Ignoring her protest, he switched it off and deftly removed the SIM card before dropping the phone in the pocket of his door.

'It'll be returned to you at the police station,' he assured her.

They drove out of the car park in silence. Unable to fight off her weariness any longer, Louise leaned back in her seat and closed her eyes. Whatever trouble Chris was in, she would soon be at the police station and everything would be cleared up. There was nothing she could do about it until then. She tried to relax, but the whole situation was worrying. Looking out of her window, she didn't recognise where they were. She hesitated to ask where they were going because the driver was so surly, but she wanted to know where he was taking her. They had left the car park about twenty minutes ago.

'Er, when I spoke to the inspector yesterday, she told me she'd meet me at the police station at Euston?' When the driver gave no response, she went on. 'So I wondered why we're going somewhere else?'

'They wouldn't have sent me to pick you up if they just wanted you to go round the corner,' he said at last.

'Yes, that's what I thought. I just wondered where we're going.'

Again, there was no answer. Louise decided the driver was odd, but that wasn't her problem. All she had to do was meet the inspector as arranged, answer a few questions, sign a statement, and be driven home. After a disturbed night, she couldn't wait to fall asleep in her own bed. The last few days had been hectic. It was nice to be sitting in a car being driven wherever she had to go. She supposed this was how rich people lived, taking taxis or employing chauffeurs. With a sigh, she leaned back and closed her eyes again, soothed by the gentle purr of the engine. She would be woken up when they arrived.

22

ALTHOUGH SHE WAS ANNOYED, Geraldine was not unduly surprised when Louise Marshall failed to turn up for their appointment at the police station in Euston. She was used to members of the public proving unreliable. This was by no means the first time a witness had lost her nerve about speaking to the police, or been confused about times, or had simply forgotten to come forward. She tried Louise's number but her phone was unresponsive, neither ringing nor diverting to voicemail. There was no need to go storming round to her house, stirring up trouble. As far as Geraldine knew, Louise's husband still knew nothing about his wife's affair. If Louise was careful, he might never find out. Geraldine would have to wait until the morning to contact her. Another day made no difference to her.

When she arrived home that evening Geraldine tried Louise's number once more, but it was still dead. The following morning, she had the same response. Instead of going to her office, she drove straight to Louise's house, off the Holloway Road. It was not far from where Geraldine lived. No one answered the door. She was no longer sure what to make of Louise's reluctance to confirm the story she had given over the phone the previous day. Chris's alibi was looking shakier by the hour.

'Not much of a love affair,' Geraldine muttered crossly when Adam quizzed her about her telephone conversation with Louise. 'She seemed so keen to give him his alibi, and now this. She's just buggered off and left him in the lurch.'

'Which means she was probably lying in the first place,'

Adam replied, 'if it really was Louise Marshall you were talking to, and if she really was his mistress. We only have his word for that.'

'And hers.'

'Based on one short phone call with a woman who could have been anyone.'

Determined to get to the bottom of it, Geraldine checked the address of Louise's workplace. The hair salon where she worked was in Camden High Street. Leaving her car at the police station, she took the train to Camden. The salon was not far away. A heavily made up girl greeted her, casting an eye over Geraldine's hair as she spoke.

'Have you been here before?'

Without introducing herself, Geraldine explained that she wanted to see Louise.

'Are you a regular of hers? Or has she been recommended to you? She's not in today, but I've got another girl who's free.' She looked at Geraldine's hair again with a faint frown. 'Is it colour you're after?'

It could hardly be a haircut. Geraldine's short dark hair had recently been trimmed.

'Is she out all day?' Geraldine asked. 'Is she in tomorrow? Can I make an appointment to see her tomorrow morning?'

The girl checked her appointment book. 'Ten o'clock tomorrow?'

Geraldine made the booking and left. She had found out what she needed to know. Louise was due back at work the next day. If Geraldine couldn't contact her at home before the next morning, she would return to the salon and speak to her there.

Adam was as annoyed as Geraldine. 'So she's giving us the run around? Oh well, I don't suppose it'll do Chris any harm to stay locked up for another day. His lawyer's been hounding me about letting him go, but he'll just have to wait.'

'Why doesn't he track down his client's witness himself and

bring her in to make her statement, if he's so desperate to get him released?'

It was a pity. The case against Chris would be virtually watertight were it not for the one fly in the ointment, Louise Marshall. Geraldine wished she would turn up and sign a statement to confirm his alibi, or else refute it. Either way, they needed to know.

'If we're going to have to start all over again, I just want to get on with it,' she grumbled to Sam.

'It's like a Sherlock Holmes mystery. The Case of the Disappearing Witness!'

'It's nothing like Sherlock Holmes,' Geraldine snapped. 'This isn't a story. This is serious. Now get back to work.'

With a grin, Sam left. Geraldine turned back to her monitor but it was difficult to start all over again, reviewing the evidence to look for a culprit, with Chris still in custody as their number one suspect. Looking elsewhere was likely to prove a complete waste of time. Geraldine went to see how the Visual Images, Identification and Detections Officers were progressing and found two officers gossiping about one of their colleagues.

'Well, Nancy said he was seen out with her again and this time...'

Catching sight of Geraldine, they fell silent and turned back to their screens. There was no point in Geraldine chastising them for procrastinating when that was what she was doing herself. The atmosphere was the same when she went to see whether the borough intelligence unit had found anything useful.

'We need to find Louise Marshall,' she said firmly, but unnecessarily.

They all knew the situation.

'Where the hell is she?' Geraldine demanded. 'She's not answering her phone, she's not answering her door, she's not at work. Where is she?'

She rarely let her feelings get the better of her at work, but she was struggling to hide her frustration.

'We've got patrols keeping an eye out, and security teams at all the shopping centres have got her description. We'll find her. Sooner or later she's got to surface. She must be somewhere,' one of the borough intelligence officers said.

'But where?' Geraldine turned on her heel and left them to it.

She remembered Celia envying her exciting life, but police work was not generally drama and danger. Mostly it was thankless hard graft.

On her way back to her office, she was stopped by a young sergeant.

'I was just coming to see you,' he said.

'Well, I've saved you the bother. What's up?'

He reached into his pocket and took something out. 'I was in the car you were using yesterday, and when I moved the seat back I noticed this on the floor under the driver's seat. You must have dropped it.'

'What is it?'

'I don't know. It looks like some sort of baby listening device.'

Geraldine's own laughter sounded hollow to her. 'Then it's definitely not mine. Someone else must have dropped it before I used the car. You'll have to find out who was driving it before me.'

Feeling unaccountably rattled, she continued along the corridor. Celia had confessed to feeling nervous about expecting her second child past the age of forty. Even if Geraldine were to meet a partner that night, she would be past forty if she ever tried to conceive. Time had all but run out for her. Not that she wanted a child, but knowing that it would soon no longer be possible was a sobering thought. Reminding herself crossly that she had never hankered after having a family, she dismissed the thought. Reaching her office, she wasn't sure whether she was pleased to see that her colleague, Neil Roberts, was back. Young and attractive, he looked up from his work with an easy smile as she walked in.

'Fancy a spot of lunch?'

She liked Neil but somehow his relaxed welcome irritated her.

'Sorry, Neil, but I just don't have time.'

'No worries,' he replied, still smiling. 'Let's take a rain check on lunch. Congratulations on your success anyway.' He turned back to his desk.

'What? Sorry, Neil, but I'm up against a brick wall with this investigation.'

He turned to her, his blue eyes troubled. 'I thought you'd made an arrest.'

Geraldine sat down and told him about Chris's alibi.

'So if the alibi checks out, he's out of the frame?'

She shrugged. It was all so complicated. That evening she went back to Louise's home and rang the bell. Once again no one opened the door. The investigation seemed to have reached a temporary impasse. She felt slightly hypocritical. She had often warned Sam against wanting to rush, and now she was being impatient herself. She decided to try again in the morning and if there was still no answer, she would check out Tom Marshall's number and call him, before returning to the hair salon. Frustrated, she went home. There was nothing else she could do that evening. She was nearly home when her phone rang. Excited, she answered, but it was not Louise.

'I wondered if you're free this evening?' Sam offered to drive over to Islington, where Geraldine lived. 'Why don't I park outside your flat, and we can walk down to the main road and get something to eat?'

There were plenty of restaurants along Upper Street. About to reply that she was tired, Geraldine answered that she was on her way home and had nothing planned.

When they had ordered their food, Sam asked Geraldine what was wrong.

'It's your mother isn't it?'

'Well, she's dead and buried now.'

'I thought she was being cremated?'

'Yes, well, same difference. She's gone.'

'Do you want to talk about it?'

'There's nothing to say. She's dead. In any case, it's not as if I even knew her.'

'I don't suppose that makes it any easier.'

'Anyway, it's not that.' Geraldine hesitated.

'What is it then? If something's bothering you, you really need to speak to someone. It doesn't have to be me.'

'Is it that obvious?'

'Only to me. I'm your friend, Geraldine. You know that, don't you? And all I'm saying is, as your friend, that if you're disturbed about something, it's best to talk it over with someone.'

Geraldine frowned. 'You think I ought to speak to a counsellor? Is that what you're trying to say?'

Sam shrugged. 'I've no idea. You won't tell me what's bothering you, so I've no idea what it is. Maybe it's nothing. If you're fed up with me pestering you about it, just say.'

Seeing how worried Sam was, Geraldine gave in and told her about Helena. 'This goes no further,' she added, regretting having shared her secret as soon as she had disclosed it.

'A twin? Oh my God! And you met her for the first time at your mother's funeral? That must be so unsettling. No wonder you've been distracted.' She paused. 'Are you identical?'

Geraldine thought about the sallow-skinned skeletal figure she had seen at the crematorium. Puffing on a cigarette, her eyes bloodshot, her fingernails bitten to the quick, her features were nevertheless familiar.

'Probably,' she replied.

'Probably? I thought you met her.' Sam frowned. 'But wasn't

it amazing? I mean, I know the circumstances could've been better, but a twin! I'd love to have a twin.'

'I think one like you is quite enough! The trouble is,' Geraldine went on more seriously, 'I don't know if I want to risk a relationship with her, which makes it awkward.'

'But don't you even want to find out about her? Meet her properly? It must have been weird, meeting at the funeral.'

When Geraldine described her twin, Sam gave her a curious look.

'Wouldn't your eyes be red if the mother you'd grown up with had just died?'

The waitress brought their food and the conversation faltered.

'Sorry, I didn't mean to pry,' Sam said at last, 'it's only that you've seemed so fed up lately.'

'It's just the case.'

'Yes, of course.'

They both knew that wasn't true, but Sam understood that Geraldine didn't want to talk about her sister any more. Neither of them mentioned Helena again, and they left soon after. Geraldine wondered if Sam was right. Perhaps she was being unfair, hesitating to have anything to do with her sister. But having met her, Geraldine could see why her mother had been worried. Helena was clearly in need of support. If nothing else, Geraldine could at least try to persuade social services to step in. But before she could seek help for her sister, she had work to do.

23

EARLY THE FOLLOWING DAY, Geraldine went to Louise's house again. Even at that time in the morning, the traffic was heavy along the Holloway Road. It was a quarter past seven when she rang the bell. The man who came to the door looked dishevelled and tired.

'Where the hell have you been...' he began and broke off in surprise, catching sight of Geraldine on his doorstep.

'Are you Tom Marshall?'

'Yes. Who are you?'

When Geraldine introduced herself, he grew anxious. 'What's this about? What's happened?'

'I'd like a word with your wife.'

He looked more surprised than ever. 'What do you mean?'

'Is your wife at home?'

'No. I thought... when you showed me your warrant card...'

'Where is she?'

'That's what I'd like to know.' Good-looking in a rugged kind of way, he had an overhanging brow and square chin that jutted out further as he spoke. 'She told me she was going to Birmingham on Monday, for a training course for her hair dressing. She was supposed to be home on Wednesday but she never showed up, and now I can't get hold of her. I don't know what's happened to her. I was thinking of contacting you lot today. If she'd been taken ill and is in hospital in Birmingham, someone would have contacted me, wouldn't they? What's happened to her? Do you think she's run off with some bloke?' He frowned. 'And what are you doing here?'

'I'm afraid I've no idea where your wife is, Mr Marshall. I came here looking for her.'

Adam shrugged when Geraldine told him that Louise had disappeared. 'That's that then,' he said. 'She's done a runner. So much for Cordwell's alibi. Let's see what he has to say for himself now.'

With Chris back in a police cell, and a team working on enhancing every frame of film they had of Louise's car on the night of the murder, Geraldine began to search for the missing woman in earnest. If they could definitely rule out Chris's alibi, they were virtually assured of a conviction. Until they had a statement from Louise, there was always a risk of her turning up and upsetting their case against him all over again.

After alerting the police in Birmingham, and the British Transport Police, Geraldine returned to the hair salon in Camden where Louise worked. The same girl was on the desk.

'Hello, it's Geraldine, isn't it? You were here yesterday asking for Louise, weren't you?'

Geraldine held her breath.

'I'm afraid she's not here again today. But if you want to be seen before the weekend, Shelley's here, and she's fabulous. I'm sure you'll be very pleased with her...'

'No, that's fine thank you.' Throwing caution to the wind, she handed the girl one of her cards. 'Please let me know as soon as Louise turns up. I need to find her. It's extremely important.'

'Detective Inspector,' the girl read aloud. 'The police are after Louise? I don't believe it.'

'No, no, not at all. We just need to ask her about something she might have witnessed. She's not a suspect. But I do need to speak to her as soon as possible.'

The girl nodded dumbly, but her eyes were alight with excitement. There was no point in asking her to be discreet.

With nothing further to go on, Geraldine made her way back to the police station. Shortly after she reached her desk,

Sam knocked on her door. The British Transport Police had confirmed that Louise Marshall had boarded her train to London on Wednesday evening and arrived at Euston station at seven fifteen as planned.

'Are they sure it was her?'

'Yes, pretty sure. Her picture was picked out by the train guard, although he only saw her briefly and could have been mistaken, but she was also apparently picked up on CCTV at Euston.'

'I want to see that film.'

'The VIIDO team are working on it right now.'

Without another word, the two of them hurried along the corridor. Sitting down on either side of a VIIDO officer, they watched the film through several times, piecing together what was happening. By enhancing the image, and using facial recognition software, it was possible to identify Louise Marshall among figures virtually indistinguishable with the naked eye. As she passed through the barrier, she stopped to talk to a man whose face was almost entirely concealed beneath a peaked cap. All that showed clearly beneath it was a dark beard.

'Is it just me, or has he disguised his face?' Sam said.

'Do you think he's wearing a false beard?' the VIIDO officer replied.

'Where did she go next?' Geraldine asked.

They carried on watching. The man took Louise's case and she followed him out of the station.

'This was a prearranged meeting,' Geraldine said.

'Not necessarily,' the VIIDO officer told her. 'Look at this.'

She rewound the tape a short way and enlarged a few frames. The man could be seen putting a piece of paper in his pocket.

'What is it?'

'Wait.'

The officer picked one of the frames and enlarged it until they could read what was written on the paper.

'Oh my God, he was waiting for her,' Sam said. 'He was holding a sign with her name on it. So she didn't know him.'

Geraldine and Sam exchanged puzzled glances.

'A stranger who went to pick her up. Who the hell was he? How did he know she was going to be there? Where did they go?' Geraldine asked, leaning forward impatiently.

The film shifted from the station footage to a street camera that showed them crossing the road. If it hadn't been for the case the man was dragging along, it would have been impossible to track their progress along the crowded street. As it was, following them was tricky. There were several pedestrians pulling luggage, and more than once Geraldine realised she was watching the wrong blurry figure. After a few minutes, their two subjects entered a car park. Once again the film altered but the VIIDO officer had done a brilliant job of picking them up again. Climbing into an old car, they drove out of the car park. Leaving the city centre, the driver headed for the suburbs.

'He drove west along the North Circular Road but we lost him in the back streets in Edgware,' the VIIDO officer said. 'We're looking for him. He can't stay out of sight forever.'

'So we got the car registration number?'

'Yes.'

Geraldine and her colleagues exchanged a smile. Sam went to follow it up and Geraldine watched the film again. Before long Sam returned, looking dejected. The registration number belonged to a car that had been written off and sent to a scrapyard a couple of weeks ago. They checked the information Sam had been given against the car in the film. The registration numbers matched. Someone had removed the number plates before crushing the car to which they belonged. Whoever had picked Louise up at Euston couldn't be traced through the vehicle he was driving.

Geraldine brought Adam up to speed. She had already made a detailed report of the latest development, but they both liked to discuss what was happening.

'So what exactly do we know about this man who met Louise at Euston?'

'Only what we can glean from the CCTV film. I'm going to get an estimate of his height and weight, and compare an analysis of his posture and gait with Chris's, and also check out her husband's height and weight, because he knew she was arriving back at Euston on Wednesday evening.'

'Surely Louise would have recognised her lover or her husband if one of them met her at the station?'

'Maybe she did. They could be in on this together. We don't know where Chris was on Wednesday evening. We don't know what he might have been up to. And we don't know where her husband was on Wednesday evening either.'

'So it could have been either of them,' Adam said. 'Tom, or Chris, or someone else entirely. She could have chosen to disappear, or been taken away and silenced. We have absolutely no idea what happened to her.'

'We know she was driven to Edgware. We have to discover where she went from there.'

'Well, let's get hold of that information before we question either of them again. It's all well and good, detectives on the television claiming to know when people are lying, but here in the real world we can only really guess. And that won't get us very far in front of a prosecuting barrister.'

Geraldine smiled. 'It would make our job a lot easier if we could read people's minds!'

'Let's get the results of those analyses. We need some verifiable information, not just speculation.'

It sounded like a criticism, even though Adam had been speculating as much as her. When he nodded at the door to dismiss her, she was momentarily irritated by his peremptory tone. Remembering that he had only recently been promoted to detective chief inspector, and was not much older than her, Geraldine relented.

'Don't worry,' she said, 'we'll sort out this mess soon enough.'

Intending to reassure her senior officer, she was afraid her words sounded patronising. Without waiting for a response, she turned and left his office. Sam agreed with Geraldine that Louise must have arranged to be picked up at Euston so she could disappear. They went over the possibilities. Louise's husband had known she was due in at Euston at seven fifteen. Geraldine wondered if he could have picked her up in disguise, so the CCTV cameras at the station wouldn't reveal his identity.

'But why would her husband be in on it?' Sam asked. 'I thought the reason she didn't want to come forward in the first place was because she didn't want him to find out about her affair?'

'Maybe she confessed, or she could have made up some story to get her husband to spirit her away, in disguise. Until we find her, we won't know what's going on. But we do know she got cold feet about giving Chris an alibi. Is that because she's afraid of her husband finding out, or because she was lying about being with Chris on the night of the murder?'

'I don't think it was her husband,' Sam said.

'We need to find her.'

'She can't stay hidden away forever.'

Geraldine stepped up the search for the missing witness, circulating her picture to all police forces and security guards across the UK. Despite her reassuring words to Adam, she was worried. With Louise's refusal to stand by her story, their suspect was as good as convicted. The case was solved. Geraldine should have been pleased, but her brief phone conversation with a woman claiming to be Louise kept playing on her mind.

24

THAT EVENING GERALDINE DECIDED to question Louise's neighbours, in case anyone had seen her since her return to London. Meanwhile Sam was going to fetch Chris and bring him to the police station where his walking could be filmed. A search warrant had been issued, and a team were being despatched to go through every inch of Chris's house. It was a long shot, but they were hoping the search team would find a false beard and peaked cap.

'It would certainly help,' Sam said.

She looked excited at the thought of discovering the disguise worn by the man who had picked Louise up at Euston.

'If it *was* Chris,' Geraldine replied.

None of them were really in any doubt about Chris's guilt now that his witness had vanished, but Geraldine couldn't understand why Chris would want Louise to disappear when she was the only person who could give him an alibi. Sam thought that was obvious. Louise was getting cold feet and Chris wanted to persuade her to back up his alibi, whether or not it was true.

'That just sounds a bit far-fetched. I mean, her husband's already wanting to know where she is, and Chris and Louise were desperate to keep their affair a secret, weren't they? Something about this is all beginning to feel a bit odd.'

Crawling along in the early evening traffic, Geraldine decided she might as well speak to Tom Marshall again after questioning his neighbours. Although he only lived three miles away from her, unless she went to see him in the middle of the night, the journey through heavy traffic was tedious. Turning off the Holloway Road, she parked at the end of the Marshalls' road and began knocking on the doors on either side of their house, before moving on to houses further away. No one she spoke to seemed at all interested in talking to her. Several of the neighbours had no idea who Louise was. The questioning proved a complete waste of time.

Finally she rang the doorbell of the Marshalls' small terraced house. Tom came to the door straight away.

'Have you found her?' he demanded, his face creased in a worried frown.

'We're looking for her.'

She hesitated to admit the police were taking his wife's disappearance seriously, but his suspicions were already aroused.

'I don't get it,' he said. 'Louise went missing on Wednesday night, barely two days ago. Why is a detective inspector interested in my wife's running off? I would have thought you'd have more important things to worry about, like looking for criminals.'

Geraldine nodded. 'You're quite right. Looking for her would normally be a matter for the missing persons' bureau, nothing to do with us. We wouldn't be investigating your wife's disappearance at all if we didn't think she could help us. We need to speak to her in relation to another matter, a serious crime.'

Tom stared at her. 'You mean she's a witness? An eye witness to a crime? And now she's disappeared.' His expression altered and he took a step forward. 'Jesus Christ, do you think someone's bumped her off to silence her? I had no idea. I thought she'd run off and left me. What happened? What did she see?'

'No, Mr Marshall, you've got this all wrong. Please, calm down. Your wife didn't witness a crime. No one wants to silence her. We think she might be able to help us with our enquiries by confirming one of our suspects' alibis.'

Tom paused, thinking. 'You mean some woman's been accused of bumping off her bloke, and she told you Lou was cutting her hair when the murder took place?'

'Something very like that, yes.'

'Was that in Birmingham? And where is Lou?'

'That's what we'd like to know. But the fact that a serious crime is involved means that she might be in some danger without knowing it, so we need to find her as soon as possible.'

'Something's happened to her, hasn't it?' he replied. 'She's disappeared. Something's happened. That's why she's gone missing, isn't it? Christ, I thought she'd run off and left me, but she's never gone off like that before, and now, just when she's needed to give some poor woman an alibi, she's disappeared. She's in trouble, isn't she? You've got to find her.'

Geraldine assured him they were doing their best.

'There are a few questions you could help us with,' she went on cautiously.

He nodded, staring eagerly at her. 'What? What? Tell me!'

'First of all, can you tell me how tall you are?'

He looked surprised by the question. 'What?'

'How tall are you?'

'Just over six foot. Why?'

'Can you be more specific?'

'What? No. You'll be wanting to know my shoe size next.'

'That would be useful, yes.'

He frowned. 'Eleven.'

'Thank you.'

'What the hell's that got to do with my wife?'

As vaguely as she could, Geraldine gave a convoluted account of how Louise had been sighted on CCTV accompanied by a man.

By now Tom's eyes were almost hidden by his heavy brow. 'OK, I get it. This guy she was with has abducted her to stop her giving someone an alibi, and you want to find out if it was me.'

'We need to eliminate you from our enquiries,' Geraldine admitted. There was no point in trying to pretend otherwise.

'Well, it wasn't me who took her. I don't know where she is. But I want you to tell me where she was seen. And when. I'll find the bastard who's taken her, if you don't get on with it. Bloody hell, what have you been doing? Find him! Why are you wasting time talking to me? I don't know where she is, do I?'

Geraldine found his protest convincing. Nevertheless, she intended to reserve her judgement until she received corroboration that Tom and the bearded man at Euston station could not be one and the same man.

'One more question, please. Where were you between seven and eight on Wednesday evening?'

He gave a surly smile. 'I was at home, on my own, waiting for my wife to call me to say she was on her way back to Holloway station and did I want to walk down and meet her, and help her with her luggage. And no, there's no one who can confirm that because I was here on my own.'

Hoping to catch him out in a lie, she asked whether he had been at home on his own the following evening as well. She knew he hadn't answered the door.

'Thursday? I was playing cards with some friends. We meet every Thursday.'

He gave her contact details for his three friends, assuring her they would confirm his whereabouts on Thursday evening. Thanking him, Geraldine left. Once again, her enquiries had been fruitless. While Louise continued hiding herself away, Chris's alibi remained unconfirmed.

25

UNSHAVEN, PASTY-FACED AND PUFFY-EYED, Chris glared at Geraldine across the interview table. Considering what he had been through, she shouldn't have been shocked at the change in his appearance. All the same, she was dismayed at how ghastly he looked. It was not so much his soiled clothes and dishevelled appearance that surprised her as the furtive air he had acquired. She tried to think back to her initial impression of him when he had arrived at the police station to report his wife missing. He had seemed worried and uneasy, and had been a bit of a mess, but he hadn't looked guilty. If she had met him for the first time now, her conclusions might have been very different. It was hard not to be influenced by his bedraggled presence, however hard she tried to remain impartial.

Attempting to analyse her response to Chris's appearance, she wondered whether she had been unfair to her twin sister. After all, as Sam had pointed out, it was natural that Helena's eyes should look red at her mother's funeral. Helena had been brought up by their birth mother. Geraldine should have taken that into account. Preoccupied by her own concerns, she was afraid she had judged her sister too harshly. She had already resolved to redress that, but now she wondered if waiting until the investigation was complete was just procrastinating. She decided to contact Helena after work and arrange to meet her that weekend. They could meet on neutral territory. There was no need for Geraldine to divulge her address straight away. She felt nervous yet unexpectedly relieved by her decision, as though a weight had lifted from her shoulders. She must have been feeling guilty without even realising it, not least because she had been ignoring her mother's dying wish that she look out for her sister.

A constable had been despatched to the scrapyard with a photograph of Chris, in hopes that someone would remember seeing him there. Everyone who worked at the scrapyard was shown the photograph and the same question was put to each of them. But the fact that no one remembered seeing him didn't prove that he had never been there.

'What about a bloke with a big black beard?' the constable had asked.

'We get some blokes with beards, yes,' the manager had replied.

It was pointless. Without anyone recognising Chris from his photograph, they couldn't prove he had been there. All Geraldine could do was try and bluff a confession out of him.

'You took some licence plates off a wrecked car,' she hazarded.

Chris looked puzzled. He shook his head but didn't answer. His lawyer leaned over and murmured to him. Chris shook his head again and muttered in reply. Geraldine couldn't hear what either of them said, but she could imagine the conversation. After a brief exchange, inaudible to everyone but the two men, the lawyer looked directly at Geraldine.

'Is my client now being accused of stealing car parts? He has no idea what you're referring to. Whatever next, Inspector? Are you going to accuse him of joy riding? What on earth would he want with car licence plates?'

Chris looked scared, but the lawyer knew she was just casting about, hoping to snare a confession. If she had any proof, she would have produced it by now.

'Is this accusation based on any evidence?' the lawyer pressed on.

Geraldine turned to Chris. 'Do you admit to removing the licence plates from a car at a scrapyard?'

'No, no, I didn't do anything of the sort,' Chris said. 'I never stole any licence plates. I never stole anything from a car. I don't know what you're talking about. I've never even been to a scrapyard.'

Still hoping to catch Chris unawares, Geraldine threw out her next question without pausing. Conscious of the lawyer watching her through half-closed eyes, she knew an ill-considered response was unlikely. If Chris was unsure what to say, he would turn to his lawyer for advice. Nevertheless, she pressed on.

'What happened to your wife, Chris?''

He shrugged miserably. 'I don't know. I don't know. I don't know what's happened since… since she was taken'

It was a slightly odd turn of phrase.

'Taken from you?'

'Killed,' he said quietly.

'It's painful for my client to acknowledge,' the lawyer chipped in without opening his eyes fully.

'Were you thinking about Louise when you said she was taken?' Geraldine asked.

'What do you mean?' Chris looked round at his lawyer who shrugged his wide shoulders and sat, poised to intervene. 'What's happened to Louise?' Chris sounded as though he might burst into tears.

'She's missing.'

'Oh my God. What are you saying? Has Louise been killed as well?'

'We don't know what's happened to her.'

Once again, Chris looked so pitiful Geraldine would have felt sorry for him if he hadn't been suspected of murdering his wife. Psychopaths could be very convincing. She refused to allow him to engage her sympathy.

'She was your alibi,' the lawyer muttered, audibly this time.

'Where is she?' Chris asked, in apparent bewilderment.

Geraldine asked him again where he had been at the time of

his wife's murder. Seeing Chris's distress, the lawyer insisted on taking a break.

'I need to talk to my client,' he said firmly. 'If his witness has gone missing, you should be considering who might stand to gain from her disappearance.'

'If she really is a witness to his alibi,' Geraldine replied.

'You know she is. You spoke to her yourself on the phone,' the lawyer blustered, but he appreciated the gravity of the situation. 'I need to speak to my client,' he repeated.

Before they stood up to leave, Geraldine told Chris that his house was being thoroughly searched. If there was any shred of evidence to link him to the death of his wife, or the disappearance of his mistress, the search team would find it.

'Find Louise,' was all he said in response. 'Please, find Louise.'

As soon as Geraldine arrived home, after a thoroughly unsatisfactory day, she called the mobile number registered to her sister's name. The line had been disconnected. On a hunch, she tried the number still registered in her mother's name and Helena answered.

'Is that Helena?'

'Who's that?'

Geraldine felt an unpleasant sensation, as though her stomach was dropping. 'It's Erin.'

Geraldine focused on keeping her voice steady as she had been trained to do in situations of extreme stress.

'Erin who?'

'Erin your sister.'

'Oh yeah. What you after? She didn't leave anything, nothing worth having.'

If their mother had owned anything of value, Geraldine suspected Helena would have sold it by now. She frowned, mentally chastising herself for jumping to conclusions about her sister again.

'I'm not after anything,' she said quickly.

'Oh yeah? What you phoning for then?'

Helena's speech was slightly slurred. She was probably drunk. Geraldine regretted not having poured herself a large glass of wine before making the call. She kept going.

'I thought we might meet?'

'Why?'

'Because we're sisters, for God's sake, twins. It's not my fault we've never met before. I really tried to meet my – our mother, but she didn't want to know. And I only found out about you after she died. Until then I didn't even know you existed. I just want to meet you and maybe we can – I don't know, I just thought maybe we could meet. Helena? Helena? Are you still there?'

She was not sure at what point Helena had hung up.

26

DISTRESSED ABOUT HER TWIN sister, Geraldine slept little. Sam's comment bothered her. She should have been more sympathetic towards her sister at the funeral. Because Geraldine had never had an opportunity to get to know their mother herself, somehow she had underestimated her sister's grief. Helena's experience in losing their mother had been very different to her own. Although Geraldine hadn't been deliberately insensitive, she couldn't help feeling guilty.

Disturbed by the hostility that had sprung up between them, she resolved to continue making friendly overtures. It was going to take time to develop a relationship with her sister, who seemed as wary of entering into a relationship as Geraldine was. If an unknown sibling had treated her as coldly as she had treated Helena at the cremation, Geraldine might also have rejected any subsequent approach. No longer suspecting her sister of wanting to take advantage of her, she was keen to gain Helena's trust.

Saturday morning brought a setback when a member of the Visual Images, Identification and Detections team assured them that the bearded man who had met Louise at Euston station was under six feet. The officer passing on the information had very straight fair hair cut in a neat bob, with a long fringe. Peering at them with bright blue eyes, she looked no more than twenty, but she spoke with an air of authority that suggested she was considerably older. For most of the film it was impossible to be precise about the bearded man's measurements as he was leaning forward or moving around, but there were three or four frames where he was clearly standing up straight. In addition, it had apparently been possible to work out his shoe size.

'Are you sure?' Geraldine asked. 'His shoe size? Really? I mean, there's no room for error, is there? This isn't just informed guesswork?'

The officer explained that, by measuring the length of the bearded man's feet when he was standing beside objects whose dimensions were known, they were able to ascertain that his shoes were size eleven. Geraldine was surprised it was possible to gauge the measurement so exactly. It was also frustrating. Chris was five foot nine, but his shoes were size ten. Tom wore size eleven shoes, but he was over six foot tall. The evidence seemed to rule them both out.

'Are you quite sure the man Louise met at Euston station was under six foot?' Adam asked.

'Yes. He's standing upright in several frames so we were able to measure his height to within an inch. He's about five ten.'

'About?' Geraldine repeated, exasperated. 'How can you be more specific about his shoe size than his height?'

The blond woman gave a tolerant smile. 'He's no more than five eleven, and no less than five nine. That's as specific as we can be on the basis of the information we've been able to gather from enhancing the images. But he's definitely not six foot. We viewed several shots of him standing upright.'

'So you're quite sure he's under six foot?'

'Yes, quite sure.'

'Chris wears size ten shoes,' Adam said gloomily.

'Oh, the man in this CCTV film isn't the one you've been questioning,' the blond officer officer replied cheerfully. 'We're sure of that. We compared the films of them walking. It's possible to match walking patterns very reliably these days, and gait has become a really useful clue to identity. An advantage of gait recognition is that we can ascertain identity from a distance, so it's useful even where the image resolution is quite low, like you have here. We took the walking pattern from the CCTV film and mapped it onto your suspect's walking pattern. The mapping's done electronically so there's no room for error. We're able to examine standard measures like stride length and speed, and any distinctive elements relating to the physiology of the individual, slightly unequal limb lengths or a turned-out femur, individual characteristics like that. You'd be surprised how many different features distinguish people when they walk. It's not just stride, but the way the head is held, the slope of the shoulders, the hand movements, there are multiple permutations that make everyone distinctive. When you factor in posture, it's really not that difficult to identify gait, especially in summer. If the man we were watching had been wearing a long raincoat, for example, his posture might have been more difficult to observe. As it is, we can be certain your suspect and the man you filmed at Euston station are different people.'

'How sure are you?'

'Enough to testify in court that it's not a match. From the gait alone the recognition software's well over ninety per cent accurate, but taking the suspect's height into account as well, I'd say it's an absolute certainty.'

'Bugger,' Adam muttered.

'Are we really going to have to start all over again, looking for someone else?' Sam asked.

Adam scowled.

After some discussion, they agreed that they would have to rethink their suspicions of the victim's husband. It made very little sense that Chris would have taken Louise and hidden her away anyway, because she was the only person who seemed able to provide him with an alibi. If he *had* picked her up, he would have brought her straight to the police to confirm his alibi.

Before they could say anything else, a constable came in to tell Geraldine someone was asking to see her. Going to the entry hall she was surprised to see Helena perched at one end of the row of plastic chairs, her legs tightly crossed, her arms wrapped round her chest.

'You've come to find me?' Geraldine tried to sound pleased, although she was nervous about seeing her sister while she was at work.

Helena stood up. She looked no healthier than the first time Geraldine had seen her. When she removed her scarf, Geraldine saw she had cut her straggly hair. Her make-up failed to conceal her bad complexion, which was pockmarked with acne scars. Only her eyes were attractive, as large and dark as Geraldine's own, their expression impenetrable. Where Geraldine was tall and slim, but strongly built, Helena was skinny, but there was no mistaking the similarity between them.

'You told me you was filth so I went in my local station and showed them a photo so's I could find you.' She stood in front of Geraldine, her face split in a grin. 'So, this is where you hang out.'

Concealing her unease, Geraldine returned her sister's smile. 'This is where I work, yes.'

It was five to one. Geraldine looked at Helena's arresting eyes, plastered in heavy make-up, and hesitated. She could hardly return to her desk and leave her sister standing there. It was time for lunch anyway.

'Come on, there's a nice little place not far from here where we can get lunch, and it's not expensive.'

Quickly Geraldine led the way out of the police station before anyone noticed them.

27

LOUISE HADN'T SLEPT FOR long. Too groggy to feel scared when she first opened her eyes, awareness of her situation hit her like a blow to the head as she woke up fully. The room was spinning. She fell back on the mattress, trembling and crying. Closing her eyes, she waited for the giddiness to pass. She wasn't sure how long she had been trapped in this room, lying on a hard mattress. For a while she lay still, gazing upwards, waiting for her nausea to pass. She knew the position of every crack and cobweb on the ceiling.

After a while she leaned over the side of the bed and threw up. The pattern on the threadbare carpet had become so familiar she could picture it with her eyes shut, red and beige, with a stylised floral design repeated at intervals, interspersed with patterns that seemed to twirl and writhe under her gaze. The window in the white wall was covered in a mesh of criss-crossing metal bars. The door didn't even shudder when she kicked it as hard as she could. She had tried rattling the handle but nothing happened.

Since she had been locked in the room, her kidnapper hadn't uttered a single word. His silence unnerved her even more than the humiliation of squatting over a stinking metal bucket. When he returned, she shuddered at the cheap white plastic mask he wore over his face. It made him look inhuman.

Trying to ignore the stench from the bucket, she considered her situation. She tried to feel encouraged that he was hiding his face. If he didn't want her to be able to identify him, that must surely mean he was planning to release her. The thought of leaving her fetid prison made her tremble.

Escape was impossible with the door and window firmly secured. All she could do was wait for him to return. Dreadful though his presence was, the fear that he might never come back was worse. If anything happened to him and no one came and found her, she would starve to death, or die of dehydration.

Her situation was all the more difficult to bear because she had no idea what was going on. She struggled to remember how she had come to be there. Her captor had addressed her by name when he had approached her at Euston station. He seemed to have known when her train was due to arrive. Although her incarceration felt like a terrible mistake, it did actually seem to have been the result of a deliberate plot. But she had no idea why it had happened. She wracked her brains to work out what could have led to her being targeted in this way.

At first she had been petrified. But as the hours crawled by, she stopped caring that he might be going to kill her. Too desperate to feel afraid any longer, her fear turned to fury. As soon as she heard the key turn in the lock, she sprang from the bed and stood facing the door, knees bent, poised to leap at him. Catching him off guard, she was determined to barge past him and race down the stairs. If she was fast enough, he might not catch her.

Slowly the door swung open to reveal a figure dressed in black. He was wearing black leather gloves and, as before, his face was concealed behind a white mask. With a screech, she hurled herself at him. Instead of staggering aside, he grabbed both her wrists in one of his hands and pushed her back into the room. Detaining her with one hand, he turned and locked the door.

'I don't know why you're keeping me here,' she panted, seething with disappointment and rage. 'What do you want with me? I'll tell you whatever you want to know if you'll just let me go. Please, please, let me go. I can't bear to stay here like this any longer. It's disgusting. It's making me sick. It stinks in here.'

The man could have been deaf for all the response he gave. Slowly he put a fresh bottle of water on the floor, and a brown paper bag of food. As he turned to leave, she reached out and clutched his sleeve.

'Don't leave me here alone,' she cried out. 'Please, don't leave me here alone. I can't bear it.'

Pulling away from her grasping fingers, he spun round to look at her. Through narrow slits in his plastic mask she caught a glimpse of light reflected off his eyes. They glittered coldly as he spoke for the first time since he had brought her there.

'You're not alone,' he whispered. 'You'll never be alone again. You're with me now. You're going to stay here, and I'll keep you safe. I won't let anyone frighten you.'

'*You're* frightening me.'

'You know that's not true.'

'Why are keeping me locked up in here? Why won't you let me go?'

'I have to protect you.'

'What do you mean? Who are you protecting me from?'

'From yourself. Don't be frightened. Not any more. I won't let anyone take you away from me. You're safe here. This is where you belong, here with me.'

'What are you talking about? I don't even know you.'

Without warning he raised his arm and hit her a stinging blow on the side of her head. Shocked, she fell back onto the bed.

'Don't say that!' he hissed. 'Don't ever say that again. You're staying here, where you're safe. With me.'

Terrified, she cowered against the wall. The hard mattress quivered as the door closed. A few seconds later she heard footsteps pounding down the stairs. With a groan, she rolled over onto her side and gave way to hysterical weeping. When she recovered from her crying fit, she tried to make sense of what was happening, but the whole situation was crazy.

Clearly her kidnapper was insane. He claimed to know her, but there was nothing familiar about him. She was sure she had never met him before. He had brought her there in a case of mistaken identity, and there was nothing she could do about it.

Now he had gone, she tried to think about her situation. Either this was all a dreadful mistake or her kidnap must be connected to Chris and the telephone call she had received from the police inspector. She tried to remember the conversation. The inspector had wanted to know whether she had seen Chris the previous Thursday. Louise remembered little of their ensuing conversation, apart from the inspector asking to see her on her return to London. The following morning Louise had received a call to say she would be picked up at Euston by a police driver.

With hindsight she realised it was odd that the driver had neither been in uniform nor driving a police vehicle, but she had thought nothing of it at the time. The police often used unmarked cars. They didn't all wear uniform. It had been a mistake not to ask to see the driver's identity card, but she had been expecting someone to meet her, so it hadn't seemed necessary to challenge him at the time. She should have been more careful, but it was too late to change that now. In any case, he could have shown her his membership card of a local gym and she would have been none the wiser. They had met in a busy station, and he had been in a hurry to leave, on the pretext that they shouldn't keep the detective inspector waiting. Of course, Louise understood now that the reason for their rushed departure had been very different. He hadn't wanted to be seen, or picked up on a surveillance camera.

There was no point in going over and over her mistake in her mind. The man who had kidnapped her was violent. She had no idea what his rambling threats meant. Either he was on drugs or else he was insane. Either way it came to the same thing.

Somehow she had to get away from him before he really hurt her, but that wasn't going to be easy. Struggling to maintain her composure, she broke down in tears again, and cried until her head hurt and her eyes were so swollen she could barely see.

28

HELENA SEEMED REASSURINGLY DOCILE. Even so, at the last minute Geraldine changed her mind. Instead of taking her sister to the local café, where a few of her colleagues might be having lunch, she drove her to a small restaurant not far away. Geraldine had been there once before with Sam. The food was reasonable, and cheap. Without wishing to be stingy, she didn't think Helena would appreciate a sophisticated menu.

The place wasn't as pleasant as Geraldine remembered it.

'This is nice,' Helena said, looking around and smiling, as they sat down on plastic chairs.

She removed her scarf. Her eyes no longer inflamed, with her greying hair dyed black she looked almost exactly like her twin. Geraldine breathed a silent sigh of relief that she hadn't taken Helena to the café nearest to the police station. Anyone seeing them together could be in no doubt they were twins, virtually identical. If Helena gained a stone in weight, it might be difficult to tell them apart.

After studying the menu, Helena ordered the all-day full English breakfast. Then she leaned forward and stared intently at Geraldine.

'Now, first things first, we got to talk about mum's will.'

It was strange hearing Helena talking about their 'mum', when Geraldine had only really spoken to her birth mother once. She wasn't sure how to respond. It was more than simple caution when dealing with an unknown sibling. She had spent years interrogating liars and criminals, ferreting out their secrets when they were doing their best to hide the truth. She had developed an instinct about people. Now her intuition screamed at her to be wary of Helena. But it was hard to disentangle her professional savvy from her troubled emotions. She nodded uneasily, perturbed by gazing into eyes that could have been staring out of her own face, her own yet not her own.

'I heard from the lawyer,' Helena said briskly, her expression sharp. 'Has he contacted you?'

'No. I haven't heard from anyone about her will. I didn't know she'd left one.'

Helena's face flushed with anger. 'What do you mean you don't know she'd left one? Didn't she...' she broke off, biting her lip. Then her frown cleared. 'I don't have to tell you nothing. And if the lawyer don't know where to find you, there's nothing you can do about it, because you don't know who he is, or where he is. It's all meant to be for me anyway. Not for you. There's nothing for you. You never even knew her, did you? So I don't know what makes you think you can just turn up and get your hands on a share of what's mine. It's all supposed to be mine. That's what she wanted. You can't go against her wishes, not now she's dead.'

With a sigh, Geraldine understood that Helena had been expecting to keep all of their mother's property for herself. Right at the last minute Geraldine had appeared, and Helena was afraid she would be entitled to inherit half of their mother's estate.

'Helena, I'm not interested in anything she had. Like you said, I never even knew her. I only met her once. Although that was her choice, not mine.'

'So you keep saying,' Helena muttered.

'It's true. But I don't suppose she had much to leave anyway,' Geraldine went on.

'It may not be much to you, but it's a lot to someone who's got nothing.'

'Well, you can have it all. I don't want anything. Helena, I never even knew her. Why would I want anything of hers? It's not like it would have sentimental value for me, is it? Although I would like a few photos if that's all right with you.'

'What do you want them for?'

Geraldine shrugged. She didn't admit that she had kept a photograph of her mother hidden in her beside cabinet ever since she had discovered she was adopted. If Helena didn't understand why she might want to have a few pictures of her mother, there was no point in trying to explain. Right now she was trying to convince Helena that she wasn't trying to take a share of their mother's estate.

'I just wondered what she was like, that's all.'

'Well, you ain't going to find out much from a few old photos.'

Geraldine nodded. Her sister was probably right. She waited while Helena finished eating.

'Was that good?'

'It was all right.'

As Helena reached for her tea, the sleeve of her baggy cardigan slipped off her shoulder. She pulled it up again quickly, but not before Geraldine caught a glimpse of red puncture marks on the inside of her elbow.

'So what was she like?'

'Who?'

'Our mother,' Geraldine said patiently. 'What was she like?'

Helena shook her head. 'What do you want to know?'

'Tell me something about her. Anything you can think of.'

'I don't know what you want me to say.'

'I just want to know what she was like. Was she a good mother?'

Helena screwed up her face, considering. 'She was tight,' she said at last.

'What do you mean?'

'She had money stashed away that she wouldn't let me have. I know because I heard her talking on the phone. Well, she's dead now and no one can stop me getting what's mine.' As though she realised what she was saying, she changed her tack. 'It wasn't much dosh. Not enough to share. Anyway, I don't want to speak badly of her. She was my mum and she's dead, but you don't know what she put me through, how she made me suffer. She never thought about me and what I might need. It was all about living healthy with her. And look where that got her.'

Thinking about the letter their mother had left her, Geraldine understood that Helena had demanded money for drugs and their mother had refused. She didn't ask any more questions, but waited to hear what else Helena would say. Her sister remained silent, staring at the table, perhaps lost in memories of their mother. At least she had her memories. All Geraldine had was one faded photograph, a letter asking Geraldine to take care of her sister, and the recollection of one brief meeting. It was not much.

'What now, then?' Helena asked when Geraldine had paid.

Geraldine offered to give her sister a lift to a station. She was taken aback when Helena replied that she had nowhere to sleep that night. Geraldine explained that it wasn't possible for her to put her sister up. Her flat was small, and she only had one bedroom. In reality, she had a perfectly serviceable second bedroom currently in use as a study and general store room for all sorts of junk. She even had a spare bed. There was no reason why Helena couldn't sleep there, but Geraldine suspected if she allowed Helena to stay for even one night she would struggle to persuade her to leave. She felt uncomfortable about lying to her sister, but she had been forced into it.

'I can drop you at a station if you like, but then I really do need to get back.'

There was no sign of Helena when Geraldine left work that evening. She looked around carefully as she drove out through the barrier. In a way it was Geraldine's own fault that Helena had been able to find her. There had been no pressing need for her to reveal that she was a detective inspector. She had volunteered the information in order to force her sister out of her car. With hindsight she regretted having said anything. Helena had been quick to make use of the knowledge. That was worrying enough. If Helena ever discovered where she lived, any chance of them gradually developing a relationship might be ruined.

29

ON SUNDAY AFTERNOON, GERALDINE watched Chloe laughing and chattering, her cheeks pink and glowing, her eyes bright with excitement. Celia looked healthy too. The contrast between Geraldine's two sisters was stark. She couldn't imagine introducing her twin to Celia's family. Unlike Geraldine, Celia had probably never encountered anyone like Helena. Besides, Celia had a lovely five-bedroomed detached house in Kent. She could hardly plead lack of space if Helena wanted to move in. Whatever happened, Geraldine resolved to keep the two strands of her family apart. They weren't related. There was no reason why they should ever meet. Helena was already threatening to disturb Geraldine's carefully constructed routine. She wouldn't allow her to intrude on Celia's life as well.

After tea, Chloe disappeared upstairs.

'She says she's doing homework,' Celia said, 'but she'll be on the phone, chatting with her friends half the night. She'll only come off the phone for supper and then she'll be up in her room again. She'll still be at it when I go to bed. Every night I have to tell her to get off the phone and go to sleep.'

'Give her a break. You remember what it was like to be a teenager.'

'She's not a teenager.'

'No, but she will be soon. She's just preparing herself, and you should too.'

'Oh please don't start giving me advice. I'm so sick of people telling me what to do all the time.'

Geraldine frowned. 'Who's been telling you what to do?'

'Oh, first the doctors were on at me, and then the midwife, and whatever they say, Sebastian fusses...'

'Are you all right? Is there something wrong?'

'I'm fine. At least I've stopped feeling sick all the time.'

'You don't sound fine. Are you sure you're OK?'

Celia sighed. 'I'm just fed up with having to be so cheerful, telling everyone I'm fine, when all the time I'm feeling so knackered I could cry. And if I say the slightest thing to suggest I'm not OK, Sebastian tries to cart me off to the doctor. All he does is worry about me, and it's driving me nuts. I mean, there's nothing wrong with me. I'm pregnant. It's not an illness. But the way he carries on, you'd think I was suffering from a terminal disease. I'm sick of him fussing.'

'You just need to rest.'

'I know. You're right. And I shouldn't go on like this. All I ever seem to do is complain when I see you. I'm sorry, but there's no one else I can talk to like this. You know that, don't you? There's no need for you to listen to me, really. You can go away and get on with your life, and forget everything I said. It's not important. I'm just getting it off my chest.'

Geraldine assured her she could talk to her any time she wanted. 'That's what sisters are for.'

Celia smiled. 'Thank you. You're really good to me.'

Geraldine gave an embarrassed laugh. 'I don't think so. I'm hardly ever here, for a start.'

That had once been true, but since Celia had fallen pregnant for the second time, Geraldine had been making an effort to visit her regularly.

'That's not true. I know how busy you are. You come here as often as you can, and I do appreciate it, really I do. Honestly, I couldn't wish for a better sister. Don't laugh. I mean it, Geraldine. Ever since mum died, you've been there for me.'

As her only biological daughter, Celia had always been close to their mother whose death had affected her far more than Geraldine. Conscious of that, Geraldine had done her best to support Celia through her grieving. Now she was pregnant, once again Geraldine felt she should make some effort to visit her as often as she could.

'You're the best sister anyone could wish for,' Celia insisted.

Remembering Helena, Geraldine felt like crying.

She didn't stay for supper. Celia was tired, and Chloe was in her room. Pretending she had to get home to do some work before the end of the day, she left. The truth was, she was tired too.

Arriving home she made some supper, and flicked through the television channels. A film title caught her eye, *The Third Man*. Even the television reminded her of Louise's elusive kidnapper. She switched the television off and was about to stand up when her phone rang.

Geraldine hadn't said a word to anyone but Sam about her newly discovered twin sister. All afternoon she had struggled against the temptation to share the news. Normally quite emotional, Celia had become more volatile than ever since she had become pregnant. In addition to that, she might resent sharing Geraldine with Helena who was not only Geraldine's blood relative, but her twin. On balance it seemed sensible not to tell Celia about Helena, at least until after the baby was born. Having restrained herself from blurting her news out to Celia, Geraldine confided in Ian straight away.

'I'm not sure I want anything to do with her. Is that very terrible of me?'

'I don't know what to say, Geraldine. I mean, she's your sister.'

'But we're strangers all the same. I can't just invite her to come and live with me. She...'

'What?'

'Well, she smokes, for a start. And I suspect she's a user. She certainly looks like one.'

Ian was silent. She could imagine him frowning at the other end of the line.

'I mean, I'd like to help her, of course I would. If I could get her into rehab, I'd do it like a shot. But I have to protect myself too. Is that wrong?'

This time Ian's reply was prompt. 'No, of course not. And of course you can't have her staying with you. Not if she's an addict.'

'Well, I don't know that she is, but...'

'Don't go jumping to conclusions. Wasn't that what you always used to tell me when I was a sergeant, back in Kent? Find the evidence first.'

Geraldine thought about her sister's skinny frame and bony fingers, and the marks she was almost certain she had spotted on her arm. It was a relief to let her guard down and tell Ian everything.

'The thing is, I'm pretty sure I saw the marks, but she pulled her cardy back on again so quickly, I'm not a hundred per cent certain.'

'Why don't you ask her?'

'What for? She's not likely to tell me the truth, is she?'

'You don't know that.'

'I do know.'

'You're making assumptions again.'

'And anyway, I'm not sure I want to get involved with her.'

If Helena was a heroin addict, the chances were that she would soon follow their mother to the grave. Geraldine knew she was selfishly seeking to protect her own feelings, but she couldn't help thinking that the less she had to do with her sister, the better. Yet even as she was speaking, she knew she couldn't turn her back on her.

'Oh, bloody hell Ian, what am I saying? She needs help. I can't very well refuse, can I? But I won't take any responsibility for her situation or for what happens to her.'

30

WHEN GERALDINE DROVE TO work on Monday morning she was annoyed to see Helena standing on the street outside the police compound. Pretending not to notice her, she drove through the barrier and went inside. Helena didn't follow her. Geraldine doubted that would be the end of it. She should have been pleased that Helena wanted to have a relationship with her. Sooner or later, she would have to deal with her, but in the meantime, she needed to focus on finding Louise, and establishing whether Chris was guilty or not. Her own family problems would have to wait.

About an hour after she arrived, she received a phone call from a solicitor contacting her about her mother's will. It was an irritating interruption, but at the same time there was not much she could do to further the investigation. Teams of uniformed constables were out questioning Louise's neighbours, family members, work colleagues and clients, looking for her. The search of Chris's house was still ongoing. Other officers were studying CCTV film from the area where the bearded man's car had disappeared. All Geraldine could do was wait for the results of all the searches.

'We'd like to read the will later on this afternoon, if that's convenient for you. I know it's short notice, but the other beneficiary is impatient to get on with it.'

Geraldine noted down the details. The sooner the matter was out of the way the better, as far as she was concerned. Once Helena was in possession of everything their mother had left, she might stop turning up outside the police station. In time they would hopefully establish a close relationship, meeting up regularly as sisters, but for now Geraldine wanted Helena to stop hounding her at work. She had considered giving her sister money, but was sure that however much she handed over, Helena wouldn't be satisfied. If she was a user, as Geraldine suspected, all of Geraldine's savings might be spent supporting her addiction, which would help neither of them.

The lawyer's office was in East London. Driving there, Geraldine regretted not having travelled by train. The traffic was dire. She was afraid she wouldn't arrive in time, and reached her destination with only minutes to spare. Buzzed in, she ran up a narrow staircase between two shops and found the office on the second floor. A middle-aged woman ushered her into an inner room where Helena was already seated, waiting. The lighting in the room was bright. With the furrows on her forehead lit up, Helena looked older than her forty years. Drumming the fingers of one hand on her knee, she seemed nervous. She looked round when Geraldine entered but her eyes darted away again almost at once, as though she couldn't bear to look at her. A young man in a suit was seated behind a desk, leafing through a folder. He looked up as Geraldine entered the room, his direct gaze contrasting with Helena's jittery expression.

'Ah, you must be Erin Blake?'

'Yes. I'm sorry to cut it so fine. The traffic was awful.'

'Her name's not even Erin,' Helena interrupted. 'She changed it.'

'I was adopted,' Geraldine explained, sitting down.

'Yes, I see that,' the lawyer said, glancing down at his papers. 'And Helena remained with your mother.'

'That's right,' Geraldine replied quietly. 'The doctors didn't expect her to survive for long. She wasn't a strong baby.'

'That's crap,' Helena said.

The solicitor turned his attention to the will. Helena leaned forward as though that would help her concentration. But when it came to it, the terms of the will were simple. Milly Blake's estate was to be split equally between her two daughters. Geraldine gazed around the cramped office. It was a very small room, dominated by the solicitor's large wooden desk and a row of tall metal cabinets along one wall.

'That's a load of shit,' Helena burst out. 'Mum told me she was leaving it all to me. Everything. To me.'

The solicitor raised his eyebrows. The will was perfectly clear. As the executor, he explained that he would oversee the division of the estate. As he continued talking, Helena turned to Geraldine, her eyes bitter.

'She can have the lot,' Geraldine interrupted the lawyer.

'What?'

'She can have everything.'

'Erin, your sister is claiming that your mother promised to leave everything to her, but that contravenes the terms of the will which she drew up, and signed, while she was of sound mind. I understand your disappointment, Helena, but your mother's wishes are clear. The estate is to be divided equally between you and your sister.'

'I want Helena to have it all,' Geraldine repeated firmly. 'I hardly knew our mother. It's only fair that Helena should have everything. That's my decision. If you insist on splitting the estate, I'll give my half to her anyway, so she might as well have it right away. I'm happy to sign any legal document you want to draw up to make this binding. Don't worry,' she added, turning to Helena, 'I won't change my mind.' She looked at the solicitor again. 'I never expected to inherit anything from my birth mother. Helena did. Let's stick to what we both thought would happen. It's fairer that way, and it will avoid any arguments.'

'It's my place to follow Milly Blake's instructions.'

Helena looked surly. 'Well, it's not like she's going to know, is it?'

The solicitor turned to Geraldine. 'Are you sure?'

She nodded. 'Yes, I'm sure. I won't change my mind. And now I'm sorry, but I've got to go. Please, do whatever you need to do. I'll sign my half away whenever you send me the documents.'

With Helena protesting that her sister couldn't leave before the agreement had been signed, Geraldine hurried from the room. She hoped she hadn't just precipitated Helena's early death from an overdose.

31

LOUISE WASN'T SURE HOW long she had been lying there. She had finished the large bottle of water, and eaten all the bread. She had tired herself out banging on the door and shouting at the window. At last, she had flung herself down on the bed where she lay for hours, drifting in and out of sleep. The masked man didn't return for a long time.

The room was dark. Only a strip of light was visible beneath the door, illuminating the frayed edge of the carpet. The hours and days since she had arrived had merged into each other in a blur, so she decided to start trying to keep track of the time. Marking off the days would help her to get through her ordeal. She had nothing to write with, but if she could find a nail or some sharp object, she would be able to scratch her arm on each new day. Starting in one corner, she searched the room but found nothing she could use. In the end, she resorted to scratching the soft skin inside her upper arm with the nail on her index finger. Having made a mark for the first day she counted, she pulled her sleeve down. Keeping it secret gave her a sense of control over her situation.

Looking around the room again, she noticed the wallpaper was peeling away from the wall behind the bed. With a vague idea that she might record the days on paper, she knelt down and began picking at the edge. At first it came away quite easily. She pulled as gently and smoothly as she could, afraid of ripping it. After a moment, it tore off completely. As she stared at the scrap of paper, an idea struck her.

As long as no one knew where she was, there was no chance

she would be rescued. Her situation had seemed hopeless, but now she had some paper and an empty water bottle. She hadn't yet worked out how she was going to write a message to send in a bottle, but it had to be possible. If she could break the window, she might be able to squeeze the plastic bottle between the metal bars and throw it down into the street. She would address it to DI Steel, the police inspector. While she was wondering what to say, and how to write it, she heard a door slam a long way off, and footsteps coming up the stairs. Hurriedly she folded her precious slip of paper and hid it in the pocket of her jeans.

He stood in the doorway, like a figure in a nightmare. She swallowed hard, and tried to study him calmly. He was quite tall, and probably slim, although it was difficult to judge his physique beneath his jacket. His face was concealed behind a white mask, but the rest of his head was visible. He was Caucasian, with mousy brown hair beginning to thin on top of his head. There was nothing much to help her convey an image of him to the police when she escaped, but she made a mental note of the little she could see.

His voice, too, would be hard to describe, as he only spoke in a hoarse whisper. She thought he was deliberately disguising his voice. Perhaps she knew him. She resisted the urge to rush up to him and tear off his mask, afraid that he would react violently. Clearly he didn't want her to see his face. Once she knew who he was, he might feel compelled to kill her.

'What do you want from me?' she muttered.

She could feel herself shaking. Aware that this could be the end of everything for her, she cleared her throat and tried to speak to him again. Her voice came out in a feeble rasp.

'Tell me, what do you want?'

The man took a step towards her. 'Follow me,' he whispered.

'I'm not going anywhere until you tell me where you're taking me.'

He shrugged. 'Do you really want to stay here? I thought you didn't like it here.'

'No! No! Wait! Don't go! I'll come with you. I just want to know where you're taking me.'

He advanced into the room. She backed away from him, staring into the dark eyeholes in the mask.

'What are you so frightened of?' he asked in his curious whispering voice.

'Who are you?' she yelled.

She made a sudden lunge. Her fingers scrabbled under his chin. She knew it was rash, but she couldn't bear to look at the mask any longer. She needed to see a human face.

As her fingers grappled with the slippery plastic, she felt a sudden crushing pain in her stomach. Her assailant was breathing heavily, his fist poised to punch her again. With a cry, she staggered backwards and fell on the bed. With one bound, he was beside her, both fists raised.

'Stop! Stop! You'll kill me!' she gasped.

The pain was excruciating.

'It's for your own good,' he panted, but he didn't hit her again.

As he dropped his arms, she seized her chance. Doing her best to ignore the burning agony in her stomach, she made a dash for the door. Flinging it open, she hurled herself through and slammed it shut.

Trembling with terror, and retching with pain, she leaned back on the door for support, pushing against it with all her strength. She knew it was futile to try and run, but fear made her reckless. Her only hope of escape was to leave the house before he realised she had moved from the other side of the door. Silently she stepped forwards. Gathering her strength, she launched herself forward. Whimpering with pain, she rushed down the stairs. The front door was ahead of her, at the far end of a narrow hallway. Bent almost double with pain, she stumbled towards it.

She had nearly reached the door when she felt an arm round her neck, squeezing her throat. With his other hand he grabbed both of her wrists. Her legs shook violently as he shoved her forwards.

'Open the door!' he whispered.

He released one of her hands, twisting her other arm behind her back.

'Open it!'

Overwhelmed by the pain in her stomach, she couldn't move to reach for the handle. He tightened his grip on her neck.

'Open it!'

She dared not refuse. Besides, she wanted to leave the house. Once they were outside, there might be other people around and she would be in with a chance of attracting attention. She might even be able to escape. With a burst of hope, she opened the door. They shuffled forwards together, and she heard the door slam shut behind them.

It was dark outside, except for pools of orange light glowing beneath street lamps. He grabbed hold of her hands once more, and kept her in a tight head lock as they hobbled across a narrow front yard, like some lumbering four-legged creature. He pushed her through an open gate to a car parked outside the house. Dragging her round to the back of the car, he released her hands and opened the boot.

'Get in.'

With his arm still pressing against her windpipe, she struggled to speak. 'What?'

'Get in.'

She glanced around frantically for a weapon to hit him with. There was nothing. Below her she could see his feet. With a faint grunt, she lifted one knee and stamped down on his foot as hard as she could. He gave no sign that he had even noticed her feeble assault. She was in too much pain to move again. All she could manage was a feeble shout for help.

Moving his hand from her throat and slapping it over her mouth to silence her, he repeated his order. Shocked, she tried to pull away from him, but he clamped his hand more tightly on her mouth, forcing her head backwards. She was afraid he would break her neck.

Without warning, he kicked the back of her knees. She collapsed. As she lost her footing he manoeuvred her into the boot, pushing her head down so she didn't knock herself out. She wondered why he cared about hurting her head when the pain in her stomach was crippling her.

As darkness closed in on her she lay curled on her side, too shocked to cry out. Her knees were pressing so tightly against her chest that it was difficult to breathe. As she tried to control her panic, the floor beneath her vibrated, there was a resounding roar, and the car began to move. Terrified she was going to suffocate, she lay immobile. Even the slightest movement seemed to send a knife slashing into her guts.

With every jolt of the car, she prayed for death to release her from her searing pain. Eventually she passed out. When she came to, the car had stopped. She lay perfectly still, waiting. Nothing happened. She tried to turn round, but any movement was agonising.

Convinced she was going to die, she was determined to do whatever she could to prevent her killer getting away with it. She couldn't betray his identity to the police, because she had no idea who he was. He had been careful to avoid any contact with her, and had worn gloves whenever she saw him. All she knew was that he was white, and his hair was brown. It wasn't enough. She could only think of one thing that might help the police. Gathering as much spittle as she could, she drooled on the floor of the boot, turning her head to spit in as many places as she could. Having daubed the interior of the car boot with her DNA, she lay still, gasping with pain.

At last she closed her eyes and allowed darkness to fill her mind, as she slithered into an ocean of pain.

32

GERALDINE WAS ALREADY ON her way to work on Tuesday morning when she received an urgent message. The search team had discovered the murder weapon on Chris's property. He had been taken straight to the police station where he was currently awaiting questioning. Before interviewing him again, Geraldine wanted to see for herself where the weapon had been found. She turned her car round and put her foot down.

'Where's the weapon?'

It had already been sent off for forensic examination. Excitedly, the constable who had found it described how he had been searching in the shed when he had come across a chisel, the tip of the blade encrusted with what could have been dried blood.

'I could be wrong,' he added.

His bright eyes and flushed face were all the confirmation Geraldine needed that the young constable was convinced he had found the murder weapon. As they were talking, the message reached them that the substance on the chisel was indeed human blood. They would shortly know if it matched the victim's.

'If it's not hers,' the constable said, 'then whose is it?'

Before she left the premises, Geraldine asked him to show her exactly where he had found the bloody chisel.

'It wasn't like it was dripping with blood,' he explained as he led the way across the muddy grass to a dilapidated wooden shed at the end of the garden.

'You did well to spot it,' she replied and his face turned a deeper shade of red.

It was dark inside the shed. The constable shone his light around to reveal a lawnmower, a few white plastic chairs stacked together, and an assortment of rusting garden tools propped against the sides of the shed. Apart from the lawnmower, everything looked disused. There were no DIY tools to be seen.

'Show me exactly where it was.'

The constable stepped forward and pointed. 'Just there, on the floor, between the rake and the spade. You can see a few flecks of dried blood.'

He shone the torch on the spot. From the doorway the chisel would have been hidden, but anyone stepping inside the shed would have spotted it straight away.

Walking back to the house, Geraldine looked around the garden. The grass needed cutting and the flower beds were overgrown with shrubs and weeds. It didn't surprise her that the garden tools looked as though they hadn't been touched for a while.

'Describe the chisel,' she said.

'It was – a chisel. About thirty centimetres long, end to end, with a blade about four centimetres in width with a bevelled end, and the handle was black plastic.' He shrugged. 'It was a common sort of chisel, I think.'

Geraldine nodded. 'Good. Let's see what forensics have to say about it.'

By the time she reached the police station the forensic team had already confirmed the blood group matched that of the victim. The width of the chisel blade was consistent with it having been used to inflict Jamie's fatal head wound. The DNA test result would be back shortly. In the meantime, only one thing was bothering Geraldine as she prepared to question the suspect again. She couldn't understand how the chisel had escaped notice a week earlier, when the police had searched the premises for a murder weapon.

'Did no one look in the shed?' she asked Sam. 'Check it for me.'

Sam reported back that the shed had been searched the previous week.

'And no one saw the murder weapon then?'

Sam shrugged. 'The answer's in the question. Perhaps it was hidden behind something? We did a more thorough search this time, now we know he did it.'

Geraldine frowned. The chisel hadn't been well concealed.

'At that time, there was no evidence to suggest Chris had murdered his wife. Only the fact that he was her husband made him a suspect at all,' Sam pointed out.

'And the fact that the murder weapon was right there, under our noses,' Geraldine retorted.

But she supposed Sam was right. The chisel could have been overlooked the previous Monday.

'But why would he have left it there?' she added. 'Wouldn't you have got rid of it as soon as you could?'

Sam frowned. 'He knew we'd already searched the shed...'

Geraldine raised her eyebrows. 'Not much of a search,' she muttered.

'If I was him, I might well leave it somewhere the police had already looked, and were unlikely to look again. He might even have put it there after we'd looked in the shed.'

Geraldine thought Sam's last suggestion was probably right.

Chris looked up miserably as Geraldine entered the interview room. His corpulent lawyer at his side barely acknowledged her presence.

'Good afternoon, gentlemen,' she said pleasantly, and paused.

'Oh, get on with it, for Christ's sake,' Chris burst out.

He seemed more nervous than on previous occasions. His eyes darted around, flitting past Geraldine and back again, as unsettled as a fly buzzing around a room.

Geraldine adopted a conversational tone to begin her

questioning. 'Did you do much DIY around the house?'

Chris glanced at his lawyer who sat, eyes half closed, giving no sign that he was listening to the interview. As before, Geraldine was certain he was paying close attention.

'Answer the question.'

'I don't understand what it is you want to know.'

'Did you do any DIY in the house? Putting up shelves? That kind of thing. Any woodwork?'

Chris gave a nervous laugh. 'No. I'm not what you might call handy. I wasn't one for DIY. I barely know how to wire a plug. But I don't see what that's got to do with my wife's death.'

For answer, Geraldine put an evidence bag on the table. Chris stared at it. 'What's that?'

'I think you know very well what it is. It's your chisel.'

'What?'

'We found it in your shed.' She leaned forward, enunciating her words very slowly. 'It has your wife's blood on it.' She sat back again, and turned to speak to the lawyer. 'The width of the blade is consistent with its having been used to inflict the fatal blow. We're looking at the murder weapon.'

She turned back to Chris who was staring at the chisel in horror.

'I never owned a chisel in my life,' he mumbled.

The lawyer frowned. 'I'd like to speak to my client.'

Geraldine smiled at him. 'I'm sure you would. You two must want to discuss his confession. A crime of passion, I expect? But murder nonetheless, with a chisel bought especially for the purpose. Because you weren't one for DIY, were you, Chris?'

33

GAZING AROUND THE SMALL whitewashed cell with its cold metal toilet he shivered, wondering if he was looking at his future. He tried to imagine what it would be like to spend a long time in a confined space, day after day, year after year, never going out to the pub or a football match, never again walking along the street on a sunny day, or feeling the touch of another human being on his skin. He didn't know if prisoners were allowed the occasional beer while they were serving their sentence.

In here everything was unfamiliar, but even at home nothing had been the same without Jamie. They had been married for five years and had lived together for three years before that. Eight years was a long time to be with someone else. Throughout their time together, not a day had gone by without them seeing one another, not a night had passed when they hadn't slept in the same bed. He stared disconsolately at the scratchy blanket on his narrow bunk. Jamie had insisted on pink sheets and a duvet decorated with a sprinkling of tiny pink flowers. It wouldn't have been his choice, but he hadn't minded. It was only bed linen.

'Choose whatever you want,' he'd told her.

But nothing he did had ever seemed to please her. Her constant misery had ruined his life. With her, he had never been allowed to feel happy. Even with her death she was taking away his freedom. He tried to forgive her. None of this had been her fault. But it hadn't been his fault either.

Louise's betrayal was more difficult to forgive. He tried

not to dwell on it. Thinking about her made him so angry, he wanted to slap her. She could so easily have saved him. After all the love he had shown her, she had abandoned him in order to keep their affair secret.

'Let me speak to her,' he had pleaded with the police. 'I'll make her see that she has to tell you the truth.'

But no one listened to him, because no one cared. In their eyes he was a murderer. It was difficult to control the slow anger burning inside him. One day he was afraid it would erupt. And he was going to a place that specialised in punishing violent behaviour.

Somewhere far off a voice was yelling obscenities. Another poor sod in a police cell. He sighed, remembering the sound of his wife's voice. Doing his best to block out the shouting, he lay down on the hard bunk and stared at a compass stencilled on the ceiling, wondering what it was for. After a while he closed his eyes, trying to recall the last time he had seen his wife alive. He remembered how violently she had struggled, and his frantic efforts to restrain her. He had never wanted to hurt her.

As long as he lived, he would never understand how their relationship had gone so terribly wrong. He had done his best to love her. It wasn't for want of trying that he hadn't made her happy. Looking back over the years they had spent together, fighting and making up, and, inevitably, fighting again, he couldn't remember a time when she had ever seemed content. He had never accepted that he was responsible for her suffering. But maybe it had been his fault after all.

Strictly speaking, they ought never to have been matched by an online dating agency. He had mistakenly added twenty years to his age. Anyone checking his details should have spotted the error straight away, but the site had let it pass. He'd noticed it as soon as his profile went online, but he hadn't thought it mattered. At twenty-three, and painfully inexperienced with women, he hadn't really expected to hear from anyone. When an attractive thirty-year-old woman had responded, he had almost not dared to reply. He had been astonished when, if anything, she had seemed amused when he had confessed his blunder, laughingly calling him her toy boy.

To begin with the nickname had irked him, but he had been too shy to complain. After a while he had no longer cared, because he had fallen in love with her. For a while nothing she did could upset him. He couldn't imagine ever taking offence at anything she said.

By the time he had realised how badly he had misjudged her, they were too deeply involved for him to extricate himself. Although he knew there was something unhealthy about their relationship, he couldn't bring himself to leave her. Instead, he had asked her to marry him. It had been a crazy impulse.

Musing over their love affair – if that was really what it had been – he cursed himself for having allowed sexual attraction to lead him into such a disastrous marriage. He had always known it wouldn't play out well. But he had never expected it to end like this, with him being accused of murdering her. He still couldn't understand how it had happened.

Rage against his incarceration dissolved into grief. In spite of her faults, he had loved his wife so much, his longing for her made him cry. She was a beautiful woman, and she had cared for him enough to marry him. The hope that they might one day find happiness had kept him going through difficult times. The finality of her death had snatched that hope away. Knowing he would never see her again, he sobbed uncontrollably.

34

THE CASE WAS AS good as closed. Adam ticked off the points he was making on his fingers. Geraldine stared, mesmerised by the delicate movements. If she hadn't seen who they belonged to, she might have mistaken them for the slender hands of a woman.

'First of all, the suspect lied about the whereabouts of his van on the night it was used to transport his wife's body. We know it was no longer in the garage. We have the paperwork to prove it. That alone ought to be enough to secure a conviction. Secondly, it appears his mistress has thought better of providing him with an alibi for the time of his wife's death, and has done a runner. We've been looking for her for five days now, and she clearly doesn't want to speak to us. And thirdly, we found the murder weapon in the suspect's garden shed. Let's see a clever lawyer argue his way out of that lot!' He grinned. 'Well done. Despite a few hiccups along the way, we got there in record time.'

Geraldine cleared her throat. 'Just to play devil's advocate for a minute, you know we can't prove he was driving the van at the time it was used to carry his wife's body. So in answer to your first point, someone other than Chris could have been at the wheel. I'm just saying it's possible. Then secondly, Louise might have disappeared because she doesn't want her husband to know about her affair. She's terrified he'll find out. She didn't want to say anything about being with Chris at all, until I'd reassured her we wouldn't approach her husband. But when she did speak out, she was clear that she had been with Chris at the time his wife was murdered.'

'We have no evidence that the woman you spoke to was Louise Marshall. Anyone could have been speaking to you on her phone. Or Chris could have forced her to lie and say she was with him, and then she thought better of it once she got away from him.'

'We know she was in Birmingham when I spoke to her,' Geraldine pointed out. 'She was already away from him.'

'But you can't argue with the discovery of the murder weapon in his shed.'

Geraldine shook her head. 'A weapon that somehow escaped our notice when we visited the premises four nights after the murder took place.'

Adam scowled. 'That's a blunder, there's no getting away from it. Who the hell missed it first time round? Their bloody incompetence has wasted a hell of a lot of time. They deserve to be hung out to dry.'

Geraldine assured him the matter was being looked into. In the meantime, they were in agreement. A decent defence lawyer might be able to raise doubts about Chris's guilt. It would be best if they could convince him that it would be in his own interest to confess.

'She was your wife,' Geraldine said, in as reasonable a tone as she could muster. 'There should be no question in a jury's mind that this was a crime of passion. We all understand that you never intended to kill your wife.' She glanced over at the lawyer as though she was speaking on his behalf as well. 'Things just got out of hand, didn't they? What happened, Chris? It's time to get it off your chest. You can't deny the truth indefinitely. So come on, tell me what happened. Were you having a row? She provoked you, didn't she? There's really no point in continuing to lie about it, because the truth is obvious to all of us.'

Chris sat stony faced, his arms folded, his eyes fixed on the table.

'We know you killed her. If you refuse to tell your side of

the story, a jury is bound to think the worst. You'll go down for life, for premeditated murder.'

She paused, but again the suspect said nothing.

'Let's start with the chisel,' Geraldine suggested. 'How do you account for the fact that you never did any DIY around the house, and you had no other woodwork tools, yet you had recently gone out and bought a chisel?'

Chris looked up in surprise. 'I never bought a chisel in my life.'

'Do you have evidence my client made this purchase?' the lawyer asked, opening his eyes.

'We found the murder weapon in your shed.'

'Were my client's fingerprints on the handle?'

'I never bought a chisel,' Chris repeated doggedly.

'Yes, you did, and we'll find out where and when.'

'So you have no evidence my client purchased the murder weapon, or ever handled the murder weapon,' the lawyer said.

It was proving more difficult than she had expected to coax a confession out of Chris. Every time she pressed him, his lawyer spoke for him. Geraldine appreciated that he was only doing his job, but she wished he would shut up and let his client speak for himself.

'We have all we need to get a conviction,' she assured him.

'Then surely you have no further need to continue with this interview,' the lawyer replied.

Geraldine tried a different line of questioning, accusing Chris of having killed his wife because she had found out about his mistress.

'Did your wife threaten to tell Louise's husband about the affair? Is that why you argued with her? You fought, and things got out of hand, didn't they? Or did you and Louise plan the murder? Had your wife been threatening her?'

'I've no idea what you're talking about,' he protested.

'You told us you were with your mistress while your wife was being murdered,' Geraldine said.

Chris nodded his head. Whether from shame or fear, he seemed unable to speak.

'But you lied about that too, didn't you? Just like you lied about your van being in for repairs on the night of the murder. In fact, everything you've told us was a lie, wasn't it?'

'I was with Louise that evening. I'm not lying. Ask her, she'll tell you. She won't lie about it forever. She must understand how important this is. Bring her here, and let me speak to her.'

'Where is she, Chris?'

Frowning, he rattled off her address. 'Or she'll probably be at work right now. In any case, it might be better to speak to her there. You know she's terrified her husband will find out about us. But she'll tell the truth, I know she will.' He sounded desperate. 'Go on, ask her. She'll tell you where I was that night. Ask her.'

The police station was bustling on Wednesday morning. Reports were being finalised, expenses claims checked, statements logged, desks cleared, while they discussed where they were all going for a celebratory drink after work. After all their worries, Chris Cordwell had been arrested within two weeks of murdering his wife. It was a speedy result.

Geraldine tried to share the general sense of exultation, but she felt uneasy. They still hadn't managed to trace Louise.

'She's taken herself off somewhere,' Adam reassured her, a touch of impatience in his voice. 'There's no law against that, is there? Think about it. We've got no proof the woman you spoke to on the phone really was Louise, or if it was her, that she was telling you the truth. And even if she chooses to come forward at a later date, she's hardly going to be regarded as a reliable witness in court. I don't think we need to concern ourselves with her any more.'

Geraldine tried to go along with what everyone else seemed happy to accept. All the same, she determined to continue chasing up any leads that might help her to find Louise. Something about her disappearance didn't make sense.

'And when things don't stack up, it usually means there's something wrong,' she told Sam.

The two of them were sitting in Geraldine's office, tying up a few loose ends.

'Hallelujah!' Sam said, when Geraldine agreed to join the rest of the team for a drink to celebrate the successful outcome of their investigation. 'You've finally accepted that we've got the right result. About bloody time!' She grinned.

Adam called them all together for one last meeting in the major incident room. Everyone squeezed in, chattering happily. The atmosphere felt more like a party than a police station. It seemed that only Geraldine had been reluctant to leave her desk.

'I've still got so much to do,' she muttered.

'What's your rush?' Sam asked her. 'The paperwork can wait until tomorrow.'

'I heard that,' Adam laughed. 'Come on, I want everyone to celebrate a job well done.'

Now they had Chris safely behind bars with enough evidence to convict him, Adam was more relaxed than Geraldine had ever seen him look before. He looked around, smiling, and thanked the team for their hard work.

'And now, no more worrying about paperwork tonight.' He smiled at Geraldine. 'Let's go and celebrate. We can start the tidying up first thing tomorrow. Come on.'

35

JEREMY WAS FED UP. The weather had been fine, but the forecast promised rain. The local news was depressing. Another teenager knifed to death, suspected terrorist activity, an investigation into an alleged paedophile ring, a gang turf war, a threatened train strike, and all the politicians seemed to do was burble on about 'taking action' to help other countries. What about charity beginning at home? There were any number of people needing help. Himself, for a start. His life was rapidly going down the pan and he could see no way out of the mess. He hadn't shared the news with his wife yet. Unfortunately, he hadn't been in his job for long enough to qualify for a redundancy package, so he couldn't even claim that crumb of comfort when he arrived at the office to discover he was out of work again.

His wife had been very understanding the first time it had happened, but kindness didn't pay the bills. Her wages alone would barely keep a roof over their heads, and even if she could earn enough to keep the wolf from the door, he didn't want to have to rely on her for money. The second time he had lost his job, her reaction had been less sympathetic.

'It's not my fault,' he had told her. 'It's a case of last in, first out.'

He went for just one drink before heading home. Paltry comfort, but that was all he could afford. It would have to be his last indulgence for a while. He left the pub feeling more miserable than ever. The sky had clouded over while he had been indoors. Putting off the moment when he would have to face his wife, he took a detour across a patch of scrubby grass. A sign called it a park, although it was too small to warrant that description.

A grassy slope led down to a children's playground. A woman sat slouched on a bench beside it. She appeared to be watching the swings and roundabout, although there were no children playing there. Curious, he observed her as he walked by. She was slumped in an awkward position, her head lolling forward on her chest, fast asleep in the shade of the overhanging trees. He walked on.

He hadn't gone more than a few steps further along the path when it began to rain, so he turned back. The woman was sitting on the bench, in the same position as before. She was sitting very still and he noticed she wasn't wearing a coat. Wondering if she was all right, he called out to her.

'Are you OK?'

She didn't answer. Jeremy hesitated. It was raining more heavily now, and he wanted to go home. He was getting wet, but so was the woman on the bench who still hadn't stirred. He began to feel uneasy. Close up, he could see that she looked quite young. If he disturbed her, she might turn on him in a drug-crazed state. She could be violent. For the first time, he began to feel vulnerable, aware that he was alone in this apology for a park with an unknown woman. She might be waiting for someone like him. The papers were full of allegations of attacks and rape. He had wondered more than once whether there were young women who deliberately set out to accuse innocent men of assault, just for the compensation. Not that anyone would benefit from trying to sue a penniless man.

'Are you all right?' he asked again. 'You know it's raining? You're getting wet.'

Approaching the bench, tentatively he reached out and shook her by the arm. Immediately the woman pitched forward. There was a dull thud as her head hit the tarmac on the path. She made no sound. She didn't even twitch at the impact.

'Oh shit,' he yelled, startled and terrified at what had just happened.

He should have realised straight away that the woman was dead. He glanced around. There was no one else about. Screened by the trees and shrubs, they were probably out of sight of anyone in the block of flats that bordered the grassy plot. In front of him, on the far side of the children's playground, drivers sped along the road too fast to notice what was taking place a few yards away from them. All the same, it was possible someone had seen him. He might even have been caught on a CCTV camera, shaking the woman's arm. Panicking, he fumbled with his phone and stammered that he needed the police. He was no doctor, but he could see there was no point in calling an ambulance.

He felt as though he had been waiting for hours when, finally, a police patrol car drew up outside the park. Two uniformed policemen jumped out. Jeremy carried on shouting and waving his arms, even after they had spotted him and had begun striding across the grass towards him. Catching sight of the woman lying on the ground, they stopped abruptly. One of them stepped delicately forward while the other shouted at Jeremy to move away from the woman. Backing off, he watched the policeman kneel beside the woman and put his fingers on her neck, craning forwards to check whether she was breathing. Jeremy should have done that himself, instead of just assuming she was dead.

'Is she – is she going to be all right? I didn't call an ambulance. Should I have called an ambulance? I thought she was dead. Her face looked... She fell...'

He turned away, shaking.

'I'm afraid it's too late for an ambulance,' the policeman said, straightening up. 'Who was she?'

Jeremy shrugged. 'I've no idea. I just came across her, sitting here. Then it started to rain so I asked her if she was all right. I touched her...'

'Touched her?'

'Yes, shook her arm, just gently, to wake her up. I thought she'd fallen asleep and hadn't noticed it had started raining.'

He tried to explain how the woman had fallen forwards, off the bench, when he had jogged her arm. The words sounded strange. He had done nothing wrong, but he couldn't help feeling overwhelmed by a terrible sense of guilt.

'I don't know who she is,' he repeated. 'I've never seen her before. I was only trying to help.'

His pity for the dead woman was swept away by fear. The police might think she had been alive when he had come along and assaulted her. In fighting him off, she could have slipped and fallen, hitting her head on the ground. And there was nothing Jeremy could do to prove his innocence.

He was led away to sit in a police car, out of the rain. He called his wife to explain why he was going to be home late. Time, which had seemed to crawl so slowly while he had been waiting for the police to arrive, suddenly sped by. As if by magic, a large white tent suddenly appeared. A team of white-suited people materialised and were soon busily examining the ground, taking photographs, and filling plastic bags. Eventually Jeremy was driven to a police station to make a statement. Sipping tea, he calmed down and found he was able to put his memories of the incident into a coherent order. As it turned out, it was lucky that he had only been able to afford one drink.

36

THE NEXT MORNING, GERALDINE was clearing up her desk, mentally preparing for her next interview with Chris, when her phone rang.

'Geraldine Steel?'

'Yes.'

The call was from Holloway Road police station.

'We've got something for you.'

'Oh yes?'

If there had been another murder, there was no reason why Geraldine should be summoned to work on the case when she had barely completed the investigation into Jamie's death.

'It's the missing girl you've been looking for, Louise Marshall.'

'At last. She's wasted a lot of our time. I've been trying to get hold of her for days.'

'Yes, it seems she wanted us to contact you.'

'All right then,' she said. 'I'll go and see her now. Is she at home?'

'I'm afraid it's too late for that.'

'What do you mean?'

'Louise Marshall was murdered early yesterday morning.'

Geraldine took a deep breath, considering the implications of this news. 'Murdered?'

'Yes.'

'But – I thought you said she wanted to contact me?'

'In a manner of speaking. Listen, Geraldine, this is a bit complicated, and well, it's a bit odd. But in view of the connection, we're handing the case over to you. I think you'd better come along and see what we've got.'

He gave her the address where the body had been found, and she went to take a look at a small rectangular area of muddy grass surrounding a children's playground. Bordered along one short edge by the Holloway Road, and along the opposite edge by a side road, the area was overlooked by a five-storey block of flats. As she walked past, Geraldine glanced at a battered slide and roundabout, both painted yellow, and a pair of swings. Beyond the playground, a white forensic tent had been erected. Geraldine passed through the cordon and put on her protective clothing before she entered the tent.

A Scene of Crime Officer greeted her. 'The body's gone off to the mortuary, but we're still checking the site for evidence of the killer.'

'Was she killed here?'

'No. We think she was killed elsewhere and brought here during the night. The park isn't well used so it's been possible to identify several individual tracks of footprints. One set of prints is interesting. A man limped quite noticeably to this bench from the road. On the way here his left foot made deeper indentations in the muddy ground than the right one. However, on the way back, both feet made roughly equal indentations in the mud.' He paused. 'It looks as though he was carrying something heavy on his left shoulder on his way here, because he ran more lightly back to the road afterwards. It's only a theory,' he added hastily.

'A theory that fits.' Geraldine nodded. 'That's great work and I'm sure the footprints are going to help you find the killer, but this isn't my case. Still, it's a relief to have this tied up, because we've been looking for Louise Marshall. She was supposed to be giving our suspect an alibi. I suspect she was killed a week ago. At least we know now why she never came forward.'

'Well, no, not really. She's been dead between twenty-four and forty-eight hours. The post mortem will be able to give us a more accurate time frame for her death. She was outside overnight, exposed to the rain, which makes it hard to be precise. But she hasn't been dead for more than two days.'

'She couldn't have been dead for a week?'

'No. Two days, three at the most.'

'How was she killed?'

'You'll have to wait for the post mortem to be sure.'

'What size were the footprints of the person who might have been carrying her?' Geraldine enquired.

She had a horrible feeling she already knew the answer.

'Size eleven.'

Geraldine nodded. The bearded man who had picked Louise up at Euston station had size eleven feet. So did Tom Marshall, but they knew he hadn't met his wife at Euston.

When Geraldine asked the Scene of Crime Officer about Louise having wanted to contact her, he shook his head. He knew nothing about that. Puzzled, Geraldine drove to the police station in Holloway Road. She introduced herself and a detective inspector came hurrying out to speak to her. Tall and long limbed, with an earnest expression, he led her into his office and handed her a sheet of paper.

'What's this?' she asked as she unfolded it.

'That's a printout of a screen shot of a message found in the pocket of Louise Marshall's jeans. It was written on a piece of torn-off wallpaper. The original was a bit delicate due to the damp, because it was in her pocket overnight, outside.'

Geraldine unfolded the paper and studied the message. All she could make out was her own name, 'DI Steel'. After that, it was just a scrawl.

'It looks like someone was trying to send me a message, but how can you be sure who wrote it, even if we could read what it says? It's just a scribble. It barely looks like writing. I know it was found on her, but anyone could have written it and put it in her pocket. Someone who killed her, perhaps.'

She wondered if the killer might be taunting her. They had

found the missing witness, and all they had to show for their search was her dead body.

'We haven't got the actual paper here, it's with forensics but they've matched the prints and confirmed she wrote it with the tip of her right index finger. It's written in her blood.'

37

GERALDINE STARED AT THE printout. After refusing to come forward to confirm her lover's alibi, it made no sense that Louise would contrive to send Geraldine an incomprehensible message from beyond the grave. She stared at the clumsy writing. It looked as though it had been written by a child.

After thanking the sergeant, Geraldine went straight to the mortuary. She needed to have as complete a picture as possible of what Louise might have been trying to tell her before she took this new development back to Adam. She had a suspicion he would dismiss her scruples. Louise was immaterial to the case now anyway. All the evidence pointed to Chris's guilt. If they could only be certain Louise had been lying to protect him, there would be no problem. But if Louise had been murdered by the hypothetical third man, it raised an uncomfortable question about the identity of Jamie's killer.

As she drove, she turned over the possibilities in her mind. It was possible that Louise had changed her mind about giving Chris an alibi. If that was the case, the only person who stood to gain by her death was Chris himself. Having killed his wife, he might well have wanted to silence Louise before she brought his final lie crashing down around him. But he had been in a police cell when her dead body had been carried to the park.

Another possibility was that someone else had killed Louise in order to destroy Chris's alibi. If Louise had been alive, the whole issue of Chris's alibi could have been cleared up.

Meanwhile, Geraldine was the only person to have heard Louise confirm it. There had been something deeply worrying about Louise's subsequent refusal to come forward to substantiate or retract her story. It was ironic that finding the witness they had been searching for was now threatening to cause more, not less, confusion.

'I thought you'd be along before this,' Miles greeted Geraldine, the lines around his eyes crinkling in a smile above his mask. 'She left a message for you.' Before Geraldine could answer, he launched into an account of the death. 'She was found out in the open, but when she died she was curled up in a very small space. To begin with I thought it might have been a box or a chest of some kind perhaps. She was lying on dark grey fabric of some kind, judging from the fibres we found. Forensics have confirmed that these fibres come from the kind of felt commonly used in cars. So it's not a great stretch to assume that she was transported to the park in the boot of a car.'

'So presumably she was killed somewhere else, and then put in the boot of the car and driven to the park?'

'No, she was alive before she went in the car boot, assuming that was where she was.'

'Do you have any evidence for that, or is it just another theory?'

'Look at this scraping on her back. Post mortem someone seized hold of her under her arms and dragged her out of the cramped space where she was lying. Rigor had not yet set in. Her T-shirt must have been pulled up against the edge, which scraped her back. There's no indication of any bruising or scratching in the other direction. It was a small space. She could only have got in there without post mortem injury if she had manoeuvred her way in there herself while she was still alive.'

Geraldine gazed down at the body for a moment, envisaging Louise being forced to clamber inside the boot of a car. Lying on her front, she looked far too long to fit into such a small space.

'She must have been threatened to make her wriggle into a confined space like that,' Miles said. 'She was lying in there for several hours before she died.'

'Did she suffocate?'

'Not exactly. Car boots aren't airtight and there's no sign of suffocation. She would probably have starved to death if she'd been left in there, but she died of her injuries long before then.'

'What injuries?'

'She'd been badly beaten while she was alive.'

Miles nodded at his assistant who helped him turn the body over. The grazes Louise had sustained in climbing into the boot were minor compared with the hideous bruising on her abdomen.

'Her internal injuries were so severe that the additional pressure of her knees pressing against her while she was curled up so tightly was too much. I could go into more detail if you want, but that's the gist of what happened.'

'Can you deduce anything about her killer?'

'I'd say her attacker must have had considerable physical strength, but it's possible her assailant was a woman. Of course we don't know that the murder was intentional.'

'But it was murder all the same.' Geraldine frowned. 'Even before she was put in the car, it looks as though someone wanted to prevent her from coming forward.' She turned to Miles. 'What can you tell me about the message she attempted to leave?'

'I found traces of paper under her nails matching the scrap of paper she wrote to you on. It was soft thick paper. The lab is still looking at it, but it was almost certainly wallpaper.'

'What did it say?'

They gazed helplessly down at the body.

'Well, she can't tell us,' Miles said at last. 'But maybe

forensics can decipher it. They're doing all sorts of tests on it. I daresay they'll work their magic.'

'I want to know as soon as anything comes through.'

'Well, there's no point in asking me,' Miles replied. 'I'm just the pathologist.'

38

WHEN GERALDINE ARRIVED AT Hendon, Adam summoned her. He looked slightly sour.

'Because of the connection with the Cordwell case, Louise's death has been passed on to us.' He sighed. 'I must say this could complicate matters. At any rate, there's no longer any question of ever being able to use her testimony about Chris now. We never had a formal statement from her. The CPS will want a report on your telephone conversation with a woman alleging to be Louise, but we won't be able to prove it was her now she's dead.'

'The two cases must be linked,' Geraldine said. 'Whether Chris killed her by accident while attempting to preserve his alibi, or someone else killed her in order to destroy his alibi, the two deaths have to be connected.'

Adam nodded. 'A man's wife is murdered, and two weeks later his mistress's body's discovered. Yes, they're connected all right. So, what's your thinking?'

Geraldine outlined her various theories, but she had nothing useful to add to what they already knew. They turned their attention to the discovery of Louise's body.

'She was found in an open space?' Adam scowled. 'Did nobody see anything? It's overlooked by a block of flats. A team of constables spoke to local residents as soon as the body was found, but apparently no one saw anything. Someone parked a car, removed a dead body from the boot and carried it all the way across to a bench, without anyone noticing a thing. Unbelievable! Has everyone gone blind?'

Geraldine described the narrow patch of scrubby grass. The

bench was not far from the road, at the bottom of a slope, and further screened from the flats by a row of trees and shrubs. It was quite feasible that a body had been carried to the bench unobserved, under cover of darkness.

'None of the lights there work,' she added. 'There's only what light reaches it from the road. And the moon.'

She wondered whether the killer lived locally, or if he had happened to drive past the park and note it as a dark and secluded spot.

'There is one other thing,' she added.

'Go on,' he said.

Adam's shoulders slumped as Geraldine told him about the size eleven footprints that had been discovered leading to the park bench.

'The bearded man,' he said, and swore. 'This won't be over until we find him.'

Adam summoned the team together to discuss the latest development. Several officers expressed the view that Louise's murder had nothing to do with Chris having killed his wife.

'We've got enough evidence to prove he's guilty. Why do we need to reopen that investigation?' someone asked.

'We've got the killer in custody. We know he murdered his wife. Now his mistress is found dead. It looks like he killed her too,' someone else added. 'If we don't nail him, what are the chances he's going to do it again?'

'Chris was in custody when Louise's body was carried across the park,' Geraldine pointed out. 'We also know that whoever deposited her on the bench had the same shoe size as the bearded man who picked her up at Euston station.'

'The same size as Tom Marshall,' Sam said.

'But we know he didn't meet Louise at the station,' Geraldine added, 'because he's too tall.'

'Until we know anything to the contrary, we're not making any assumptions about whether this was the same killer,' Adam said. 'Presumably Louise's husband found out about her affair...'

A faint murmur flitted around the assembled team. Most of the officers on the team looked pleased. Geraldine wondered why they all seemed to think it would be easier to treat Louise's death as a new investigation. Sam unwittingly answered the question as they left the major incident room together.

'At least we've got Jamie's killer safely behind bars,' the sergeant commented cheerfully. 'We're doing the right thing, treating this as a new case. It doesn't let Chris off the hook. If he killed his wife, he needs to go down for it.'

Geraldine nodded. She was sure Louise's murder was more closely related to Jamie's death than her colleagues seemed to think. She couldn't dismiss the conviction that both women had been victims of the same killer, and that killer wasn't Chris. The trouble was, she couldn't prove it.

Later that afternoon, a call came through from the forensic laboratory. The technician asked to speak to Geraldine.

'There's a message for you.'

'Yes?'

'It's from Louise Marshall.'

Geraldine had been able to read her own name at the top of the piece of paper. 'But the rest of it was just scribble,' she said. 'Have you managed to make out anything it says?'

'Yes. That's what I'm phoning about. We're sending over a detailed report about the processes used to investigate it which you'll need for your records but, in a nutshell, we've been able to read it by examining indentations made on the paper. Fortunately the paper's relatively soft and thick, so a finger pressing on it left a faint impression, invisible to the naked eye.'

'What did it say?

'The message was addressed to you.'

'Yes, yes, I know that. But what did it say?'

She was vaguely aware of Neil glancing up at her impatient tone.

'I hope this makes more sense to you than it did to us,' the technician replied. 'It just said: "Chris was with me the night J was murdered. Killer is a man with no face." That's all.' There was a brief pause. 'I read it out exactly as she wrote it,' he added at last.

'Can you email that to me?'

'It'll all be in the report.'

'Yes, I know, but it would be helpful if you could email me the message you just read out. I'd appreciate it if you could do that right now.'

As soon as the email came through, she went straight to Adam. They studied it together.

'"Chris was with me the night J was murdered",' Adam read out loud. '"Killer is a man with no face." This doesn't change anything,' he added.

'She's confirming Chris's alibi for the night he was framed for killing his wife.'

Adam frowned. 'Or is she confessing she was there with Chris when he killed his wife?'

'No. This proves that it was Louise Marshall who spoke to me on the phone. How else would she know my name?'

'I suppose this could be taken as a written statement of what she told you, but that still doesn't mean it's true. We had no opportunity to question her...'

'And why was that? Someone made sure she couldn't talk. At least, they tried to.'

'She was his mistress. If she was in love with him, don't you think she might have lied about this? We can't be certain.'

'That's the problem. But I don't believe a woman who thought she was going to die would have spent her last efforts on writing down something that wasn't true.'

'A deathbed confession?'

'It's not a confession, is it? It's an accusation. And it's Chris's alibi.'

Adam nodded. 'Yes,' he conceded, 'you could be right. We need to go over every statement and every scrap of evidence that we've taken as proof of his guilt. There must be a hole in it somewhere. Someone's been lying to us.'

'Someone with size eleven shoes.'

'Yes, the other man. Find him and we have our killer, Geraldine. That's the priority.'

'And Chris?'

'Let's leave him where he is for the time being. We don't yet know for sure that Louise wasn't lying right to the end.'

Geraldine wondered about what Adam had said. She tried to envisage what it might feel like to be locked in the boot of a car, in agony from internal injuries, knowing she would probably never leave there alive. Before she passed out, she was almost certain she would think of nothing but her own survival. It was difficult to imagine what Louise had gone through.

What was evident was that she had been determined to make sure the police carried on looking for the real killer, the man with no face who had killed Jamie and was now killing her as well. Perhaps, instead of expending all her energy on banging and kicking the sides of her prison, and yelling for help, she had devoted all her attention to scratching at her skin, until she was able to scribble down a bloody message. By concealing the paper in her pocket, she would have known that if she did indeed die, her message would reach Geraldine.

'If she was locked in the boot of a car, dying, would she have given a thought to proving Chris's innocence?' Adam asked.

'I think she wanted to tell us that whoever had locked her in the boot of a car had also killed Jamie. She wanted us to keep looking for her killer. She can't have known who he was, or she would have given us the name.'

'She gave us Chris's name.'

'No. This message was addressed to me. It's a continuation of our conversation. Her message tells us that whoever killed Jamie also killed Louise. She was collateral damage. If she hadn't come forward with an alibi for Chris, I don't think she'd have been killed. Jamie's killer had to stop Louise talking to us, so we wouldn't continue investigating Jamie's death. We haven't found the killer yet. He's still out there.'

39

A WOMAN CAME TO the door. She was small, with bags beneath her eyes, and hair scraped back in an untidy ponytail.

'Is Jeremy Douglas in?'

'Oh, Jesus, what now?' the woman asked, taking a step forward.

As the porch light fell across her face, Geraldine could see that she had been crying. Tracks of tears were faintly visible on her cheeks, and her eyes were slightly puffy. Geraldine introduced herself.

'Yes, yes, I know who you are,' the woman replied, although they had never set eyes on one another before. 'It's about that poor woman he found, isn't it? Look, I don't want to sound callous, or anything, but we do have problems of our own to deal with. Do you really have to talk to him right now? He's said what he has to say.'

As she was speaking, a man came down the stairs and halted in the hallway behind her. He was carrying a suitcase.

'It's the police again, Jeremy,' the woman called out over her shoulder.

'Oh shit.' He put down his case. 'This isn't what it looks like.' He gave a nervous laugh. 'I'm not doing a runner.'

'I threw him out,' the woman interjected.

Geraldine had been wondering whether Louise had lied to protect a man she loved. It struck her that this woman might be doing the same. Perhaps it was common for women to behave like that. In a way, Geraldine had lied in keeping her affair with her married colleague a secret, but her own reasons had not been totally selfless. Once the lie had been uttered, at her colleague's insistence, Geraldine was determined not to be exposed as not only promiscuous, but also a liar. In her job it was vital that her team trusted her. But it was dodgy to start justifying dishonesty, whatever the reason.

Geraldine stepped into the hall. 'Why would you want to move out just now, when you must have realised we'd need to speak to you again?'

With an anxious glance at his wife, Jeremy cleared his throat. 'I wasn't planning on doing a disappearing act. I was going to phone the police station as soon as I knew where I was staying.'

'He's already told a police officer all about it,' the woman grumbled. 'Do we really have to go over it again?'

'A woman's been murdered, and I need to speak to your husband about it now. Moving out can wait. My investigation can't.'

They sat down in a small front room. Geraldine listened attentively to Jeremy's rambling explanation of how he had stumbled on the dead woman. Geraldine had read his earlier statement. Although differently worded, his latest account matched it in every detail. The only information he added was the reason for his walking in the park.

'I didn't want to go straight home, you see,' he said, looking miserably at his wife. 'I knew how she'd react.'

'How do you expect me to react? That's twice in six months,' his wife muttered darkly.

Geraldine stood up. The look of relief that crossed Jeremy's face was not lost on her. It was a pity so many people automatically felt stressed when questioned by the police, even when they had done nothing wrong. There ought to be a name for the syndrome, she thought, as there was for white-coat blood pressure. The reaction of innocent members of the public could be similarly misleading.

'There is just one more thing.'

'Oh God, it's bloody Columbo,' Jeremy's wife muttered.

'What size shoes do you wear?'

'What?'

'Your shoes,' his wife repeated. 'Oh don't be so dumb, Jeremy. They've found some footprints by the body and they want to know if they're yours.'

'Oh, I see.'

Looking faintly worried, Jeremy told her that he wore size nine shoes.

'Here, take a look.'

He pulled off one of his shoes and held it out to her, upside down, so she could see the number on the underneath.

'Thank you. That's all I need to know. I'll see myself out.'

As she crossed the narrow hall, she heard the couple start arguing again.

'Where the hell do you think I'm going to go now, at this time of night? It's getting late.'

'Who's fault is that? If you'd left when I told you, instead of faffing around upstairs, you'd have found somewhere by now.'

Listening to Jeremy and his wife arguing reminded Geraldine of her friend, Ian. He had taken to calling her quite often since his wife had left him. Appreciating that he was lonely, she liked to think she was helping him to cope with his unexpected solitude. That evening, she settled back on her sofa and called him.

'How's things with you?' he asked her when he had finished his account of his latest woes.

Geraldine began to talk about the latest developments in the case.

'I thought it was all sorted,' he interrupted her.

As briefly as she could, Geraldine told him about the discovery of Louise's body.

'Well, I don't have all the details, of course, so I'm not really in a position to comment,' Ian said when she had finished, 'but from what you've just told me, I'd say it sounds like he could have been framed all along for murdering his wife. The killer could have had the whole thing planned out, using Chris's van and his bin and all that, only then your witness turns up with an alibi. The killer panics. He has to shut her up, whatever it takes.'

'Why would he wait? Why not kill her straight away?'

'Maybe he didn't have the opportunity right away.'

'But she disappeared,' Geraldine pointed out.

'In hiding from the killer she knew was pursuing her?'

'And all the time we thought she was hiding from us because she didn't want her husband to find out about her affair.'

As soon as she spoke, Geraldine realised her blunder. Ian's estrangement was still raw. She began to stammer an apology.

'No, that's all right,' he said heavily. 'I'm going to have to deal with it. I need to move on.'

'There's no chance of a reconciliation?'

'She's carrying another man's baby, Geraldine.' There was a pause. 'I'll get over it. Life goes on and all that. I'll take it like a man. It's not as if anyone's died.'

Remembering how cheerful and positive he had always been when they had worked together, Geraldine felt an almost overwhelming sadness. Even the most deserving of people were not protected from pain and misfortune. More than anything, in that moment, she wished Ian was with her so that she could comfort him.

They rang off, and Geraldine mulled over Ian's responses. Without any involvement in the initial investigation into Jamie's death, given an overview of the facts he had immediately concluded the two murders were related. Whether or not Chris had been deliberately framed for his wife's murder, Geraldine was sure they were hunting for one killer. And all they knew about him was that he had no face.

40

GERALDINE AND SAM SET off early to see Louise's widower. On the way, Geraldine discussed her concerns.

'I've been thinking, and there are a few things I just don't understand.'

'You're lucky. There are lots of things I don't understand. Just about everything, in fact.'

'I'm serious, Sam.'

'Go on.'

'Well, let's say the man who picked Louise up at Euston station was her killer...'

'And before killing Louise to eliminate Chris's alibi, he had probably killed Jamie and framed Chris for it.'

'Yes, but if that's the case, why did he wait? Louise disappeared from Euston station on Wednesday evening but she wasn't killed until the following Monday. Why did he wait five days to kill her?'

Sam shrugged. 'You're always trying to understand why killers do what they do. You can't, Geraldine. They're nuts, all of them. Anyway, maybe he spent a few days trying to persuade her to keep her mouth shut. Or perhaps he didn't intend to kill her at all. He beat her up, didn't he? But she was still alive when he put her in the car. She wasn't strangled or hit on the head.'

Geraldine nodded, considering. Everything Sam had said was possible.

'What I'm struggling to work out is how the killer knew she was going to be at Euston station at seven fifteen that

Wednesday evening. It must have been someone she knew. But we've been through her phone records, and the records of the hotel where she was staying, and checked all her emails, and the only person she told about her travel arrangements was her husband.'

'And you,' Sam pointed out.

'Very droll.'

'Her husband must have told someone.'

'You're right. That's the only explanation. Let's see if he mentioned the time she was due back in London to anyone.'

It was going to be a difficult visit. Although he would doubtless be distraught on hearing that his wife was dead, at least the uncertainty was over. His wife had been missing for a week. Not knowing what had happened to her must have been excruciating for him. His worst fears were about to be realised, but once he recovered from the initial shock, he would be able to try and move on. As long as Louise was missing, he had been stuck in a kind of nightmarish limbo.

Tom came to the door looking as though he had not slept or washed for a week. His hair was a mess, he was wearing a crumpled T-shirt, and his feet were bare. His glazed eyes opened wider when he caught sight of the two detectives and he took an involuntary step towards them. A whiff of body odour reached Geraldine, and when he spoke she noticed his breath smelled stale.

'Have you found her? Is she all right? Where is she?'

'Let's go inside and sit down,' she replied quietly.

More often than not, that was all she needed to say, but Tom was evidently not a man to jump to conclusions. Either that, or else he was clinging to hope. There was a third possibility. He might be concealing his guilt behind a mask of distress.

'Is she all right?' he demanded more urgently.

'Please, let's go inside and sit down.'

With a sigh that was almost a sob, he turned and led them

past a kitchenette. Geraldine glimpsed a sink full of dirty plates, and used pans on the hob. At the back of the house they sat down in a small cluttered living room.

'Well?' he asked her. 'Have you found her yet?'

'Tom, I'm afraid we've got some bad news for you,' Geraldine said.

He opened his mouth to respond, then closed it again. Lowering his eyelids until his eyes were only open a slit, he sat perfectly still, while Geraldine told him his wife was dead.

'And they found her in a park, you say?' he repeated dully after a moment. 'I don't understand. What was she doing there?'

As gently as she could, Geraldine explained that Louise had not died from natural causes.

'You mean she was killed? Someone left here there?'

'Yes.

'Who was it? I hope you've got him behind bars, because if I get my hands on him...' he broke off. 'I'm not a violent man, Inspector, but I loved my wife.'

'We'll find him, Tom, we will. It's only a matter of time.' Geraldine watched the bereaved man closely while she was speaking. He didn't seem afraid. On the contrary, he looked almost pleased.

'You'll think me unnatural, but I'm almost relieved, you know?' he said, as though reading her thoughts. His voice shook. 'I thought if you told me she was dead I'd be devastated, but... you know what was the worst of all this? I'll tell you. It was waiting, hoping no one was hurting her. She used to get so scared, with all the terrible things in the news... At least now I know she's not suffering...'

He broke off abruptly and dropped his head in his hands, his shoulders heaving, his body shaken by silent sobs.

'What happened?' he asked at last, as his fit of crying died down.

There was something incongruous about this rugged man breaking down in tears. Geraldine wondered if he was pretending to feel upset. But his height didn't match that of the man Louise had met at Euston station. If Tom really was involved in his wife's death, he had gone to a lot of trouble to cover his tracks. Somehow Geraldine didn't believe an angry husband would come up with such a complicated plot to kill his cheating wife. A powerful man, Tom would be more likely to hit out at her in a temper.

Geraldine hesitated. 'She was beaten.'

'Oh my God. Did she die straight away, or…'

The recently bereaved often asked that question. There were times when it was hard to reply.

'Yes,' Geraldine lied. She glanced at Sam. 'That is, she would have passed out quite quickly.'

'So she wouldn't have known what was happening?'

It was difficult to give an honest answer to a man pleading for his future peace of mind. Geraldine hesitated. Obviously Louise would have understood what was going on when she had been forced to climb, badly injured, into a car boot. She would doubtless have been terrified, but she couldn't have known for certain that she was going to die.

'No, she wouldn't have known what was happening. Not exactly.'

His chin protruded further as he pressed his lips together, and his voice became hard. 'What happened to her? I want to know every detail. Was she raped?'

This time Geraldine assured him straight away that his fears were unfounded. Louise had not been sexually assaulted. Only killed, she thought to herself. When she asked whether Tom would identify the body, he shook his head.

'I haven't got much of an imagination, you see, not like some people. If I don't look at her, I won't know anything. You know she was away, in Birmingham. And then she never came back. And she still hasn't come back. I don't want to see her.' He shook his head again. 'I don't understand. Why would anyone do that to her?'

Ignoring his question, Geraldine explained that his wife had returned to London. When Geraldine told him what was known about Louise's arrival at Euston station, he frowned until his eyes all but disappeared beneath his overhanging brow.

'Tom, someone knew that Louise would be arriving at Euston station on that seven fifteen train from Birmingham last week. I knew about it, and you knew about it, but someone else knew about it and met her there. Now she's dead.' She leaned forward. 'We need to find out who else knew about her travel plans. Did you mention to anyone that she would be coming into London on that train?'

Tom stared at her. He looked shocked. Then he shook his head. 'No,' he whispered. 'I didn't tell anyone. Why would I?'

Geraldine spoke briskly. 'Your wife booked her ticket for the Birmingham conference, and her train ticket, two months ago. Think carefully, Tom. Could you, or she, have told anyone the time she expected to arrive back in London? Think.'

He shook his head. 'I didn't know what time she'd be back. She never told me. She said she'd call me when she got back to Euston, because she said you can't always rely on the trains keeping to their timetable and she didn't want to keep me hanging around at Holloway Road station waiting for her. We'd arranged that I'd walk down and meet her there, and walk her home. I knew she'd be home that evening, but I never mentioned it to anyone. Why would I? I never even told anyone she was going to Birmingham.'

'Are you sure of that?'

'Yes, I'm sure. I'm not one to chat.' He frowned, remembering. 'I was waiting for her to phone me from Euston so I could meet her at the station round the corner. But she never called.'

'Could she have told anyone else the time of her train?'

Ignoring her question, Tom burst out. 'I don't understand.

Why would anyone do that? Why don't you know who did that to her?'

Geraldine sighed. If she knew the answer to that question, Louise's killer would no longer be walking around the streets of London, free to kill again.

41

BACK AT HER DESK, Geraldine reviewed what Tom had said. He hadn't been much help, and had flatly refused to view the body. Fortunately, Louise's parents were prepared to identify their daughter. They were travelling to London from Milton Keynes that afternoon, and expected to reach the mortuary early in the evening. A local detective had been to see them to break the news, around the time that Geraldine had been speaking to Tom. She was pleased to have an opportunity to speak to them herself.

Having arranged to meet them at the mortuary, she wanted to arrive there first so she could have a word with them before they viewed the body. After seeing their daughter's body, she was afraid they might be too upset to talk to her. There could be nothing worse than viewing the dead body of your own child. Even if the couple were able to conduct a coherent conversation, Geraldine would not feel comfortable questioning them after such a harrowing experience.

Before she left the police station, Geraldine asked Sam to set up a team to scrutinise Louise's phone records and email history, focusing on the past two months. They needed to check every message Louise had sent since she had booked her trip to Birmingham. Before that, she wouldn't have known the time of her train, so couldn't have passed on information about it to anyone else. It was imperative they discovered who had known the time of her train back to London. One brief comment could nail the killer.

'Make sure they stay on it,' she told Sam. 'I know it's a long job, but it's crucial. If they have to work through the night, inject them with caffeine, do whatever it takes. Just impress on them how important this is. If there's a lead there, and we miss it, our killer could walk.'

On her way to the mortuary, she went to speak to Chris. He insisted that he hadn't known Louise was due to arrive back at Euston at seven fifteen. So there was no point in asking him whether he might have told anyone else about the time of Louise's train.

'I knew she was coming back that day, but we didn't discuss train timetables. And I didn't tell anyone she was coming back from Birmingham. I never mentioned Louise to anyone else. We kept our relationship strictly between the two of us.'

The pathology technician led Geraldine into the waiting room where Louise's parents were sitting side by side on the sofa. They were holding hands. Neither of them appeared old enough to have an adult daughter. As Geraldine drew closer she saw they looked older than she had first thought. Mrs Johnson pulled her hand away from her husband's and gave a tight smile.

'We can't believe it,' she whispered. 'We can't believe it...' Her voice petered out.

Her husband sat silently staring at the box of tissues on the table in front of them as though he might collapse if he moved. Perhaps he would. Geraldine addressed his wife.

'Mrs Johnson, it's good of you to come here...'

'What do you mean? She was our daughter.'

Her husband stirred for the first time. 'I suppose there's no possibility – I mean, it is definitely her?'

'We are almost certain.'

'Let's not hang about any more then, let's go and make sure, one way or the other. This could all be a horrendous mistake.' He stood up.

'I wonder if I could ask you a few questions first?'

'No. I'd prefer to see the body now, if possible. Let's get this over with.'

Geraldine realised she had been naive to expect them to sit talking when they had not even confirmed that the dead woman was their daughter. She turned and led them out of the waiting area and through the door into the chapel where the body lay waiting for them. The identification was immediate. With a cry, Mrs Johnson fell on her knees beside the body, and stroked her dead daughter's hair as she sobbed her name. Mr Johnson, surprisingly stoical, turned to Geraldine and nodded.

'That's her,' he said. 'That's our Louise. Come on, Emmie, don't take on so. She's out of harm's way now.'

Taking his wife by the elbow, he helped her to her feet and guided her out of the room. She was crying so hard, she wouldn't have been able to find her way unaided. Geraldine escorted them back to the waiting room and offered them tea.

'Do you know what happened?' Mr Johnson asked her. 'Can you tell us how she died?'

'It was murder, wasn't it?' his wife hissed. 'Why else would she be here?'

She glared at Geraldine as though her presence was in some way to blame for their daughter's death.

As delicately as she could, Geraldine explained that Louise had died while locked in a confined space.

'We think she may have been trapped in the boot of a car,' she added.

'The boot of a car? What the hell was she doing in the boot of a car?' Mr Johnson replied.

'I said it was murder, didn't I?' his wife repeated.

'Was there someone else involved?' he asked.

Geraldine described how they had seen a man meet her at Euston station. 'After that, we could find no trace of her. We need to find that man. He knew what time her train was arriving at Euston station that Wednesday.'

She gave them the date and the time of the train.

'Birmingham?' her mother echoed. 'What was she doing in Birmingham?'

That question seemed to answer Geraldine's question, but she persevered nonetheless.

'Did Louise give either of you any information about her journey?'

The couple looked at one another, nonplussed.

'We didn't even know she was going to Birmingham, did we, Emmie?'

His wife shook her head. 'She never said. What was she going there for?'

'She was going on a course.'

'Oh yes,' Mrs Johnson said, 'she did mention it. A hairdressing course. She's a hairdresser in London – oh,' she broke off in consternation.

'Did she tell you what time she would be back in London?'

It was clear that Louise's parents knew nothing about Louise's travel arrangements that day. They couldn't have told anyone the time of their daughter's train.

'Can you think of anyone who might have wanted to harm your daughter?'

'No.'

'Was she happy in her marriage?'

Louise's father scowled. 'Look, this was obviously a tragic accident. No one would have wanted to hurt our Lou. She was a hairdresser, for goodness sake, not a member of a gang.'

All Geraldine could do was reiterate her condolences and promise to let them know of any developments in the investigation into Louise's death.

'There'll be an inquest, I suppose?' her father asked. 'We want to know what happened.'

'That won't bring her back,' his wife said. She was crying again.

Geraldine assured them that they would be notified. She didn't add that she hoped there would be a trial, not an inquest. On her return to the police station she learned that Louise's phone and email records had so far produced no results. It was beginning to look as though Louise had told someone herself, in person. And if that person had been her killer, he was hardly likely to admit that she had told him she would be arriving at Euston at seven fifteen on the night she was murdered. The hunt for the man with no face was going nowhere.

42

GERALDINE WAS SITTING IN Adam's office discussing their progress, before a briefing of the whole team. They were both feeling frustrated. The more Geraldine thought about it, the more convenient it seemed for Jamie's unknown killer that Chris had lost his alibi. And now Louise had been murdered.

'Louise must have been killed to stop her giving Chris an alibi. Why would anyone bother to silence her, unless Chris's alibi is genuine?'

'To begin with, we don't know that Louise was murdered. We know she died in a small space, probably a car boot, although we've not had any luck in tracing the vehicle she was in yet. Chris was brought in on Tuesday morning, but Louise died some time on Monday night. So it looks as though he could well be responsible for her death.'

'Why would he want to remove his own alibi? And what about the footprints?'

'He could have been wearing the wrong shoes,' Adam said irritably. 'I think he met her at Euston station and she told him she'd decided against giving him an alibi, for whatever reason, I'm guessing because it wasn't true. He kept her locked up somewhere, while he tried to coerce her into changing her mind. Hence the injuries she sustained while he attempted to force her to agree. Whether or not he actually intended to kill her when he put her in the boot of the car is anybody's guess, and we may never find out the truth of it. But kill her he did. If we hadn't released him when we did...'

'For lack of evidence,' Geraldine pointed out.

'We need to find that car,' Adam said.

She nodded. A team of technicians were working on enhancing images of all the vehicles that had driven past the park the night Louise's body had been dumped there. It was unfortunate that there were no working cameras immediately outside the park, which would have enabled them to see if anyone had stopped there. By comparing the times cars passed cameras a few miles on either side of the park, they were able to eliminate some of the vehicles. The drivers would not have had enough time to stop, carry the body across the grass, return to their vehicles and reach the next camera along the road when they did. With such limited records, it was the best they could do. So far images of four cars had been sent for enhancement so the registration numbers could be read.

'Her death could have been an accident,' Geraldine suggested. 'Is it possible she was trying to hide from Chris because she'd decided not to lie for him after all? She might have persuaded a friend to hide her in the boot of his car and drive her out of the area so she could get away without being spotted. She must have known he'd be looking for her.'

'And this friend of hers beat her up?'

'No, that must have been Chris. She managed to escape from him but died, and that's why her friend drove to the park.'

'Instead of calling us?'

'Perhaps her friend was frightened.'

'This is all mere speculation,' Adam snapped, as she had predicted he would. 'We need more information. We could sit here talking all night but it won't get us any closer to the truth.'

Geraldine was silent. This was where she and her senior investigating officer differed. Where he insisted on working outwards from established facts, she thought it was sometimes necessary to form a feasible hypothesis and look for facts to prove or disprove her theory. Without that framework, she didn't always know what facts to look for. Between them, she and Adam made a formidable team, thanks to their different approaches. Although she would never have admitted as much to Adam, occasionally she wondered whether the same thought ever occurred to him.

'There's no denying it's very convenient for someone that Louise can't give Chris an alibi,' she said, remembering Ian's conclusions.

'Convenient for whom?'

She shrugged. 'Not for Chris.'

The identity of the bearded man who had met Louise at Euston station continued to elude them. After the briefing, which did nothing to move the investigation forward, Geraldine went to speak to Chris. He was sitting quietly in his cell, his knees drawn up to his chin, his lanky arms wrapped around his shins. He barely looked up when Geraldine entered.

'You again,' he said, sullen but not belligerent.

'I have some bad news for you.'

'Don't tell me, I'm being arrested for murdering my wife. Oh no, wait a minute, you've already done that. So what could this bad news be? I mean, what can possibly seem bad after that? It must be the apocalypse, and it's somehow all my fault. Or a meteor's about to hit the earth, and I'm to blame. Or perhaps a tsunami's about to engulf the whole of the British Isles? Because I can't think of anything that could possibly be worse than being accused of murdering someone you loved.'

'Loved?'

'Yes, loved. Oh, I know I was having an affair with Louise, and yes, I loved her too. I thought she felt the same way, God help me. It is possible to love more than one person, you know? Or is love something you know nothing about, Inspector?'

Geraldine gazed solemnly down at him. 'I'm afraid Louise is dead.'

'What?'

There was something peculiar about his reaction. Although he winced in distress, he didn't seem surprised. When he spoke, his voice was completely devoid of emotion. He could have been talking about the weather.

'What happened?'

Geraldine hesitated before explaining that she was not in a position to tell him any more. Chris's expression altered and his face flushed.

'Tell me what happened to her,' he insisted.

'I'm sorry, Chris.'

She turned and knocked on the door.

'Is that it?' he cried out as the door swung open. 'Why would you come in here and tell me she's dead, if that's all you're going to say?'

'I thought you'd want to know.'

'I want to know what happened to her.'

There was something pathetic about his pleading.

Geraldine spoke softly. 'I'm afraid Louise was murdered.'

All at once, Chris's self-control snapped. He dropped his face in his hands and sobbed. At last he regained his composure sufficiently to look up.

'That's why she never came forward,' he mumbled.

Geraldine nodded. 'So it would appear.'

'I thought...' He broke off, tears sliding down his cheeks unchecked.

'You realise you've lost your alibi,' Geraldine said gently.

'I know you won't believe me, but I loved them both,' he whispered. 'I loved them.'

The door slammed shut behind Geraldine and she walked away lost in thought.

43

HE STARED AT THE empty bed. It was heartbreaking. She had always been so frightened. All he had ever wanted to do was protect her. He regretted having let his anger get the better of him. If only he had kept his temper, she would still be there, safe and well. It was his own fault that she had gone. He understood that. But he would find her again, and next time he would be more careful. He'd look after her properly, so that she never again felt frightened or threatened. It was his responsibility to keep her safe. He wouldn't fail her again. His big mistake had been allowing her to leave the room at all. Up there she had been free from any outside threat. If only he had kept her there, where no one could touch her, she would still be safe.

He couldn't believe she had gone. He had only left her in the boot for a few hours. His plan had been to drive her out of London, somewhere remote out towards Hertfordshire. There were woods off the road to Watford that were usually deserted. He used to take her there when she was a child, before going out for tea. Revisiting her childhood haunts would have calmed her down and reassured her that he wanted only to take care of her. Instead of that, she was gone.

There was no time to sit at home, fretting. All that mattered now was finding his daughter who was out on the streets again, waiting for him to find her. She could be in danger, lost and alone. Wherever she was, she needed him. Everywhere he turned, people were trying to stop him from taking care of his daughter. But he wouldn't be thwarted for much longer, not now he knew how much she needed him.

Before he set off, blindly searching, he sat down in his neat kitchen with a mug of tea to make plans. His daughter liked to go out in the evenings. Although it would be easier to spot her in the daylight, she was more likely to be out and about, walking along the street, after dark. He would wait until dusk to go out. There were several bars and clubs she liked to frequent, but he was not sure of their names. She had talked about Covent Garden, and Camden. There had been other places, but he couldn't remember where they were. Camden wasn't far away. He decided to start there.

Finishing his tea, he washed up his cup. It only needed rinsing but he used a small squirt of washing up liquid, even though he was in the house by himself. Old habits died hard. Besides, his daughter would be back soon and he wanted everything clean and orderly for her return. He would find her in Camden and bring her home with him. This time he would not let her leave the house again, not for anything. She could beg and plead as much as she liked, and insist that she was an adult and free to live her own life, but he knew what was best for her. In time she would understand that he was only thinking of her welfare.

He was going to keep her safe. This time, they would both wear masks, just as she liked to do when she was a child. It had been one of her favourite games, dressing up and putting on the masks she made. She had always been clever like that. He smiled, because soon they would be playing her games together, and she would never leave him again.

44

THE CAFÉ NEAR ARNOS Grove station was quiet, and not very well lit. The meeting place had been Helena's choice. There were only half a dozen small tables, all of them empty. Geraldine was the only customer. An olive-skinned man behind the counter served her a coffee, and she settled down to wait. After staring at the chipped table and the grubby tiled floor for about twenty minutes, she was forced to accept that her sister was not going to turn up. Ordering another coffee, she resolved to finish it and leave. And after that she decided to wait another five minutes.

Arriving forty minutes late, Helena sat down opposite Geraldine without a word of apology. Even in the dim lighting her hair looked greasy and her face was spotty, for all her thick make-up. Her red skirt was embarrassingly short for a forty-year-old, and her black T-shirt was too tight for her skinny torso.

Geraldine offered to buy her sister a coffee. With a grunt, Helena reached for a menu. As she leaned over the table, Geraldine caught a whiff of stale cigarette smoke. The laminated sheet trembled in her hand.

'I'll have the all-day breakfast,' she called out to the man behind the counter. 'Well this is nice, innit?' she added, giving Geraldine her lopsided grin. 'Aren't you having nothing at all? This place not good enough? I expect you're used to better.' She spoke without rancour.

Geraldine shrugged. 'I'm fine. And this place is fine too. I'm not hungry, that's all.'

'Why's that then? You on uppers?'

'You know I don't take drugs.'

Helena grinned. 'Well, no need for us to get off on the wrong foot,' she said. 'It wouldn't have been right of you to try and get your hands on what mum left you, not when you were never there for her, not like I was. She always promised everything was going to come to me. She wasn't thinking straight at the end or she'd never have changed her mind, not in a million years. I thought you'd got at her to change her will at the last minute. You have to admit, it looked bad. It's not like you're stupid. You'd have thought the same in my place. All those years you never showed any interest in us and then you show up, right at the last minute, just when there's dosh up for grabs, have a chat with mum, and then bang wallop she changes her will so you get half of what's been promised to me.'

Geraldine didn't answer. There was no point in reiterating that it had been Milly Blake's decision not to meet the daughter she had named Erin, and also to change her will. The waiter brought Helena's breakfast. Geraldine was relieved to see she had a healthy appetite despite her emaciated figure.

'So,' Helena said when she had finished. 'What's the plan?'

Geraldine prevaricated, uncertain what Helena had in mind. 'I've got some work to do –'

'On a Sunday?'

Geraldine shrugged. She didn't want to talk about her work, and was sorry she had mentioned it.

'It's great you got a job,' Helena went on with fake enthusiasm. Her fingers tapped nervously on the table, the nails bitten to the quick. 'I'm really proud of you.'

Geraldine was suddenly uneasy. 'Yes, well, we must do this again soon. Now I need to be off. I'll get the bill.'

Helena's grin slipped, and she reached across the table to clutch Geraldine's arm. 'Don't go.'

'Helena, I've got work to do.'

'No, you can't go. Not yet. Sit down,' she hissed. 'I need your help.'

'What kind of help?'

'Don't look so suspicious,' Helena replied, letting go of Geraldine's arm as she sat down again. 'The thing is, I got a bit of a problem right now. It won't be for long. But I need you to bail me out for a bit, just till I get what's mine. Those fucking lawyers are still fannying about.'

'What are you talking about?'

At least Helena seemed to be asking for money, and not for help in avoiding a criminal charge.

'It's not my fault. I was banking on getting what's mine, only now they're saying no one's getting hold of mum's money until the bleeding lawyer gets his finger out. It's a fucking joke. He's there, sitting on my money, so I got to go short. How is that fair? If I had what's rightly mine, all this would go away.'

'So you're saying you want to borrow some money?'

'Don't worry. I'll pay you back soon as I get what's mine. Seeing as you're so flush, it won't be a problem. You got a job, ain't you? And you know I got money coming to me. But you got to tide me over until the estate's sorted. It's my money what they got and they refuse to give it to me. Sitting on it with their fat arses. Well screw them. I got a sister can help me.'

Geraldine wasn't sure if Helena still remembered who she was talking to. 'So you want to borrow some money?' she asked.

'That's what I've been telling you. Jesus, for a cop, you're a bit on the slow side.' Helena's grin returned, slightly uncertain now. 'Just kidding. So, that's agreed then?'

Geraldine couldn't help smiling at Helena's transparent cunning. It reminded Geraldine of the way her niece had behaved when she had been a small child. Instead of being annoying, it was curiously endearing. There was something compulsive about watching this woman who was a stranger, and yet so familiar. Born together, they had grown up in different worlds. But they were still sisters.

'How much do you want?' she asked, 'and for how long?'

Helena shrugged. 'How much you got?'

Helena was unlikely to repay her debt, for all her assurances to the contrary, but that wasn't what made Geraldine hesitate. She had an uneasy feeling that once she started lending Helena money, the begging would never stop.

'I can lend you a hundred quid,' she ventured.

Helena's wheedling tone became brisk. 'I need a lot more than that, sis, and I need it in cash, and soon. You can get it can't you?'

'How much?'

'Five grand.'

It took a lot to surprise Geraldine, but she was startled. 'I'm sorry,' she stammered, 'but I can't hand over that kind of money.'

'You don't understand. I'll pay you back, I promise, but I got to have it before tomorrow or I'm done for. I'm telling you, sis, if you don't help me out, I'm dead.'

'What do you mean? What kind of trouble are you in?'

Helena gave a hollow laugh. 'Trouble like you don't want to know about.'

'Who do you owe so much money to?'

'Better you don't know.'

'But five thousand quid – I'm sorry, I'll help you any way I can, but you can't seriously expect me to hand over that kind of money without even knowing what it's for.'

'I can't tell you.'

'I can't help you then.'

'You got to. If you don't help me, I'm dead.'

Geraldine studied her sister. She looked genuinely frightened, but Geraldine was uncertain whether to believe her. 'Why do you need it? Why so much?'

'I owe it,' Helena mumbled. 'Don't look so worried,' she added, attempting a grin. 'It's not like I'm going to use it for anything dodgy. I'm just a bit short at the moment, but

I promise I'll pay you back. You know I'm going to get my hands on a lot more than that soon, don't you? I'm going to be sorted. Soon as I get my money, you'll be first to be repaid. It's just that some of the people I owe, well, they won't wait. I been keeping my head down, see, staying out of sight. There's places I can go when I don't want to be found. Only they got to hear about mum's funeral, and that's how they found me again. And these people, well, they aren't going to wait, not now they know where I am.' She glanced around as though someone might be there in the café watching her.

'Here you are,' Geraldine said, taking over two hundred pounds out of her purse. 'I've just been to the bank. Here's ten twenties and a couple of tens. That should tide you over for a while.'

Helena shook her head. 'I'm going to need more than that. I told you, I need five grand. I wouldn't ask if I didn't have to. I got no one else can help me.'

'That's all I can spare without leaving myself short.'

'You got more in the bank, though, ain't you?' Helena said, cajoling again. 'You can go there in the morning, soon as they open.'

'Take this,' Geraldine said. 'That's all I can give you. There's no more. It's this or nothing. Take it or leave it.'

'That's harsh.' Helena glared at her.

Geraldine struggled to conceal the irritation she was feeling. 'I'm giving you over two hundred quid here. Don't bother to thank me, just let me know when you're going to pay me back.'

She put the notes on the table between them. Helena snatched them up and stuffed them in her bag.

'Oh go on then,' she said, as though she was doing Geraldine a favour by accepting the money. 'Two hundred it is then.' She didn't add, 'until the next time,' but Geraldine could almost hear her thinking it.

Wondering if she had been ill-advised to give her sister any money, Geraldine paid the bill and stood up.

'We must do this again,' Helena said.

'That would be nice,' Geraldine answered stiffly.

'If they don't get to me first. But don't worry. I won't be the kind of stiff your people give a toss about. One more dead junkie. Who cares?'

Helena stood up so violently her chair fell over backwards. Wracked with indecision, Geraldine watched her sister scurry away.

45

AFTER CHECKING IN AT work on Monday morning, Geraldine took the train to Camden High Street to speak to Louise's workmates. It was a beautiful day and she walked to the station slowly, making the most of the sunshine before she reached the underground. On the train, she jotted down a few reminders about what she wanted to say, but it was basically very straightforward. Louise must have told someone what time she would be arriving back at Euston. Whoever had been given that information had, perhaps unwittingly, passed it on to the killer. Geraldine needed to trace the messenger.

This time she went into the salon and announced herself without any preamble. The same heavily made-up girl who had been at the desk on her previous visit was there again. She greeted Geraldine by name. Impressed, Geraldine complimented her on her feat of memory.

The girl smiled. 'It's all part of the job,' she said. 'Making our clients feel they're receiving a very personal service. It makes them feel important. Now, what is it you want? I take it you haven't found Louise yet? I'm sorry, she's not been back. It's...'

'Louise won't be coming back,' Geraldine interrupted her softly. 'She met with an accident.'

The girl's eyes widened in consternation. 'What sort of accident?'

'I'm afraid she's dead.'

The girl's hands flew up to her painted mouth. 'Oh my God! What happened?'

'I can't give you any details of the case, other than to say we are treating it as murder.'

'Oh my God,' the girl repeated. 'What happened? Oh, sorry, you can't tell me, can you?'

'Listen very carefully. I need to know everything Louise told you, or any of your staff here, about her trip to Birmingham. It's very important. Can you remember what she said about it?'

The girl's forehead creased in a frown with the effort to remember. 'It focused on colouring,' she said, 'mainly highlights and bleaching.'

The content of the course Louise had attended was of no interest to Geraldine, but she listened patiently as the girl told her what she could recall about what Louise had said.

'She was terribly excited about it,' she concluded. 'It was a bit of an adventure for her, going off to Birmingham on her own. Oh my God, poor Louise. I can't believe it. I feel like she's just going to walk in through the door, any minute now. I can't believe she's gone, I mean, really gone, for good. What happened?'

'I can't divulge any details yet.'

'Was she raped?'

'No. It was nothing like that.'

'Well, that's something I suppose. But who would do such a thing? To Louise? She was a hairdresser!'

'Did she tell you how she was getting to Birmingham?'

'No. She must've gone by train, I suppose. I don't know. We never talked about how she was getting there, only about different kinds of bleach. But the course was in Birmingham, so I'm sure she would've gone by train.'

'She never mentioned her travel arrangements?'

'No. Why would she?'

Geraldine asked the same questions of the other girls working there. They all came up with the same answer. Two of the stylists who worked at the salon were not there that day. The girl on the desk obligingly called them so Geraldine could question them briefly on the phone. No one had been told anything about Louise's travel plans to Birmingham and back.

'What about her clients?' Geraldine asked, desperate to find someone Louise could have spoken to about her travel arrangements. 'Did she have any regular customers she might have chatted to about her course? Or anyone who goes to Birmingham regularly?'

The girl shook her head. 'None that I can think of.'

All Geraldine's questioning led nowhere. None of Louise's relatives or workmates were able to offer any leads. Wearily she thanked the girl on the desk and left. Her visit to the hair salon had been a waste of time. Her next enquiries would have to be in Birmingham. Back at her desk she contacted the local police force and asked them to question the organisers of the course. But it was a hopeless task. Unless she was going to trace all two hundred hairdressers who had attended the course, any one of whom might have chatted to Louise, there was no way she could do the job thoroughly. A thought struck her, and she contacted the local police to ask the organisers whether anyone else might have returned to London on the same train as Geraldine. It was going to be a long slow process of questioning and elimination, with no guarantee that whoever had known the time of Louise's train would come forward with that information. The killer had been aware that Louise was arriving at Euston on that particular train. He had been waiting for her. But Geraldine was no closer to finding out how he had learned about her movements.

'And that's not the only thing puzzling me,' Geraldine said later on to Sam, when she expressed her frustration over a pint after work.

'At least we've got the wife killer,' Sam replied with a grin, although she didn't sound sure.

'There's no need to look so cheerful about it.'

'Cheerful?' Sam laughed. 'You'll be accusing me of being gay next.'

'In any case, Louise's death raises a query over whether Chris is guilty because it looks as though someone didn't want him to have an alibi.'

'But we've got the murder weapon,' Sam protested.

'Which doesn't have his fingerprints on it.'

'He could have been wearing gloves.'

'So could anyone else. Listen, Sam, I'm not saying he's definitely innocent. All I'm saying is that it's possible someone else killed Jamie, and framed her husband as the obvious suspect, depositing the murder weapon in his garden shed after the event. Remember, no one spotted it when the shed was originally searched. Doesn't that strike you as odd?'

Sam nodded. 'So when the real killer discovered that Louise had come forward to provide Chris with an alibi, threatening to blow the killer's carefully constructed set up apart, he made it his business to get rid of Louise in order to keep Chris in the frame for his wife's murder.'

'I'm not saying that's what happened, just that it's possible. There seem to have been a few too many coincidences in this case. Something doesn't ring true.'

'The bearded man,' Sam muttered. 'He could have killed them both. First he killed Jamie, for some unknown motive, and it was easy enough to frame her husband for that. Then he had to kill Louise to stop us from discovering that Chris wasn't guilty.' She nodded. 'It does make sense. So we need to be looking for any enemies Jamie might have had.'

'Yes, someone wanted her dead. We need to go back to the beginning, and re-examine the first murder. Then we might start to get somewhere with the second one. We'll talk to Chris again tomorrow, as soon as I've run this past Adam.'

Geraldine fell silent, staring at her glass, only half listening to Sam who was talking about searching Chris's house and shed again.

'Only this time, we'll be looking for evidence that someone else was there,' she said.

Geraldine wasn't looking forward to the conversation she intended to have with Adam in the morning. She suspected that, in the detective chief inspector's mind, Jamie's case remained as good as resolved. Husbands were usually the culprit in a case like that, and there was compelling evidence to suggest Chris was guilty. But Geraldine was not convinced he was. She hoped Adam was thinking along the same lines as her. She understood that he felt pulled in different directions, committed to discovering the truth, yet under pressure to succeed in solving the case. She hoped she would never find herself in a similar position.

46

SHE WAS STANDING ON a street corner, waiting for him, as he drew into the kerb. He leaned over and opened the door. 'I thought it would be more difficult to find you,' he called out.

She smiled. 'Well, here I am.'

'Hop in then.'

He watched her as she climbed on to the passenger seat, her short tight skirt riding up her thighs. He didn't blame her. She was too young to understand the signals her clothes sent out. It was her mother's fault for letting her run around dressed like a whore. He would have words with Veronica about it later. For now, he just wanted to get her back home safely.

'I'll get you some new clothes,' he said, and was going to leave it at that.

To his surprise, she burst out laughing. 'Whatever turns you on.'

He spoke severely. 'I'm talking to you about the way you dress.'

She didn't answer. At his side, he thought he saw her shrug her shoulders. The car stank of cheap perfume. He wrinkled his nose. That was something else he would have to speak to her about. If she insisted on wearing muck like that, she could at least be subtle about it. She couldn't have reeked more if she'd poured a whole bottle of the foul sickly stuff over herself.

'So where are you taking me?' she asked when they had been driving for about twenty minutes.

'Don't worry,' he reassured her. 'We're going home.'

'OK, but you need to give me the address.'

Glancing down, he saw that she had taken a mobile phone out of her bag. He reached across. Her reactions were fast, but she wasn't expecting him to snatch her phone out of her hand.

'Here, give it back! What the fuck do you think you're doing?'

They were in a deserted side street. No one saw him toss the phone out of his window. He drove on.

'You don't need that any more. And don't use foul language in front of me,' he added.

She began swearing like a whore, rattling her door handle, but the childproof lock was on. He'd made sure of that. He knew what she could be like.

'Let me out at once!' she shouted. 'Stop the car and let me out!'

She started banging on her window.

'Don't do that!' he snapped.

She was beginning to annoy him. He took a deep breath and tried to remain calm, remembering what a temper she had. He didn't want this to turn into a full-blown argument while they were still in the car.

She turned and began hitting his arm.

'If you keep doing that, we're going to have an accident,' he warned her.

She carried on hitting him. Muttering a curse under his breath, he spun the wheel, turning into the entrance to a small park. The gates were shut, but he was off the road. He glanced around. The street was deserted in both directions.

As he whipped off his belt, her eyes widened in fear.

'No!' she cried out, 'you can't do that! I don't want you to carry on. Open the door, now!'

She grabbed her bag. While she was scrabbling inside it, he reached over and seized it. She wrestled to keep hold of it, but he was too strong for her. One of her red plastic nails flew off as he tore the bag from her grasp and tossed it on to the back seat.

'Here, give that back! That's my bag.'

She twisted round to reach for it. Grabbing both her wrists in one hand, he tied his belt around them.

'Now be quiet and stop making such a fuss, for Christ's sake. I'm only taking you home. Anyone would think I'm going to throw you into a snake pit, the fuss you're making. You'll be quite safe at home. You really don't need to look so worried. It's for your own good. Once you calm down, you'll realise this is the best thing for you. Trust me.'

'Trust you? What makes you think I'll trust you, when you've chucked away my phone and tied me up?' She spat on the floor. 'You're crazy.'

Saddened by her hostility, he shook his head.

'Come on, now,' he said, 'let's be friends. You know I'm only thinking of what's best for you.'

'You're insane,' she replied angrily. 'And we're not friends.'

'Of course we are,' he gave her a reassuring smile. 'Now come on, let's get you home and then we can play some games.'

She shook her head, muttering that she was fucked if she was going to play any fucking games with a fucking nutter. He knew she was only using that bad language to shock him. With a sigh, he reversed out of the park entrance and put his foot down again. Sooner or later she'd come round. In the meantime, he was going to take good care of her. She wouldn't get away from him again.

47

AFTER A DISTURBED NIGHT, Geraldine arrived at work feeling as though she could do with a rest. All through the night she had been fretting over whether she had done the right thing in handing over so much cash to her sister. She had an uneasy feeling she could guess how it might be spent. At the same time, she felt guilty for thinking the worst of her sister. She had no proof that Helena was a user, although everything about her jittery demeanour indicated that she was.

It wasn't only the puncture marks Geraldine thought she had glimpsed on Helena's arm. She could have been mistaken about them. But her sister's frailty and unhealthy skin, her glazed eyes and erratic conduct, all combined to build a fairly conclusive picture. And beyond the physical evidence, Geraldine's gut feeling was that Helena was an addict. She had met enough dysfunctional people in the course of her career to have developed a sense of judgement that was almost instinctive.

On top of her anxieties about Helena, she was worried about speaking to Adam.

'You really think we should release Chris and start all over again? You'd better have good grounds for wanting to do that,' he growled when she voiced her concerns.

Patiently Geraldine went over her reasons for doubting Chris's guilt. The detective chief inspector listened, his elegant features creased in a scowl that made him look like a sulky teenager. Geraldine persisted, convinced that Adam must have been plagued by the same reservations.

232

'So if what you're saying is right, it's back to the drawing board.'

'I'm not saying I'm right...'

'You may not be right, but we could be wrong,' he replied heavily.

Geraldine shrugged.

'Well, go on then, see what you can find out. But let's keep him where he is for now.'

Taking Sam with her, Geraldine had Chris brought to an interview room. It took a while to organise, as he refused to answer any questions without a lawyer present. At last everything was in place.

'Chris, I want you to think very carefully before you answer. Can you think of anyone who might have had a grudge against you, or your wife?'

The stout lawyer's eyes glittered as he grasped the implications of the question.

'Are you saying my client is no longer a suspect?' he asked, with a briskness Geraldine had not heard from him before.

'Please just answer the question.'

Chris glanced at the lawyer who nodded.

'If by that you mean did anyone hate Jamie enough to want to kill her, then no, I can't think of anyone.'

'Are you sure?'

'We're just ordinary people...' he burst out, and paused. 'We *were* just ordinary people,' he amended his statement, 'until all this happened. We didn't hate anyone, and no one hated us. We're – we were just people. We were just like everyone else, like any other married couple.'

Geraldine leaned forward to emphasise her point. 'Chris, you want to convince us you were happily married, but we all know you were having an affair. So let's be honest with each other. You weren't happy with your wife at all, were you? In fact, you were so unhappy in your marriage, you were desperate to get rid of your wife. Now, who do you suppose we imagine might have wanted to kill her?'

The lawyer leaned across, and muttered to Chris who shook his head.

'I think it was a terrible mistake.'

'She was killed in your house.'

'An intruder must've broken in by chance. A burglar. Jamie must have interrupted him, so he killed her.'

'There was no sign of a break-in.'

'Well obviously she must have opened the door, and then I guess he must've just barged in.' He dropped his head in his hands with a muffled groan.

'Are you absolutely sure you can't think of anyone at all who might've wanted to get your wife out of the way? It wasn't necessarily someone who deliberately set out to kill her. Perhaps she had an argument with someone who had been pushed to breaking point? Someone who was desperate to be free of her, and suddenly snapped?'

Chris's face reddened. He shook his head. 'I didn't kill her.'

'Did she know that you were seeing Louise?'

'No.'

Geraldine paused. There was no need to spell out the implications of what had been said.

'How can you be sure she didn't see you and Louise together? Perhaps when she was on her way home from work one day?'

Chris shook his head. Jamie hadn't worked, and, according to him, she had rarely gone out.

'She must have gone out,' Sam protested.

Chris shook his head.

Geraldine leaned forward. She spoke very gently. 'Did Jamie have problems, Chris? That must have been very difficult for you. I'm sure you did your best, but it was all too much for you, wasn't it?'

'I don't know what you mean,' Chris snapped. 'Jamie didn't have problems. Sounds to me like you're the one who's got problems.'

He was rattled. Geraldine wasn't quite sure why, and with the lawyer watching her she wasn't able to needle Chris too much.

'Chris, is there something you're not telling us?'

His reaction was out of all proportion to the question. His face darkened, and he scowled as though this was the first time she had accused him of murder.

With his voice rising in consternation, he looked and sounded as though he was panicking. 'There's nothing I haven't told you about Jamie, nothing! What makes you think I'd want to hide anything about her from you? There was nothing wrong with us. Nothing! We were just fine.'

The lawyer put his plump hand on Chris's arm to restrain him. Turning to Geraldine, he requested a break. Chris subsided, grumbling. Whatever was going on, there was something Chris was not telling them. But Geraldine had no idea what it was.

'My client's upset,' the lawyer said. 'He's overtired and overwrought. He needs a break.'

Geraldine nodded. They both knew the lawyer was insisting on a break because Chris was losing his self-control and threatening to become indiscreet. But Geraldine could not refuse his lawyer's request.

'Listen,' Chris said, when they reconvened after a break, 'Jamie didn't go out much, but that was her choice. She liked being at home. There's nothing wrong with that. She didn't go out to work.'

'What did she do? Did she have any hobbies? Who were her friends?'

'She looked after the house. That was her hobby. She didn't need friends. We were happy together.'

'So happy that you killed her,' Sam muttered.

'You seem to be confusing an accusation with a conviction,' the lawyer remarked drily.

48

'SOMEONE DOWNSTAIRS ASKING FOR you.'

It was a common enough request, but something in the constable's tone made Geraldine hesitate.

'What? Who is it?'

The constable shrugged, looking uncomfortable. 'She didn't seem to know your name...'

Neil didn't look round, but Geraldine could tell he was listening.

'You said he was asking for me.'

'She. It's a woman.' The constable hesitated. 'She's got a picture of you on her phone.'

Feeling uneasy, Geraldine stood up. Her fears were confirmed by the constable's next words.

'She's confused. She said your name was...'

'That's OK,' Geraldine interrupted him quickly. 'I think I know who she is.'

Helena was slumped on a chair in the entry hall, her eyes closed. She opened them when Geraldine spoke. At first Helena resisted when Geraldine asked her to accompany her. In a very short black skirt and bright red stilettos she could have been brought in for soliciting; her unsteady posture and smudged make-up betrayed her state of mind.

'Where you taking me? Get off me!'

Leaning forward, Geraldine put her lips close to Helena's ear in an effort to sound authoritative, while speaking too softly to be overheard. 'You don't have to come with me. I never asked you to come here. If you've changed your mind about speaking to me you can leave right now.'

Helena's hair smelt of stale beer and cigarette smoke. Inured as she was to lowlifes and misfits, Geraldine felt wretched. It was impossible to detach herself from the woman she might have been, had circumstances not dictated otherwise. Taking her by the arm, she led her sister to an interview room. She hoped that none of her colleagues had noticed their similarity. It might be difficult to ascertain that they were identical, without looking closely. But despite their differences, on a close look it must be clear they were at least related, especially now that Helena had dyed her hair.

Before either of them spoke, there was a knock on the door and the young constable opened it. 'Do you want me to come in with you?'

Wondering how much the young constable had deduced, Geraldine sent him away and invited Helena to sit down.

'What are you doing here?'

'I need to speak to you.'

'I'm at work. You can't come here again. If you do, I won't see you.'

'Never mind that. You got to help me. Listen, I only come here because I couldn't think where else to go. I knew they wouldn't follow me in here. I'm not safe anywhere else. Please, Erin, I need your help.'

'I just gave you some money.'

'I need to give them what's owed or I'm dead. They'd have been after you by now if you weren't protected by your people. But I got no one to protect me, and no one to help me. Only you.'

Geraldine hesitated. Of course some of her colleagues had relatives operating on the wrong side of the law, but this was a new situation for her and she hadn't yet worked out how she was going to handle it.

'You're lucky I left my desk to come and speak to you.'

Helena glared, muttering darkly about her luck.

'You blew the two hundred quid I gave you on drugs, didn't you?'

'Too bloody right, it was your dosh got me in this state. Always the same, innit? That was what my mum – our mum – did to me. Always give me enough to get me smashed, never enough to get the bastards off my back.'

Her complaint didn't make much sense, but Geraldine thought she might have spotted a way through the mess. If Helena was talking about wanting to escape from her current life, there was a chance she might be prepared to kick her habit. At any rate, it was worth a try.

'Listen, Helena, I want to help you. Do you understand what I'm saying? I want to help you.'

The focus in Helena's glazed eyes sharpened as she stared at Geraldine, but she said nothing.

'I'm going to pay your debt, all of it, but on one condition.'

Helena grunted and complained about there always being a catch. 'Can't you do nothing to help me without expecting something in return?'

'I'll help you, however much it takes, but I'm not going to give the money to you so you can get smashed.'

'I need the money, Erin. It's not for me. They're going to kill me if I don't give them what I owe.'

'I'll pay these people off, whoever they are, but I'll pay them directly. You won't touch the money because you'll just blow it on crack, or whatever it is you do.'

'Smack,' Helena replied. 'So you still want to help me, now you know your sister's a heroin addict?'

'Yes, I'll help you, but only if you go into rehab.'

'What the fuck you talking about?'

'You need help to kick your addiction.'

'It won't work. Once a user, always a user. I'm a loser. Jesus, Erin, this is me we're talking about.'

'That's my condition. If you don't go into rehab, you won't get a penny from me to wipe out your debt and get your drug dealer off your back.'

Helena closed her eyes. 'They'll kill me if I don't get them their money.'

'You're already killing yourself. If you don't agree to go into rehab, you'll be dead soon anyway. Listen, I'm offering you a chance here, Helena. A chance to live.'

'And if I don't agree to go into rehab, you won't hand over the dosh?'

'Exactly. Those are the terms on which I'm prepared to help you.'

'Shit, do you have to talk like that? Like you swallowed a bloody dictionary. I get it. You're clever and educated and now you want to save my life.'

'That's right.'

'That's got to be a first.'

Helena closed her eyes and appeared to fall asleep. She lay sprawled in the chair, snoring softly. Waking her, Geraldine took her out to the car park. Helena barely spoke. It wasn't clear if she understood what was happening. In the car she fell asleep again straight away. Geraldine drove her to a rehabilitation clinic she knew in North London. As the car stopped, Helena woke up and looked around, bewildered.

'Where the fuck are we?'

'This is a clinic where you can get the support you need to help you kick your habit. And after that, we can get to know one another properly, without all this. I can meet the real Helena.'

Helena laughed. 'This is who I am, Erin. There is no other Helena. I'm a druggie, a user, a junkie. This *is* the real me.'

'Well, we're here, and you know what you have to do if you want me to help you extricate yourself from all this.'

Helena seemed to wake up. Her eyes widened as she registered the elegant white stone building in front of them. 'Jesus, you are joking. I'm not going to no clinic...'

'Then you can sort out your own mess. Do you really think

I'm going to hand over five thousand quid, not to mention what this place is going to cost, if you're not a hundred per cent committed to kicking your habit? So make your mind up. Now. I'm not going to be messed around, Helena. What's it to be?'

Geraldine wasn't sure if she was being direct enough. Helena had to appreciate that she was serious. It really was a turning point in her life. Geraldine was offering her time in a private clinic where she would receive help to walk away from her addiction, something no one had ever been able to afford to do for her before. Geraldine's salary could support her sister in the clinic, even if it meant reducing her mortgage repayments temporarily, and she had the funds to pay off Helena's debt of thousands. She just hoped her sister wasn't too far gone to understand that she was being thrown a lifeline. In a way, Geraldine was rushing blindly into helping someone she knew nothing about. But Helena was her sister. She didn't really have any other choice.

49

Up until twenty-four hours ago, Cindy had been lucky, or perhaps naive. Still fairly new to the game, she had never intended to stay on the job for long. She had heard too many stories of girls being picked up by dangerous nutters. Occasionally a girl disappeared. Even among the few other sex workers she knew, several had been through terrible experiences. And there were always rumours, the stuff of nightmares. Realistically, she had to concede it was probably only a matter of time before her number came up. But she had planned to quit the job long before trouble came looking for her.

'You got to be tough as nails in this game,' one of the other girls had told her.

Still, most of the punters were OK. And as long as she was careful, she was going to come out of it on top. She wasn't the kind of girl to go off with a pervert. She was far too cautious for that. In the meantime, she was earning nicely, even after she'd given her pimp his cut. On a busy night she could make more lying on her back than she'd get in a month standing on her feet in a shop. In another few months she would reach her target. With enough money to pay off her debts, she was going to settle back into a dull day job and be satisfied for the rest of her life, or at least until she met a bloke who would support her properly.

She hadn't come up against any problems at all, until she'd climbed into a car the previous night. At first glance, the bloke had looked all right. Clean enough, decent clothes, nice wheels.

She wouldn't have got in his car if she'd suspected there was anything wrong with him. But it hadn't been long before he'd started talking strangely to her. Not dirty, but weird. When she'd tried to jump out of the car, she'd discovered she was trapped. From then on, things had gone from scary to downright terrifying. It was all well and good in theory learning how to defend herself, but this guy was strong. And her rape alarm was no use once he'd snatched her bag away from her. When he tied her wrists together, she'd given up trying to struggle against him. Sitting back in the passenger seat, she had waited for an opportunity to escape.

Eventually, they had turned into a small cul de sac where they'd drawn up outside the end house.

'Get out. We're here.'

She didn't move.

'I said, get out. Or do I have to carry you inside?'

She glanced around. It was late. There was no one else around, and no lights on in any of the other houses. As though reading her mind, he lunged forward and tied his scarf round her mouth so she couldn't cry out for help. Not that there was anyone around to hear her if she'd started screaming.

Having silenced her, he dragged her out of the car and hustled her through his front gate onto a narrow yard. She tried to resist, but he was holding onto her arm so tightly she couldn't wriggle free. With an exasperated sigh, he picked her up off her feet. Carrying her under one arm, he hurried towards the house.

'Here we are,' he said cheerfully, as he opened the front door.

He seemed to expect her to be pleased they had arrived. She glared at him. With her mouth gagged, she couldn't protest as he closed the front door on the world outside.

For weeks she had been mentally preparing to protect herself, in case she attracted the attentions of a maniac. She had rehearsed different scenarios over and over again in her imagination. Now the situation had arisen for real, she seemed to be paralysed. In any case, with her hands tied together, there wasn't that much she could do. So much for all her self-defence moves.

'Knee them in the balls,' one of her fellow workers had said. 'Works every time.'

As soon as she could, she was going to do just that. If she injured him, so much the better.

'Let's go upstairs and play a game,' he said, with a bright smile.

She grunted as loudly as she could, waving her arms as far as her bonds would allow, to indicate that she wanted to be released.

'I'll let you go, if you promise to behave,' he said.

She nodded her head.

'Good girl.'

He was speaking to her as though she was very young. With a flash of hope, she began to understand what he was after. He wanted to fantasise that she was a child. Well, she could play along with that, no trouble. She was on familiar ground with men's sexual fantasies. There was nothing dodgy about him after all. He was just a sad old paedo. If she could just calm down and work this job right, she might yet turn the situation to her advantage. The bloke had a house. He wasn't badly dressed. There could be money in it for her, if she was a bit clever. He might become a regular punter, and she wouldn't have to let on to anyone how much she was making. The more perverted his needs, the more he would pay. All she had to do was satisfy his needs. She might even be protecting some poor kid from being attacked.

'Come on then,' he said, 'you're room's ready.'

Turning, he led her upstairs, babbling about the games they were going to play. Still bound and gagged, she followed him. After the stress of the journey to his house, this was turning into easy pickings. She had been a fool to give way to panic. He had taken away her phone and her bag because they were the trappings of an adult. As a pretend child, she ought to have no control over her life. It had all become clear to her now.

He took her into a room furnished only with a plain grey bed. There were bars on the window.

'Here we are,' he said.

Once again, she grunted and lifted her arms. With a nod, he released her hands and gently removed her gag.

'That's better, isn't it?' he smiled. 'Now you can be comfortable.'

'Thank you, kind gentleman.'

He looked surprised. 'Call me daddy.'

'Thank you, daddy.'

'Wait here,' he said again. 'I've got something for you to wear.'

Perched on the bed, she pulled off her boots and undid her shirt in readiness. He still hadn't returned, so she took off her shirt completely and removed her underwear. It was inappropriate for a child to be wearing a bra anyway. She had to be careful to pander to his fantasy correctly, if she wanted to exploit him successfully. Lying on the bed, she spread her legs and waited, with everything on show. But she kept her little skirt on. That was probably what had attracted his attention in the first place.

The door opened. The man entered the room. He was wearing a clown's mask with a shiny red nose and fluffy orange hair, his expression concealed behind a huge painted grin.

'Come here and fuck me, daddy,' she said.

With a roar of rage, he ran forward. Grabbing the edge of the blanket, he threw it over her to cover her naked body. Raising his fist, he began raining blows down on her.

'You filthy little bitch. What the hell are you doing? I'm your father!'

The last thing she saw before she passed out was the gleam of his massive red nose.

50

GERALDINE PASSED AN UNEASY night. She slept in short bursts, waking frequently with a sinking feeling. First thing in the morning, she called the clinic and was relieved to learn that Helena was still there. So far so good. Leaving instructions with the clinic that she was to be contacted at once if there were any problems, she did her best to put her sister out of her mind and went into work. Her worries there weren't as distressing as her anxieties about Helena. In any case, she knew what was going on at work. Short of calling the clinic every ten minutes, she was completely in the dark about what her sister was up to. As Adam was keen on saying, speculation didn't help, so she threw herself into work, tidying up numerous loose ends in her paperwork, and signing off expenses claims from her team. Sorting out her documents, she tried to suppress unease.

'I can't see what your problem is,' Adam scolded her.

His dark hair could have been painted on it was so sleek, and his pale blue shirt looked freshly ironed. There was no Mrs Eastwood lovingly taking care of his laundry. Geraldine wondered if he did his own ironing, or whether he paid someone else to do it for him. She occasionally glimpsed the insecurity behind his composure, but there was no sign of it now. He gave her his characteristic controlled smile.

'I'm just not a hundred per cent convinced Chris did it.'

'Well, when you have something more concrete to go on, come and talk to me again.'

It was a dismissal. What made it worse was that Geraldine knew he was right, in a way. She had nothing to back up her claims. Her view was based on a hunch. She had warned her sergeants so many times to act on evidence, not intuition. Now she was making exactly the same mistake herself. With a sigh, she returned to her desk.

'What's up?' Neil asked, just as Adam had done. 'You've got your wife killer, so why the long face? You look as though someone shoved a lemon in your mouth when you weren't looking. What's wrong?'

Annoyed with herself for allowing her feelings to show, Geraldine was reluctant to admit that she was feeling wretched about her sister. There had to be a chance that Helena would kick her habit. If that were to happen, there would be no need for anyone to know about her past. In the meantime, Geraldine had to be patient.

'I'm just not convinced Chris is guilty,' she said, turning to Neil and forcing a smile.

'Really? I thought it was all over bar the shouting.'

'Yes, it seems that way.'

'Seems?' Neil was quick to pick up on her expression.

Geraldine shrugged. 'You know how it is,' she muttered.

'Last-minute doubts?'

'Yes.'

As it happened, Geraldine had been harbouring reservations about Chris's guilt all through the investigation, but she didn't want to discuss her feelings with Neil. Adam had already dismissed her misgivings as groundless and Neil might do the same. At the very least he would expect her to justify her disquiet, when all she could say was that it was just a feeling. Tedious administrative tasks did little to distract her. She decided to talk to Chris again. This time she didn't set up a formal interview, but instead went to speak to him in his cell, alone. He sat awkwardly on his bunk, a fine sheen of sweat glistening on his forehead. Without his lawyer at his side, he looked very isolated. He looked up at her with a helpless expression.

'I didn't do it,' he burst out, his voice trembling. 'I didn't. I couldn't. You have to believe me. Why is this happening to me?' His plea sounded almost childlike.

Geraldine spoke gently. 'Chris, you've been protesting your innocence. So let's just suppose for a minute, just between you and me, that you're telling us the truth...'

'I am telling the truth.'

'In that case, you really need to give me the names of anyone you think might have wanted your wife dead. You have to stop pretending she had no enemies and there was no one who could have held a grudge against her.'

'What are you talking about?' He shook his head and raised his hands in a helpless gesture, staring wildly at her.

'Tell me about any enemies your wife might have had. Who might have wanted to harm her?'

'No one. Jamie didn't have enemies.'

Geraldine paused for a second, wondering if he understood what she was talking about. 'But someone wanted her dead.'

'No. That's just nonsense. No one would have wanted her dead.'

'But someone killed her.'

'It must have been a random attack, a random nutter...'

'She was killed inside your house.'

'Random people come to the door. It must have been a random crazy caller...'

'Crazy I grant you,' Geraldine interrupted him, 'but not random. Chris, this was a carefully planned murder. Whoever killed your wife knew exactly what he was doing and how he was going to set about it. Your wheelie bin was used, and the murder weapon was deposited in your shed. Jamie's murder was carefully planned and executed. This was no chance opportunistic killer. It was someone who knew your wife and deliberately came calling when you were out. Who could that have been?'

Chris shook his head. 'No one would have wanted to kill my

wife. She had no enemies. She didn't know anyone. She hardly ever went out.'

'Was there a reason for that? Could she have been hiding from someone, someone from her past with a grudge against her?'

As she was speaking, Geraldine realised her theory sounded ridiculous. All the same, it was possible. And if Chris really hadn't killed his wife, Geraldine's suggestion should be investigated. But first she had to convince Adam that they might have arrested the wrong suspect.

Geraldine looked closely at Chris as she enquired what his wife had been like. He seemed instantly on his guard, which surprised her. Perhaps Adam was right after all, and she should stop questioning Chris's guilt.

'What do you mean, what was she like?' he asked, hedging.

'What kind of person was she?'

'Jamie was…' His eyes filled with tears and he dropped his head in his hands. His voice came out muffled. 'She was meek and good,' he said.

51

THAT EVENING, GERALDINE HAD arranged to meet her friend and former colleague, Ian. She had been pleasantly surprised to learn that he was in London. She had hoped he was there investigating the possibility of applying for a transfer to London but he explained he was attending a conference in place of a colleague who had a stomach bug. Geraldine mentioned an Indian restaurant where they could sit in a booth and chat, without being overheard.

'If you like Indian food, that is?'

'Sounds great. I'll see you there.'

Geraldine couldn't have been more excited if she had been going on a date. Ian was an old friend and she hadn't seen him for a while. They both appreciated the opportunity to talk over their current cases with an outsider who was neither involved in the case nor incapable of appreciating what it was like to be working on it. They could share each other's frustrations and triumphs with genuine sympathy.

'I wish Bev could see what I'm doing the way you do,' Ian had grumbled on more than one occasion, before his wife had left him.

After exchanging brief expressions of sympathy, he for the death of her mother, she for the breakdown of his marriage, they avoided discussing personal matters, keeping instead to the relatively safe topics of murder and detection.

'Have you thought any more about leaving York?' was the closest Geraldine approached to talking about his situation.

Not yet ready to talk about her twin, she was reluctant to pry into her friend's private affairs, for fear he might reciprocate. At the same time, she felt uncomfortable keeping quiet about someone who had become so important to her. She and Ian had worked closely together, and she trusted him more than anyone else she knew. But she needed time to work out how she felt about Helena before sharing her problem with anyone else. She was surprised when Ian told her that he was thinking of staying in York, despite his unhappy experience there.

'I thought you'd decided to move, and put your life there behind you?'

As she spoke, she did her best to hide her disappointment. She had been hoping Ian would request a transfer to London. They might have ended up working together again. Swallowing her dismay, she waited to hear what he had to say.

'The thing is, I really like York itself, the town I mean. It's a great place to live. But you're right. I was considering requesting a transfer to somewhere more exciting...'

'Like London?'

'Well, yes, exactly. I need to keep busy right now.' He raised his head, and Geraldine caught a sad expression in his eyes.

'So what's happened to change your mind?'

'They're setting up a new major crime unit where I'm based, in Fulford Road.' He grinned, his fleeting misery gone. 'Right now they're busy recruiting more officers and we're going to have more to do than ever! It couldn't have come at a better time, as far as I'm concerned. Can you imagine how Bev would have reacted if I'd told her I was going to be working longer hours? And this way I'm going to have more than enough to take my mind off what happened.'

Ian was more cheerful than Geraldine had seen him in a long time. When she commented on his good mood, he looked thoughtful.

'You know, I used to feel slightly sorry for you, and at the same time jealous of you, for being single. You had no one to please but yourself. And I have to say, much as I bitterly regret what happened, being single has a lot to recommend it. I can do what I want, whenever I want, and I'm not answerable to anyone. I didn't appreciate quite how hemmed in I was at the time, but I see now that I was living in a state of permanent guilt, all the time I was married. I can't tell you how liberated I feel now. I mean, I'd turn the clock back if I could, and still be married to Bev, in spite of what she did...' He paused and shook his head. 'The thing is, I can't believe I'm on my own and unattached again. I don't have to feel responsible for anyone but myself, and that makes me feel so free.' He smiled.

Geraldine wondered if she would ever feel that kind of freedom again, as long as Helena was alive.

'You were very young when you met,' was all she said.

He nodded. 'We were still at school. She's been a part of my whole adult life. More than a part of it – she was at the very centre of it. I've been forced to re-evaluate my entire life. If it wasn't for work, I don't know how I would have coped.'

'But you are OK, aren't you?'

'I'm fine, and I can't wait to see how things pan out with the new unit. There's nothing like work to keep your mind off your own problems.'

'What are you working on right now?'

Geraldine listened patiently as Ian told her about the murder he was investigating, before she told him about Jamie and Louise. He agreed the two murders must be connected, since both victims were in close relationships with Chris. The man who had met Louise at the station had been shorter than Chris, so he hadn't picked her up. At the same time, the fact that the bearded man had held out a sign with Louise's name on it suggested that her husband hadn't met her at Euston station in disguise either. It all came back to the mysterious bearded man. Like Adam, Ian thought that the shoeprints found near Louise's body could be irrelevant. Anyone could wear shoes that were too big, 'or even too small, at a pinch,' he added, smiling at his own pun. Geraldine couldn't help smiling back.

'But it does sound like there's a killer out there who's kept himself under the radar.'

Chatting about the bearded man with a friend who was not involved in the investigation should have clarified the various strands of the case in Geraldine's mind. Instead she left the restaurant feeling, if anything, even more confused than before. Ian had not been wrong when he had said it was a complicated case. But at least Geraldine had been able to forget about Helena for a few hours. She hoped Ian had also been able to take a break from his personal problems.

52

On Thursday morning, Geraldine received a summons from the detective chief inspector. Their suspect wanted to speak to them. Adam looked up at her from behind his desk, speechless but exultant. 'This is it,' his grin seemed to announce, 'the breakthrough we've been waiting for.'

He leapt to his feet, his excitement infectious. Falling into step beside him, Geraldine felt her spirits rise. Thrown off her stride by her problems with her sister, she had been unnecessarily sceptical of their success, but all they needed was a confession from Chris for the case to be satisfactorily tied up. And at last he seemed ready to capitulate. Even a clever lawyer wouldn't be able to get him off, once he had given a formal confession.

'I wonder why he's changed his mind.'

'His lawyer must have made him see sense,' Adam replied as he strode along the corridor beside her.

Chris stared miserably at Geraldine across the table. Wearing a dark green jacket, his squat lawyer resembled a giant toad. He watched Geraldine without seeming to blink. The atmosphere in the room was heavy with expectation. Beside Geraldine, Adam was sitting squarely on his chair, leaning back slightly in a relaxed proprietorial position.

'You said you had something you wanted to share with us?' Adam prompted the suspect.

Although he was doing a good job of hiding his feelings, his voice held a note of suppressed excitement, and his eyes were brighter than usual. Geraldine knew he was thinking this was it, the moment that would wrap the case up properly. Chris gave no response. No one spoke as they waited for him to answer.

'You want to tell us something,' Adam repeated softly. 'Take your time, and tell us in your own words.'

Instead of answering the detective chief inspector, Chris turned to his lawyer. 'I can't do it,' he muttered.

'It will help you a great deal if you simply come clean,' Adam urged him. 'Tell us what happened, and why you did it. The court will be far more lenient with you if you co-operate. I'm sure your lawyer will advise you it's best if you just tell us the truth.'

Chris didn't answer.

'You came here to confess to killing your wife. Let's get that out in the open straight away. We all know you did it, but if you take this opportunity to explain yourself, it will really help you. That's why your lawyer brought you here to record your confession. Crimes of passion are...'

'No, no,' Chris blurted out, casting a terrified glance at his lawyer. 'That's not it at all.'

'What do you mean?'

'I didn't kill my wife. I already told you I didn't kill her. Why won't you believe me?'

Adam made no attempt to conceal his irritation. 'What the hell's going on then? We came here to listen to your confession.'

The fat lawyer heaved himself up in his chair. 'My client gave you no indication that he wanted to confess to anything.'

'Why did he ask to see us then?'

'He has an additional line of defence he wishes to disclose.'

Adam flung his hands up in the air in a gesture of despair. 'What is this? First you come up with a belated alibi you didn't want to tell us about, now another line of defence suddenly and conveniently crawls out of the woodwork. Why didn't you bring it to our attention before now? And, given that you didn't, what makes you think we'll listen to it now, when it's clearly something you just fabricated?'

The lawyer smiled pleasantly. 'And yet, despite your histrionics, you are obliged to listen to what my client has to say.'

'He's not saying anything,' Adam grumbled. 'Unless he confesses, there's not a great deal he can say that would possibly interest us.'

'This concerns my client's relationship with his recently deceased wife.' The lawyer turned to Chris, nodding encouragement at him.

'Chris,' Adam addressed the suspect. 'We know you used to beat your wife.'

Before Adam could continue, Chris burst out, 'You don't know anything about me or my wife, and you don't know anything about our relationship.'

'Why don't you tell us then?' Geraldine prompted him.

But Chris dropped his head in his hands, mumbling, 'I can't. I can't.'

'We know you used to beat her,' Adam resumed.

Chris raised a tearful face. 'No. I never touched her, not in any way that might hurt her. I couldn't. I loved her.'

Adam lowered his voice. He sounded almost sorry for the suspect. 'Chris, we've found evidence of your beatings. There were traces of your skin under her nails from where she resisted your attacks. There are scratch marks on your neck. You can't continue to deny it.'

'My client's deceased wife was not defending herself,' the lawyer said.

Chris was sitting, stony-faced. Now he spoke. 'It was her. My wife used to hit me. I never hurt her. She – she – I tried to help her, but I couldn't stop it. She didn't want to be like that, but something drove her to do it. She never meant to hurt me. She was always sorry afterwards, but...' He dropped his head in his hands once more and sat, sobbing silently.

'That went well,' Adam snapped as they left the room.

'The trouble is, the story's credible. I know innocent until proven guilty and all that, but sometimes these lawyers are too bloody clever for anyone's good. If Chris didn't have legal representation, he would never have cooked up a defence like that on his own.'

'You're assuming it's not true,' Geraldine added quickly, annoyed with Adam for his intransigence. 'It's possible his wife used to beat him up. He never struck me as a violent sort of person. Quite the opposite, in fact. He seems quite a weak character. I think it's possible he's telling the truth.'

Sam thought it must be humiliating for him to admit that his wife used to beat him up.

'No man would admit to that unless it was true.'

Geraldine refrained from pointing out that Sam was hardly an expert on men's behaviour in the context of intimate relationships. She was not sure she agreed with Sam's opinion. All the same, she had to concede that a jury might be swayed by such speculation, as Adam pointed out with a scowl. All Geraldine could do was set out to talk to everyone who might have known the truth about the Cordwells' relationship.

53

EARLY THE NEXT MORNING, Geraldine drove to Chris's workplace to see what she could find out about him. Chris worked as a heating engineer, travelling round to residential properties fitting and servicing central heating systems. The company he worked for was based in Camden. It was a relatively small business, comprising a boss and his son, an office manager, and three other engineers. Geraldine went to the office and spoke to the boss first, explaining that she would like to speak to each of his employees in turn. The boss was not particularly co-operative. About fifty, balding and sturdily built, he gave the impression that he was used to getting his own way.

'Will this take long?' he asked. His face, already florid, turned a darker shade of pink. 'I need to get my engineers out. We've got customers waiting. You wouldn't be best pleased if your heating packed up and the engineer was late.'

Geraldine explained the nature of her enquiry and he shrugged. 'Terrible business. I couldn't believe it when I heard what had happened. None of us could. I would never have thought it of Chris.'

Although she was interested in what he had to say, they agreed she would speak to the engineers first as they needed to go out to appointments. The boss would be in the office all morning.

'Not that I'm not busy,' he added, 'there's always work to do. But I can take a few minutes off to speak to you. Once my lads go out, that's it, you won't catch them again until this evening.'

The first engineer was tall and thin, and monosyllabic in his responses.

'Did you ever see any sign that Chris might behave violently?'

'No.'

'Did he talk to you about his wife at all?'

'No.'

'Were you surprised to hear he'd been arrested on suspicion of murder?'

'Yes.'

Despairing of prising any information out of the man, Geraldine finally asked whether there was anything he could tell her about Chris. She wasn't surprised when he said no. The second engineer was equally taciturn. He only uttered one whole sentence, telling her that 'Chris was a decent bloke.' The third man was altogether different. Small and bright-eyed, he entered the room with a swagger and extended his hand.

'Robby,' he announced with a cheery smile. 'How can I help?'

Geraldine suspected he was more of a salesman than an engineer. Inviting him to take a seat, she asked him how well he knew Chris. He shrugged, still smiling.

'How well did I know Chris?' he repeated. 'How well did I know Chris?'

Geraldine waited.

'He kept himself to himself really,' was the disappointing reply. 'He was never in any trouble, as far as I was aware, and I never heard of any complaints against him. You could've knocked me down with a feather when I heard he'd bumped off his missus. I mean, he didn't strike me as the aggressive sort. But I didn't really know him.'

For all his attempts to be helpful, he was no more informative than the other two engineers had been. Questioning the boss was equally useless. He more or less repeated what his chatty engineer had said, but in a more long-winded way.

'He was punctual,' he said, 'and he was a good worker. I

still can't believe it. But of course you never really know what people are like, do you? You just get to see their public persona. Behind closed doors, who knows what goes on?'

It was the same with the boss's son, who looked uncannily like his father, and spoke in a similarly pompous manner, and with the office manager who, Geraldine discovered, was the boss's wife. They all reported that Chris had appeared to be mild-mannered and conscientious, while admitting that they hadn't really known him.

Next Geraldine visited Chris's doctor.

'Do you have an appointment?' the middle-aged receptionist asked when Geraldine reached the front of the queue.

Quietly Geraldine explained the reason for her visit and the receptionist said she could go in next. Five minutes later, Geraldine was facing a lively young Asian doctor.

'He was my patient, yes, and we heard about his wife,' he said. 'Is it true that he was responsible for her death?'

Geraldine told the doctor that was what they were trying to establish.

'And how can I be of assistance, Inspector?' he asked, glancing at the clock on his wall.

'Did he or his wife ever come to see you with injuries consistent with physical abuse?'

The doctor hesitated before he answered. 'These injuries are not always conclusive,' he hedged.

'But in your opinion?'

'Might this be treated as evidence?'

'Yes.'

He paused again, checking his records before he replied. 'Chris came to see me a couple of times, presenting injuries consistent with having been assaulted. The first time he told me he had been involved in a pub brawl. He had a black eye and split lip and it was pretty clear he had been fighting. I questioned him on the second occasion, and he was adamant that he had accidentally fallen down the stairs in his house.'

'What about his wife? Was she your patient too?'

The doctor checked his records again and frowned. 'She was registered with one of my colleagues here, but there's no record of her having come to the surgery with any injuries. In fact, although she was registered with us for five years, she never came to the surgery. Her records here are blank.'

'What about prior to the last five years?'

The doctor shook his head. It seemed Jamie had only once been to the doctor in the past twenty years, when she had been suffering from flu.

'Is that odd for a patient to only go to a doctor once in twenty years?' Geraldine asked.

'It's unusual, certainly, but some people are healthy, and not everyone likes going to the doctor.' He smiled.

Chris had told them that his wife didn't go out much, and had no friends. Geraldine suspected that she had been agoraphobic. She was beginning to wonder what other psychological problems Jamie might have suffered.

'Doctor, I'm investigating the murder of your patient. If she had any problems, or if there's anything at all that you can tell us about her, you really do need to share that information with me.'

The doctor shook his head once more. 'You probably know more about her than I do. We never saw her here after she registered with us.'

'Did she come here alone when she registered?'

The doctor tapped a few keys and checked his screen. 'Her husband registered with us on the same day, so I'd guess they came in together.'

While Geraldine had been talking to Chris's workmates and doctor, Sam had been talking to his neighbours. A consistent picture began to emerge of a woman rarely seen leaving her house. Several of the neighbours described Chris as polite and quiet, others claimed never to have spoken to him. None of them had heard any sounds of fighting in the house, although he had been heard raising his voice a few times. There was nothing to substantiate Chris's report that his wife had physically abused him.

Late that afternoon, Geraldine went to see the pathologist. Miles smiled when she walked into the mortuary. For once he wasn't about his grisly work but was sitting in the office with Jasmine, a young anatomical pathology technician who worked with him. They were discussing Jasmine's wedding plans. Geraldine suspected Miles wasn't as interested in weddings as she was, but he was putting on a good show of enthusiasm.

'I've just got to make sure I don't put on any weight until after the wedding,' Jasmine was saying as Geraldine entered the office.

'Hi Geraldine,' Miles looked up and greeted her. 'Did you know Jasmine's getting married?'

Geraldine had already spoken to the young technician, but she repeated her congratulations.

Miles stood up. 'I was going to call you first thing in the morning, Geraldine. I've got something to show you.'

'Must be my lucky day,' she replied with a laugh.

'I wish,' he answered, 'but the wife would kill me, and then I'd need a post mortem and I really wouldn't want any of my colleagues let loose on me.' He turned to Jasmine in mock horror. 'You wouldn't let anyone carve me up, would you? Who knows what they might uncover about my ill-spent youth?'

After a little more banter, Miles led Geraldine into the mortuary. 'Here it is.'

Geraldine looked at two bodies he was showing her, Jamie Cordwell and Louise Marshall, the two women whose deaths she was investigating. Watching Geraldine's reaction closely, Miles told her that traces of the same DNA had been found on both corpses. It wasn't a match with anyone so far involved in the case.

'So you're telling me DNA was found on both of them and it definitely couldn't have been from either of their husbands?'

'Exactly. To spell it out, it wasn't a match for either Tom Marshall or Chris Cordwell.'

'But how do you know it was the killer's?'

The pathologist shrugged. 'I don't know who the killer is. I find out everything I can from the bodies about how they died, and when they died, and where they died. But it's not for me to establish who killed them. I seem to remember that's your job.'

The unidentified DNA was a physical link between the two dead women. Apart from Chris, there was no other reason to suppose they were connected in any way. Given that Jamie rarely went out and so probably didn't come into contact with many people, it was quite likely the owner of the unidentified DNA had killed both of them. It might be a dead end, but the lead couldn't be ignored. It was imperative they discovered whose DNA it was, but that was impossible without a match.

'Can you tell me anything about this DNA, anything at all?'

'The individual is male, Caucasian, with brown hair and eyes. That might not narrow it down much, but it might help you to eliminate potential suspects.'

Geraldine sighed.

54

ON SATURDAY MORNING, GERALDINE sent a team to take Chris's garden apart, searching for any trace of DNA. It was a fairly hopeless task, but she still wondered if an elusive killer could have set Chris up by planting the murder weapon in his shed. It would make sense of the fact that the chisel hadn't been found when the shed had first been searched. It was one more piece of the puzzle that pointed to Chris being innocent. Of course, it would be virtually impossible to find traces of DNA in a garden, but searching inside the shed might prove more helpful.

In the meantime, while the shed was under scrutiny, Geraldine set to work looking for anyone who might have held a grudge against either of the Cordwells. Louise's death appeared to have been collateral damage. She had probably been killed to prevent her from giving Chris an alibi. If Jamie hadn't been murdered, Geraldine suspected Louise would still be alive.

Adam saw the investigation very differently. 'We know Chris had motive and opportunity to kill them both,' he said, addressing a meeting of the team. 'Let's start with motive. First, his wife. They were hardly happily married. Granted, we've established she was the violent one in the relationship. We should have considered that possibility from the start, instead of jumping to the conclusion that he was the aggressor in their fights, just because he was the man. But it comes to the same thing. She was physically abusive and he resisted too violently, or maybe he snapped and fought back. We need to press him on that point and find out what really went on between them on the night she was killed. Who else would have known where the bin was?'

'Anyone could have seen it outside,' Geraldine said.

'As for Louise,' Adam continued, ignoring the interruption, 'we know Chris was relying on Louise to give him an alibi for the night his wife was murdered. When she refused, he panicked. He might not have intended to kill her, but things got out of hand.'

When Geraldine reminded him that Louise had tried to leave a message giving Chris an alibi, while she was dying, Adam dismissed that as speculation, impossible to prove.

'Just because it was written in her blood proves nothing. We can't be sure what she was trying to tell us. We do know the only name she wrote down in her blood as she was dying. We've got enough here to build a case against Chris Cordwell,' he went on. 'But if you can find any evidence to indicate that he's innocent, I want to see it, and sooner rather than later.'

Geraldine decided to search through all the interviews and data, hoping to discover a new lead. All she had to go on was the thought that if Chris was innocent, then someone must have framed him. So far she had come across nothing that suggested he had any enemies. No one seemed to have even disliked the mild-mannered man, or to have had much to do with his reclusive wife.

'She must have left the house sometimes,' Sam grumbled.

'Unless she was agoraphobic,' Geraldine pointed out.

'The doctor didn't say so.'

'He said there was nothing else he knew about, but he didn't know much about her because he never saw her, and her most recent medical records were from her adolescence.'

Geraldine had intended to visit Helena that evening, but by the time she finished what she was doing it was growing late, so she decided to carry on working for another hour or so, until she was too tired to carry on. There were a lot of documents to scan through. She was about to pack it in for the night when she spotted something she thought could be interesting. The accusation had cropped up before, but she hadn't paid much attention to it at the time. On the face of it insignificant, in the context of looking for someone with a potential grudge against Chris it raised a question mark. With very little expectation, she looked up the file and read through the report.

Chris had been accused of abducting a young woman from outside Cockfosters station not long before the death of his wife. The missing woman's father had noted down the registration number of Chris's van, and reported him to the police. The case against Chris had been dismissed straight away, but as she read the notes, Geraldine grew increasingly excited. Chris had never denied being at the station. His wife had confirmed that she had been in the van with him. They would never be able to discover whether she had been lying to protect her husband.

But another scenario occurred to Geraldine as she cast about for possibilities. Believing that Chris had snatched his daughter, it was just plausible that the missing woman's father had taken matters into his own hands. There was a chance he might have killed Jamie and framed Chris for her murder, as an insane act of revenge for the loss of his daughter. Bizarre though it seemed, it might be worth looking into. The officer who had filed the original report about the alleged kidnap was not at work that evening, but would be there in the morning. Although she was interested in this potential lead, Geraldine decided to wait until she had spoken to the officer concerned before taking her suspicions to Adam. All she had now was a tenuous supposition.

It was difficult to go home and put her new theory out of her mind for the rest of the evening. Without any evidence, she was reluctant to share her idea with any of her colleagues. Keen to talk it through, she called Ian Peterson. He was so full of the major crime unit that was being established in York that she hesitated to raise her idea with him.

'So, how's your investigation going?' he enquired at last.

'Oh, fine,' she heard herself answer. 'I just called to find out how things are going there.'

She hung up and was putting some dinner in the oven when her phone rang.

'Erin, it's me.'

'Helena? How are you doing?'

'I need help.'

'What? Where are you?'

'I don't know.'

'Aren't you at the clinic?'

'No. I had to leave. They knew I was there. I had to get away. Erin they're coming for me. You got to help me. They're going to kill me if I don't get the money to them tonight.'

55

HAVING AGREED TO MEET Helena outside Arsenal station, Geraldine drove straight there. Uncertain what to expect, she waited anxiously. The street outside the station was quiet at that time of night. It would have been very different after a football match at the stadium just around the corner. She hadn't been able to get much sense out of her sister's paranoid rambling over the phone, but one thing was clear. The night wasn't likely to end well. Helena had said her life was in danger. Given the kind of people her sister consorted with, Geraldine didn't think she was exaggerating. The drug dealers to whom she owed money were growing impatient. Geraldine had just lost her mother. She didn't want to lose her sister too.

She had been waiting for about twenty minutes when a skinny figure tottered out of the station. She paused, looking around uncertainly. Catching sight of Geraldine waving, Helena scurried over to her.

'Here you are,' she said as she flung herself into the car, as though Geraldine had been keeping *her* waiting.

'What's this all about?'

'Get away from here. Drive to your house. We can talk there.'

Geraldine refrained from pointing out that she didn't live in a house. Reassured that Helena didn't know her address, she made no move to start the engine.

'We're sitting here until you tell me what's going on.'

'Stay here if you like, but I'm telling you he'll find us soon. And then you'll be done for too. You think you got some God-given protection just because you're a pig? He won't know who

267

you are. And he won't care neither. He'll shoot. No questions.'

Responding to the urgency in Helena's voice, Geraldine turned the key in the ignition and pulled away from the kerb.

'Start talking, or we're going straight back to the clinic, which is where you should be.'

Helena scowled. Without straggly locks framing her face, her likeness to Geraldine was more obvious than ever. Talking rapidly, Helena launched into a convoluted account of how she had been befriended by a man called Benny.

'Course, it's not his real name. He likes bennies.'

Geraldine grunted to indicate she understood Helena was referring to the sedative Benzodiazapine. When she asked for Benny's real name, Helena said she had no idea.

'He's just Benny.'

Geraldine thought she could probably trace the man known as Benny from his street name.

'Where does he live?'

Helena could tell her nothing about the man she called Benny. All she could say was that she had believed he genuinely liked her. Geraldine knew the end of the story long before Helena stopped speaking.

'The fucking scumbag fleeced me for everything I had, and now he knows I'm due to inherit what mum left, he's after every penny of that too.'

'So he's your pimp and your supplier, and you owe him a great deal of money,' Geraldine summed up as Helena finished her account.

It was a squalid story, but hardly unusual.

'That's about it, yes. And if I don't get him his money, he's going to kill me.'

'He's just trying to frighten you.'

'Well, he's succeeded. But this ain't a game, sis, he really is going to kill me. I know him, and I know exactly what happens to anyone who owes him.'

'You don't have to refuse to pay, just stall him. Explain about your situation. You're going to come into money soon. He'll just have to wait.'

She knew what Helena was going to say, and knew that her sister was right. People like Benny didn't wait.

'He ain't going to lose street cred over me,' Helena said with a bitter laugh. 'And besides, he's pissed. He'll kill me for the hell of it, just because he can. He don't give a fuck. You got to help me, Erin.'

She explained she had arranged to meet her supplier near to Arnos Grove tube station.

'I got to take the dosh in a bag and hand it over without no one seeing. I got a bag here. I put everything I got in there. You got to put up the rest. It's got to be another four and a half grand or I'm dead.' She held up a faded leather bag, as though that would persuade Geraldine to help her. 'I got to meet him there tomorrow night at eleven. If I don't show up he'll find me. He always gets people. I been on the run from him for months. No way is he going to let me get away from him again. I mean it, sis. If you don't help me, I'm dead.'

There was nothing else for it. Geraldine drove Helena to a small pub with rooms that she knew of in Soho, explaining that Benny might trace her if she stayed at Geraldine's flat. Helena acquiesced at once. In fear for her life, she wasn't bothered about where she was going to stay, as long as she was safe. Having dropped Helena off, settled her in a bedroom and paid the bill in advance, Geraldine left, promising to return the next day. First she would need to go to the bank and draw out nearly five thousand pounds in cash.

With serious reservations about what she was doing, Geraldine set off home. She knew she ought to inform the drug squad about her meeting with Benny, but she was reluctant to draw their attention to her sister. She decided instead to follow Helena's lead and find out more about Benny. All she needed was to see him, and take a photograph of him, and she should be able to see him apprehended, protecting herself and Helena at the same time. Determined to protect her sister, she went to bed and slept uneasily.

Her handbag stuffed with cash, she took the train to Oxford Circus and walked from the station to the pub where she had left Helena. She was nervous, with so much cash on her, but it was important to behave as though nothing unusual was happening. Besides, it was her money. So far she had done nothing wrong. Once she knowingly handed the cash to a drug addict who intended to use it to pay a dealer, she would be straying into questionable territory. But Helena was her sister.

She went up to Helena's room and knocked on the door. There was no answer. The door was unlocked. Expecting to find her sister asleep in bed, she found the room was empty. She checked the bathroom. There was no sign of Helena. She ran back downstairs, hoping to find her sister at breakfast, but she was not in the small dining area, or in either of the bars. Helena had disappeared.

56

WITH A SICK FEELING in her stomach, Geraldine went up to the bar and asked if the girl knew where Helena had gone.

'Are you Erin?'

'Yes. Is there a message for me?'

The girl behind the bar nodded and fished an envelope out of the till. 'She left this for you. She said it's really important.'

Registering the barmaid's wide staring eyes, Geraldine took the envelope. Taking pains to conceal her unease, she ordered a coffee and took her drink over to a small round table in a corner of the bar. Only then did she take out the note that her twin had left for her, and look at what was perhaps the most disturbing message she had ever read.

'You got to do it. I'm sick. He'll be in the car park. If you don't say nothing, he'll think you're me. If you don't, I'm dead.'

Geraldine sipped her coffee thoughtfully. There was no way she ought to even consider carrying out the request. All her instincts screamed at her to report this rendezvous to the drug squad. But the cash Helena needed was in her bag. If she carried out this one generous act, there was a chance she and Helena might begin to forge a relationship. It would take time, and a lot of patience on both their parts, but the possibility was coming tantalisingly close. Helena's desperation had opened up a way for Geraldine to try and gain her trust. It had to be worth the attempt. If Geraldine refused to help her sister, that might be the end of their relationship. They were strangers. Fate had given Geraldine this chance to connect with her lost twin. Regardless of the risk, she had to do what Helena asked.

With her thoughts in a whirl, she went home and changed into her scruffiest clothes. Wearing old jeans and a loose T-shirt that made her look skinny, she made up her face to look very pale and smudged her eyeliner until it looked as though she had grey bags under her eyes. After messing up her hair with oil and a dusting of talcum powder, she hurried to the station and caught a train to Arnos Grove. Arriving at the car park with five minutes to spare, she looked around. There was no one else in sight. Everywhere she looked she saw only shadows and empty cars. As she hesitated, at the periphery of her vision she thought she caught a flash of movement. She spun round. Someone stirred in the shadows.

Geraldine started forward. 'Helena?' she whispered.

Squinting in the half light, she made out a hooded figure. As her eyes grew accustomed to the darkness, she saw a man shuffle forwards. Cutting across the shadow, a narrow shaft of light from a street lamp fell on him. From beneath his hood, pale eyes gleamed at her. She caught only a glimpse of an unshaven face before he shifted out of the light.

'You got it?' a hoarse voice asked.

Geraldine hesitated. The hooded figure took a step towards her. He was holding a gun.

'Helena,' he growled, 'don't fuck with me. You owe me. Take three steps towards me and drop the bag.'

'I'm not...' Geraldine broke off, her thoughts whirling. 'Is that you, Benny?'

'Don't fuck with me, you stupid whore. Who d'you think it is? You think I'd send one of the boys?' He spat on the ground. 'Now give it here if you want to walk.'

Geraldine glanced at the gun. Benny had mistaken her for Helena. He might shoot her, whatever she did.

'Give it here,' he repeated. 'Three steps.'

Geraldine's fingers tightened on the handle of the bag until the hard leather dug into her palm. Without moving her head she looked around, but there was no sign of anyone else in the car park. With desperate resolve, she stepped towards the man and held out the bag. In one minute this would be over, and she could begin to build what might develop into the most important relationship of her life. Benny shuffled forwards, one arm extended. When she was a foot away from him, she leaned down slowly and placed the bag on the ground. As she straightened up he lunged for it. In that instant, a bright light snapped on.

'Put your hands in the air! Don't move!' a voice shouted. 'Hands in the air where I can see them.'

Geraldine froze.

Benny swore, swivelling frantically on his heels. 'What the fuck...'

'Don't even try, Benny,' the disembodied voice called out. 'We've got you surrounded, you and your whore there, so you'd best come quietly. Now drop the gun, nice and steady, and put your hands up, where I can see them.'

Benny spat on the ground. 'It was Monkey told you I was here, wasn't it?' he growled. 'I never did trust that fucker.'

The gun fell on the ground with a faint clatter. As Geraldine went to whip out her identity card, another voice yelled at her to raise her hands in the air. Understanding what might happen if she tried to explain, she obeyed the order. As she did so, her wrists were seized in a firm grasp. Before she could say anything, she heard handcuffs snap closed and her arms were securely trapped.

'Wait,' she cried out firmly, confident the arresting sergeant would respond to the authority in her voice. 'You're making a mistake.'

The sergeant gave a bark of laughter. 'Save it for the interview. Once you've been charged you can complain all you like.'

'Listen, you've got this all wrong. Look in the inside pocket of my jacket.'

'It's Benny all right,' another member of the drug squad called out. 'Hello, Benny,' he went on in a conversational tone. 'I told you we'd get you one day, didn't I? So, what's in the bag, Benny?'

'Fuck off, it's mine. Keep your hands off it. I'm telling you, it's mine, all above board. Don't you touch it.'

Out of the corner of her eye, Geraldine saw Benny struggling to free himself from his arresting officer's hold.

'Come on, let's get you in the car. Come on, move it. Mind your head.'

'This isn't the first time I've been in a police car,' Geraldine muttered as she was pushed over to the waiting vehicle.

'Well, let's hope it's the last time,' the officer who had cuffed her said.

Geraldine felt as though she had been slapped in the face.

'You need to check my ID…'

Geraldine's announcement was greeted with a snort of laughter. Controlling her agitation, she allowed the sergeant to lead her over to the car. It was difficult to know what to do, given that she had been caught in a deserted car park handing thousands of pounds to a notorious drug dealer. Although she was reluctant to tell her colleagues about her sister, it seemed there was nothing else for it. She had faced tricky situations before, but never anything like this. Whatever happened, it was going to be difficult to talk her way out of this problem.

Head down, she sat in the back of a police car taking her to the nearest police station. All the while they stopped and started in the late London traffic, her mind was racing. She couldn't decide what to say when challenged about her reasons for her actions. The prospect of confessing everything to Adam and throwing herself on his mercy made her cringe, but she couldn't think of an alternative. She bitterly regretted having agreed to have anything to do with Helena's illicit activities. But it was too late to change her mind. And she still had no idea where Helena had gone.

57

'ARE YOU SERIOUS?' GERALDINE wasn't sure, but it sounded as though Ian was trying not to laugh. 'You are pulling my leg, aren't you?'

'No, I'm not.'

'And they actually arrested you?'

'Yes, I just told you. That's what happened.'

'Bloody hell. I wish I'd been there to see it. I can't believe it. You, of all people.'

Geraldine bristled. 'What's that supposed to mean?'

'Just that you're always so conscientious and...' He broke off.

This time there was no doubt. He was laughing.

'This isn't funny, Ian. I've been suspended.'

'Suspended?' His altered tone indicated that he was taking her seriously at last. 'What the hell happened?'

Geraldine took a deep breath. 'I gave a known drug dealer five thousand quid that I'd just taken out of my own bank account.'

'What? How come you didn't know who he was? And what were you doing handing over that much money anyway? Don't tell me it was cash? Bloody hell, Geraldine, didn't you check...'

'I knew exactly who he was and what I was doing. It was an arranged handover.'

Ian laughed. 'This is a wind-up.'

'It's true, Ian.'

There was a pause before he said flatly, 'I don't believe you.'

'I'm serious. I've been suspended pending an enquiry.'

'I'm not surprised.'

Geraldine felt tears prickling her eyes. She had been sure Ian wouldn't believe she had strayed on to the wrong side of the law, even if no one else trusted her. His next words reassured her somewhat.

'So what's the story? What's behind all this? What on earth could have possessed you to do that?'

'You don't think I've become a user?'

'Don't be ridiculous. There's something behind this, I'm quite sure, but I'm damned if I can work out what the hell you thought you were playing at. What's happened, Geraldine? This is to do with your twin sister, isn't it? So, what can I do to help?'

Struggling in earnest not to cry, Geraldine took a deep breath. 'It's a long story.'

'I've got all night.'

Slowly at first, and with increasing desperation, Geraldine told Ian how she had tried to help her twin sister. She did her best, but she could tell Ian didn't understand why she had paid off the dealer.

'I did it to help my sister,' she insisted, aware that her explanation sounded crazy. 'I thought if I paid him off, she'd be more likely to trust me, and be ready to have a relationship with me.'

'You thought you could buy her affection?'

'No,' she protested miserably, aware that he was right. 'It wasn't like that. Not really.'

'What was it like?'

She shrugged, glad that he couldn't see the tears sliding down her cheeks.

'And what happens now?' he went on, suddenly brisk.

'I've been suspended while the DCI considers what to do. So far nothing's been decided, but I suppose if I don't resign they'll boot me out. If I'm lucky they'll let me go quietly,' she added sourly.

Having spent years establishing herself as a successful detective, one moment of insanity had put an end to her long career.

'No,' Ian interrupted her. 'You can't leave. Go and speak to your DCI. Ask him to let you continue, even if it means going back to being a DS. It wasn't so bad, was it? You'd have to leave the Met, but there are other forces. Listen,' he went on, his voice warming with enthusiasm, 'you know they're in the process of setting up a major crime unit here in York. I told you about it, didn't I? Well, they're recruiting right now. We need experienced officers. You could leave London and all that behind you, and come up here. Work in York. It's not a bad place to live. I think you'd like it. And what else are you going to do if you leave the force altogether? Imagine waking up every morning with absolutely nothing useful to do. It'd drive you nuts, Geraldine. At least think about it. We need good officers up here. We're really stretched right now. Someone with your experience would really help. You can't just throw away all your skills, not when they're needed.'

After she had hung up, Geraldine resisted opening a bottle of wine. She had a lot to think about. Apart from considering her own future, she was worried about Helena. Having tried to pay Benny off, and seen him arrested, Geraldine had still had no word from her sister and could only hope that she was safe from any repercussions following Benny's arrest. There had only ever been one way Geraldine had been able to cope with personal troubles, and that was to throw herself into her work. Whenever she had felt her own life was a mess, at least she had been able to strive to achieve justice for the dead. If that sense of purpose was taken away from her, she wasn't sure how she was going to cope.

The following morning, she called Adam and begged him to allow her to carry on working. He flatly refused.

'You're lucky you're not being thrown out on the spot,' he fumed. 'You must see that the desire to protect a long-lost sister doesn't give you licence to flout the law. It's no defence. Only your outstanding record, and the fact that you weren't directly involved in any illegal activity, is keeping you from instant dismissal.'

Back at home, Geraldine automatically started reviewing the case. Lacking access to the full records gave her an overview that turned out to be very helpful. There was one possible lead she had intended to follow up, before the disaster with Helena had occurred. She called Adam but he was very brusque with her. She had expected he might reject her suggestion, since he had been convinced all along that Chris was guilty.

'You're no longer working on the case,' he snapped.

There was not much Geraldine could say to persuade him to listen to her. As soon as he hung up she phoned Sam, but her colleague didn't answer the call. Annoyed, she tried again, stabbing at her sergeant's name on the list on her screen. This time Sam's phone went straight to her voicemail. After they had developed what had felt like a genuine friendship, Sam was blanking her. Frustrated, Geraldine suspected every officer on the team had been warned not to speak to her. Not only was she accustomed to working with the backup of a team, but without access to the case records it was going to be very difficult for her to pursue her new line of enquiry. She struggled not to give in to despair. There had to be a way to climb back out of this catastrophe, but she couldn't see how.

She was still considering her options when her home phone rang. She didn't recognise the number. With a cautious flicker of hope, she took the call. It was Sam.

'Why didn't you answer your phone?' Geraldine blurted out, irritated.

'You know I couldn't.'

'Why are you calling me?'

Down the line she could hear the hesitation in Sam's voice. 'You called me. I couldn't just ignore it. I wanted to speak to you, as a friend I mean, just to see you're OK. You are all right, aren't you? I just want to know you're all right, but I couldn't speak to you at work. You know we've been advised not to talk to you while you're – under investigation.'

'Where are you?'

'I'm at Emma's office, using her phone. I can't contact you, not officially. I'm calling as a friend, Geraldine. Are you all right?'

'Yes... no. Oh, what do you think?'

'Geraldine, what the hell happened?'

'What have you been told?'

'Nothing. Only that you've been suspended. No one's told us why. Not a word. What happened, Geraldine? I won't tell anyone but please, let me know what happened.'

Geraldine related the events leading up to her suspension.

Sam reacted angrily. 'That's outrageous,' she fumed. 'You were only trying to help your sister. I thought we were supposed to help other people. I thought that's what the job was all about.'

'Never mind all that right now. I need you to do something for me.'

'Don't ask me to do anything illegal.'

'No, I won't. Don't be daft, Sam. And I haven't broken the law. Not really. Not yet anyway.'

'What do you want me to do?'

Quickly Geraldine explained what she needed. 'Don't email me,' she finished. 'Meet me in the toilets at the McDonalds by Kings Cross station at six o' clock tomorrow. No one will spot us there.'

To begin with, Sam was reluctant to co-operate. 'It's more than my job's worth to be discovered passing on information like that.'

'You'd better make sure you're not discovered then,' Geraldine retorted sharply before she hung up.

58

BY THE TIME HE'D realised his mistake, it had been too late to save the woman. The blanket having slipped off, he had pulled it back over her bruised chest and torso. Her head had been lying at an awkward angle, with dark purple marks on her neck left by the pressure from his fingers. She lay perfectly still, her mouth hanging open, her blank gaze fixed on the ceiling.

For a long time he had stood beside the bed staring at her through his clown's eyeholes, wondering what to do. At last he had ripped off his mask and placed it carefully over her face to hide her distorted features. Tufts of fluffy orange hair rested on the pillow, a splash of bright colour above her grey shroud.

He turned and left the room, locking the door behind him. Things were getting out of hand. He couldn't keep repeating the same mistake without risking getting caught. It was so unfair. The woman's death wasn't his fault, but he was bound to be blamed for it if anyone found her. He had never invited her to come to his house. *She* had approached *him*. It was understandable that he'd thought she was his daughter. It was a natural mistake to make, when she'd been so keen to get into his car. How was he supposed to have known that she was a stranger?

The more he thought about it, the more aggrieved he felt. It was all her fault. He had no reason to reproach himself. If anyone was a victim in this situation, it was him. A complete stranger had targeted him, climbing into his car on the pretext of being his daughter. If it had all ended badly, she had only herself to blame. She ought never to have tried to trick him like that. She would have to be disposed of, but that could wait. His priority now was to find his daughter.

Time was passing, and Beth was still out there. He had to rescue her. He had a plan, and this time he would make sure it succeeded. When they were reunited, he would be able to take care of her again, like he used to do when she was a child. And she would care for him again. They needed each other. He had tried calling her, but he couldn't get through. In desperation, he set about searching her room. The drawer of her desk was locked, but it was a child's desk with a flimsy catch. Forcing the blade of a knife between the top of the drawer and its frame, he pushed and joggled it up and down until there was a click. Holding his breath, he pulled the drawer open. There was nothing inside.

He printed out a recent photo of her and slipped it in his wallet. That evening he would start showing it to everyone he could find in Camden, returning night after night until he had an answer. It didn't matter how long it took, he was going to find her.

With the photo safely stowed, he carried her old box of costumes into the kitchen. Dressing up had been her favourite game. She used to beg him to play with her, insisting he put on ridiculous outfits and spoke in funny voices. The papier-mâché masks she had made were splitting and crumbling, but there were plastic masks in the box too. The clown mask had gone, but there were several animal masks. He laid them carefully on the table. When she came home, she could choose whichever one she wanted. He pulled out several old frocks and colourful ties, and a piece of net curtain she used to wear on her head, pretending it was long hair. He smiled at the memory. Closing his eyes, he pictured her flouncing around the kitchen with a curtain hanging off the top of her head. The image was so real, he could almost believe she was there with him, pirouetting around the kitchen.

He was going to find her soon, and bring her home.

59

SEATED WITH A CLEAR view of the Ladies, Geraldine waited anxiously, a cup of coffee on the table in front of her. It was unnerving to think that she and Sam were no longer colleagues, even stranger to acknowledge they might never be allowed to work together again. At exactly six o'clock, Sam entered McDonalds and joined the queue. Only customers were given the code for the toilet. Geraldine made no move to attract her attention. Without so much as a glance in Sam's direction she kept her in sight, at the edge of her line of vision.

Unlike Geraldine, who had only bought a coffee, Sam tucked into a burger and chips. Geraldine waited, increasingly nervous for Sam more than for herself. They weren't sitting together, but the longer they remained in the same café the greater the risk they would be spotted. It wouldn't take a genius to work out that it was no coincidence they were there at the same time. Although they had done nothing wrong, if another officer happened to see them it would be impossible for Geraldine to communicate with Sam.

Miserably she fidgeted with her coffee while Sam finished her meal. There was nothing she could do to force Sam to hurry. Eventually Sam disappeared into the toilet. Geraldine followed at once. With a grim glance around, Sam handed over a manilla folder stuffed with papers.

'It's all here,' she muttered.

Sam had taken a risk in printing out the documents, because it would have been impossible to pass on information electronically without leaving a trace. This way, she could claim she wanted to study the hard copies herself, if anyone challenged her. Geraldine stowed the folder in her bag, and left without another word. It was dangerous to linger. Only when she was back in the privacy of her flat did she take out the folder. Before opening it, she brewed herself a pot of coffee and then settled down on her sofa to leaf through the contents of the file.

It contained copies of interviews with Chris, reports on what his neighbours and work colleagues had said about him, and other associated information stored on the database. Sam must have spent hours gathering it all together, and she had done so with amazing promptness. Geraldine hoped she hadn't aroused suspicion. With a sigh, she opened the folder and took out the first sheaf of papers. This was the only thing that could keep her sane.

Having sat up most of the night studying everything Chris himself had said in his various interviews, she fell asleep. So far she had uncovered nothing new, but her mood of despair had lifted. Ian was right. She needed her work. If she could relocate to York, perhaps even taking a demotion to sergeant would be better than leaving the job altogether. Waking at midday, she turned her attention to what others had said about Chris. Again, there was nothing to suggest he was innocent.

Only Geraldine had actually spoken to Louise, and heard her give him an alibi before she had disappeared. Adam had suspected Geraldine was mistaken in believing what Louise had told her. Louise had certainly sounded convincing over the phone, but Geraldine had to concede that Adam was right to dismiss that reported brief conversation as insufficient evidence to exonerate Chris. They couldn't even be sure it had really been Louise speaking to Geraldine on the phone. Chris could have persuaded another woman to call Geraldine, claiming to be Louise. If he had done so, that pointed to his being responsible for Louise's death to prevent her from coming forward and revealing the truth.

Having read through all the documents relating to Chris's arrest, Geraldine turned her attention to his earlier history. He had no form. Until recently, he had never had anything to do with the police at all. But two months earlier, he had been questioned in connection with the disappearance of a young woman. Her distressed father had reported her missing to the police. His daughter, Bethany, had called him from Cockfosters station at midnight to say she had fallen asleep on her train. Having missed her stop, she had phoned her father for a lift home. He had answered the summons, but when he had arrived at the station, his daughter wasn't there. Noting down the registration number of a van he had noticed driving out of the station as he arrived, he had passed that information on to the police.

Geraldine read the entire report through several times. The van that had been spotted leaving was registered to Chris Cordwell. He had insisted that the woman Bethany's father had seen in his van had been his wife. Once again, the only person who could have confirmed his story was now dead. Geraldine felt a rush of adrenaline. Chris had never been involved with the police before. Now in the space of two months, he had been accused of abducting a woman, and of murdering his wife. The allegation of abduction hadn't been pursued, due to lack of evidence, but something felt wrong.

60

IT WAS EARLY AFTERNOON by the time Geraldine began to suspect the two crimes of which Chris had recently been accused were connected. She brewed herself a pot of coffee and reviewed the earlier report. The more she thought about it, the more convinced she was that the episodes must be linked in some way. She called Emma's phone.

'Hello, Emma, it's Geraldine here. I work – used to work with Sam. This might sound like an odd request, but could you ask Sam to call me as soon as she can? I'd call her myself but...'

'That's OK,' Emma interrupted her quickly. 'Sam told me what happened.'

There was a pause. 'It's OK,' Emma went on. 'I'll get her to call you.' She hesitated. 'Sam thinks what happened was terrible. I mean, what happened to you. She knows you don't deserve it. She's mad about it. She thinks it's really shabby, what happened to you.'

Geraldine gulped. 'Actually, it's more complicated than that. But thank you. Please tell her that means a lot to me.'

'It's probably better if I don't say anything. She's already really wound up about it. We're trying not to talk about you any more.'

'But you will ask her to call me?'

'Of course. Is there any message?'

'No, I just need one more piece of information, if she can get it to me.'

'I'm sure she will.'

When she rang off, Geraldine surprised herself by bursting into tears. Sniffing fiercely, she wiped her eyes and returned to her files. Unable to settle, she rang the rehabilitation centre, hoping that Helena might have turned up there, but they hadn't seen her since she had first walked out.

'She was here voluntarily,' the woman on the line pointed out.

'Yes, I know. I just wondered if she might have come back.'

That evening, Sam called her on Emma's phone. With access to the database, she was able to call back in five minutes with the information Geraldine wanted.

'Who is she?' Sam asked.

'Just someone I need to talk to, to settle something for myself.'

'Do you want me to come with you?'

'Better you don't know anything about it,' Geraldine answered. 'Don't worry. I'm not doing anything stupid or dangerous. It's just a query I want to clear up. But if I do discover anything new pertaining to the case I will need to pass it on to someone. Adam's told me I'm not to have anything more to do with it, so you'll have to claim this was your line of enquiry. But let me see if it leads anywhere first. It's probably nothing.'

'I'm intrigued!'

For the first time in days, Geraldine smiled.

It was too late to make a visit, but first thing the following morning she went to see the woman whose address Sam had given her. Veronica lived in a block of flats off Hanger Lane in Ealing. It was not far from North Ealing station, and Geraldine thought she might be less conspicuous if she took the tube. Her car would be relatively easy to trace. Avoiding facing the cameras at the station, she made her way off the train and walked along a winding side street to her destination. It was a fairly narrow road, with cars parked on both sides. She was glad she had decided to take the train.

Reaching the address Sam had given her, she rang the bell. No one came to the door. Rather than go all the way home and return in the evening, she walked back to a parade of shops by the station and took a seat towards the back of a café. She waited there for a couple of hours then moved to a large old pub a few doors along. No one took any notice of her as she waited for the day to pass. Ordinarily she would have questioned the sense of what she was doing, but now she had no other demands on her time. The hours passed until she began to feel uneasy and crossed the road to another café. When it closed at half past five, she returned to the pub for yet another coffee. At seven, she walked back up the road to Veronica's house and rang the bell. This time the door opened almost straight away.

'Veronica?'

'Yes?' The woman standing in the doorway eyed Geraldine suspiciously. 'What do you want?'

Aware that she had no identity card on her, Geraldine tried to sound confident as she introduced herself as a detective inspector. Technically she still was, although she had been suspended. To her relief, the other woman did not ask to see her ID.

'I'm enquiring about your stepdaughter, Bethany.'

Veronica's face dropped. 'Has something happened to her?'

Geraldine was quick to reassure her. 'As far as I know, Bethany's fine. This is about her father, Daniel Saunders.'

Veronica shook her head. 'Daniel's not here. Dan and I divorced years back, and I remarried a long time ago.' She shook her head. 'Dan was – is – a lovely guy, but – look, you were asking about Bethany. Perhaps you'd better come in and tell me what this is all about.'

Under normal circumstances, Geraldine would have considered pointing out that Veronica hadn't asked to see her ID. As it was, she followed her into the house without a word.

'Like I told you, Dan's a lovely man, but he's got a problem with his daughter. The trouble started, I suppose, when his wife died. Bethany was barely six when it happened and it hit them both very hard, as you can imagine.' She shook her head.

'How sad.'

'After that it was just the two of them for four years, so they grew very close. I didn't realise just how close they were. When I met Dan I thought I could help. I mean, I was in love with him, but marrying him meant taking on the child as well, and Bethany was very difficult. But I thought I could win her round in time. I felt sorry for her. The poor child had lost her mother, after all. But eventually I had to accept that losing her mother wasn't the real cause of her problems. It was Dan.'

'What do you mean? If there's any abuse...'

'Oh no,' Veronica interrupted quickly. 'At least not in that way. There was nothing improper. It's just that he indulged her in every way possible and she became completely wild – drugs, drink, men – you know. Really wild. He was desperate, but he never put his foot down, never said no. If she'd had a bit of discipline in her life, she might have managed it better, going through puberty without a mother. I tried, God knows I tried, but a stepmother isn't the same, not after all that time. Maybe if I'd been more supportive of her it would have worked out, but, well, anyway, Dan and I split up over it.'

'That must have been hard for all of you.'

'It was, at the time. Oh, I'm not bitter about it any more. Far from it. I feel sorry for them both, especially poor Bethany. She was a victim in all this, a victim of his overbearing protectiveness. He wanted to know everything about her life – where she went, who she was seeing, what time she was leaving the house, where she was going, when she'd be back – this went on well into her twenties. She was twenty-three when we divorced, and he was still on at her all the time. 'I've lost your mother, I couldn't bear to lose you too,' he used to say to her, as though letting her out of his sight meant risking her life. She tried telling him to mind his own business, and they had some terrible rows. So after a while she just lied to him about what she was doing. I didn't blame her for that. If he'd had his way, she'd never have left the house.'

She broke off. Geraldine nodded, doing her best to look sympathetic.

'He was crazy,' Veronica resumed. 'He treated her like a six-year-old when she was twenty. In his head, he was stuck with her as a small child. I'm no psychiatrist, I can't explain it, but somehow in his mind she never grew past the age she was when her mother died. And her emotional development was stunted by all his smothering. He wanted her to be totally reliant on him for everything. It was horrible to watch at close quarters. If I'd known how he was suffocating her, I never would have married him, but I had no idea how unhealthy their relationship was until I was there all the time, living with them. Once he married me, any pretence at normality slipped. He insisted I join in his insanity. Of course, I refused. She wasn't my daughter, and in any case, it was no good for her, the way he carried on. I never thought she'd have enough spunk to walk away from him. But she did. In the end, she did.'

'What happened?'

'About three months ago she came to see me.'

Veronica described how Bethany had begged for help to escape her father.

She said she wanted to get right away, leave the country, but she couldn't manage it alone. She was afraid her father would find out if she tried to book a flight out of the country. Veronica had agreed to do what she could to help Bethany, who wanted to go to New York. She said she had a friend there.

'I didn't ask too many questions. She's twenty-seven. If she wanted to go to New York, she was perfectly entitled to go there, as far as I was concerned. I was only too pleased to help her get away and live her own life. It wasn't an easy decision for her, but she told me if she didn't escape soon, she would die enslaved to her father. And she was probably right. So I bought her ticket and she sorted out her documents and went. I drove her to the airport. She's in New York now, as far as I know, and good luck to her. God knows how she's coping, but at least she's having a shot at growing up. It was a shabby thing for her to do to Dan, going off like that without a word, but I still think I did the right thing, helping her. She wouldn't have got away from him otherwise. He would never have let her go. I'm telling you, where his daughter's concerned, he's completely insane. You'd think he was normal if you met him, but he's not. He's really not.'

Geraldine listened carefully to Veronica's account of her stepdaughter's trip to America. She was not sure if this was relevant to the case she was investigating or not.

'And her father has no idea where she is?' she asked.

Veronica shook her head emphatically. 'She made me promise not to tell him. She's afraid he'd follow her there and find her and try to drag her home.'

'But in the meantime, he doesn't know where she is.'

'Don't you see? This is the only way she can feel she's free of him?'

'What if he thinks she's dead?'

Veronica looked solemn. 'I think that's what she's hoping. In a way, she wants to be dead to him. That's the only way she can be free to live her own life.'

Geraldine thought it sounded extreme, but she didn't say so. When she asked where she could find Dan, Veronica insisted she first promise not to tell him where Bethany was.

'I can't make any promises like that,' Geraldine replied. 'If you refuse to give me his address, I can find out from the borough intelligence unit.' Veronica didn't know that Geraldine no longer had access to any information the police force could supply. 'Either way, we'll find him and contact him, so you might as well tell me where he is.'

She made a note of his address and stood up to leave.

'Or you might find him at the garage where he works,' Veronica added.

With a start, Geraldine heard her name the garage where Chris had taken his van for repairs.

61

Trying to make sense of what she had just heard, Geraldine left. In view of what Veronica had said, it seemed possible that Daniel had killed Jamie and framed Chris for the murder, in the mistaken belief that Chris had abducted and killed Bethany. He had committed the murder with the double satisfaction of knowing that Chris would not only lose his wife, but that he would be convicted of the murder himself. If Geraldine's suspicion was true, he had exacted a terrible revenge on the man he believed had killed his daughter. And all the while, Bethany had been in New York.

But Daniel couldn't have killed Louise, because there was no way he could have known she was arriving at Euston station at seven fifteen on the night she disappeared – unless there was some connection between them that Geraldine knew nothing about. It was maddening that she was unable to question Chris to find out whether he or Louise had known Daniel. All Geraldine could do was prompt Sam to speak to the suspect for her. In the meantime, she wanted to find out as much as she could about the man who had accused Chris of abducting his daughter.

It was too late to visit him at work, and she was reluctant to go to his home. Any hint of a complaint against her conduct right now might jeopardise any faint hope she still had of remaining on the force. Even though she tried to convince herself she no longer wanted to continue working as a detective, she was desperate not to scupper any chance that she might be allowed to stay. There was nothing more she could do that day. She hesitated to contact Sam again, but she had to pursue what could be a significant lead. Hoping she wasn't pushing her luck too far, she called Emma's number.

Sam sounded wary when she came to the phone. 'I can't do any more copying,' she began.

'No, don't worry about that. I mean, what you did was brilliant, and more than enough. I just called to thank you.'

'That's OK. How are you doing?'

'Yes, I'm all right. Have there been any developments?'

Sam told her that the case against Chris was being compiled and the suspect had become taciturn.

'He hardly speaks to us now, but Adam doesn't care. He thinks we've got enough evidence against him. To be honest, it all seems fairly cut and dried now. Chris isn't even bothering to protest any more.'

'Has he confessed?'

'No, not in so many words, but he isn't denying his guilt either.'

Not denying guilt was not the same as confessing to it.

'There is one thing I need you to do for me,' Geraldine said.

'I'm not sure I ought to be...'

'Just this one last thing,' Geraldine replied.

She was counting on Sam appreciating how difficult it was for her to have to beg where previously she had been able to command. Predictably, Sam caved in straight away.

'Oh, go on then. What is it?'

Geraldine explained that she wanted Sam to question the suspect about a man called Daniel Saunders.

'Daniel Saunders?' Sam repeated.

'Just ask him how well he knows him.'

'How am I supposed to do that? I mean, I can't just throw it in. Oh, and by the way, tell me about a man called Daniel Saunders. What if he doesn't want to talk. I told you, he's not being at all co-operative. I think his brief's warned him he's going down, and he's in an almighty sulk. I'll be lucky if I can get him to say two words.'

'Try goading him. We have to find out if he knew Daniel Saunders.'

'You need to give me a bit more than that, Geraldine. I need to know who this man is, and how he's supposed to fit into the case. I mean, is he a witness? If so, you really need to share what you've found out. You can't go carrying out an investigation on your own.'

'Listen, Daniel Saunders is the man who accused Chris of abducting his daughter.'

'Oh yes, I remember. It came to nothing though. There was no case to investigate.'

'Not for us, but what if Daniel was convinced he was right in his suspicions? What if he went to Chris's house to look for his daughter, only while he was there he killed Jamie and left Chris to take the blame for her murder? A wife for a daughter.'

'OK, there's motive, of a sort, I suppose, although it sounds pretty crazy.'

'When is murder not crazy?'

'But how is he supposed to have done it?'

'This is where it all becomes interesting.'

'Go on, I'm listening.'

Aware that she didn't have much time, Geraldine hurriedly explained that Daniel worked at the garage where Chris's van had been taken in for repairs. 'So it's not a huge leap of imagination to suppose he might have spotted the van, recognised the registration number, and realised he had found the man he suspected of abducting his daughter. It could have been Daniel who drove the van on the night of the murder.'

'But the van was back with Chris on the night of the murder.'

'Only according to the paperwork in the garage, which could have been doctored after we left.'

'OK, I'm following so far. So the idea is that Daniel killed Jamie and framed Chris, all in the name of revenge.'

'Yes. It's unlikely, I know, but it's possible. Only then Louise turned up to give Chris an alibi so Daniel had to get rid of her.'

Geraldine paused. 'That's where I come unstuck.'

'Because there's no way Daniel could have known Louise was going to arrive at Euston when she did.'

'Unless he knew Chris, or Louise. That's why I want you to question Chris, without anyone realising what you're up to – you'll have to say it's something you thought of. Whatever you do, don't mention you were talking to me. And then you need to speak to Louise's husband again, and find out if he knew Daniel. Perhaps he took his car to that garage. Somehow there has to be a link between Daniel and Louise which meant he knew she was expected at Euston on the seven fifteen train.'

Sam was reluctant to follow up the lead. Adam was confident they had arrested the killer. They were hoping to get a confession out of Chris but, even without one, the case against him was more or less watertight, at least in terms of his wife's death. Louise was more problematic.

'That's the point,' Geraldine interrupted her friend. 'Daniel Saunders might help us to clear up the second murder. It has to be worth a try. But I really need to know of any possible connection between him and Chris. Just ask him, Sam. Ask him how well he knew Daniel Saunders and let me know exactly how he responds, what he says, how he looks...'

'OK, I know how to question a suspect,' Sam interrupted her irritably.

Geraldine smiled. 'Thank you. Call me tomorrow and let me know what he says. Please, Sam. This is really important.'

Geraldine hardly slept that night. She waited all morning for the phone to ring. Sam wouldn't be able to call her from work, but given how important this was, Geraldine hoped she would call her as soon as possible. By late morning she had still heard nothing, and was struggling to control her impatience. There was nothing she could do but wait. She made a few calls trying to trace what had happened to Helena, but could discover nothing. Everything in her life was conspiring to frustrate her.

Finally her phone rang, at lunch time.

'Did you speak to him?'

'Yes, I tried,' Sam replied, 'but there was no point. He's completely unresponsive. It's like he's given up. He knows he's beaten.'

'Did he react when you mentioned Daniel Saunders' name?'

'No. But, to be fair, he didn't respond to any questioning.'

Geraldine thanked Sam, but they had nothing more to say to one another.

'I hope the situation gets resolved soon, one way or another,' Sam said after an awkward pause. 'All this waiting around in limbo must be driving you nuts.'

Geraldine didn't admit that she had been keeping herself busy studying the files Sam had given her.

'There is one other thing you could do for me,' Geraldine said. 'Nothing to do with the case.'

'What's that?'

Geraldine explained that she hadn't seen her sister since Helena had voluntarily left the rehabilitation clinic. There was very little Sam could do to help, but she agreed to ask around and see what she could discover. Geraldine had to be content with that. With so much to worry about, and more enforced inactivity, she thought she might go stir crazy. It was a few weeks since she had last seen her adopted sister. In desperation, she picked up the phone.

62

CELIA WAS SURPRISED TO hear from Geraldine on a Tuesday.

'I'm kind of at a loose end,' Geraldine confessed.

'Is everything OK?'

'Oh yes, of course. It's just that I'm in between cases right now and haven't got anything pressing to do this afternoon.'

'So you sorted out the double murder you were working on?'

'Yes.'

'Honestly, Geraldine, I don't know how you do it.'

Geraldine forced a laugh. They had been through this same conversation many times before. 'I do it because it's my job,' she replied. She almost broke down and confessed that was no longer true, but she didn't want to worry Celia. In any case, her problem might yet be resolved. It was unlikely, but while the possibility remained that she might be reinstated, there was no point in giving up hope. 'Anyway,' she went on, 'I'm free this afternoon and wondered if you fancied a visit?'

'This afternoon?'

Geraldine regretted her rash offer at once. She never made last-minute arrangements with her sister. Celia was bound to suspect something was wrong.

'That would be lovely,' Celia gushed, wiping out all Geraldine's concerns. 'I'm so bored sitting around all day like a beached whale. You know the doctors have told me to take it easy, but it's driving me round the bend. You can't imagine what it's like, having nothing to do all day.'

Geraldine muttered sympathetically, privately stung by the irony of the situation. Half an hour later, she was behind the wheel of her car, speeding out of London. Putting her foot down, she felt a sense of freedom, and remembered what Ian had said about leaving the Met. He was right. There were other police forces. As she left the cramped streets of London behind her, a plan began to form in her mind. Continuing in her present post had become untenable, but she might be able to persuade Adam to support her relocation to a more humble post in a different area of the country.

York was a long way north, but that might not be a bad result. Celia wouldn't be happy about her moving so far away, but she would deal with that objection if it arose. For now, it was enough to hope she might still have a future in a job she loved. Working as a detective sergeant hadn't been so bad. Ian was right about that. In any case, if she moved out of London, taking a cut in her salary would be virtually irrelevant. She could sell her flat. With her savings and the equity on her flat in Highbury could be enough for her to buy a decent flat in York outright. Mortgage free, she might even end up financially better off than she was now.

By the time she arrived at Celia's house, Geraldine was feeling far more positive than she had been since her traumatic arrest. With any luck, her career was not over, but merely shifting into a new gear. It would be hard to revert to the role of sergeant, but it was preferable to any other future she could imagine for herself. Not much over forty, she wasn't ready to give up yet. Life would go on for her, and she would continue to serve the cause to which she had dedicated her whole adult life. Nothing would really suffer from her demotion, apart from her pride.

Celia was pleased to see her. Not for the first time, Geraldine felt a stab of guilt that she visited so infrequently. She determined not to mention the possibility of her moving further away. It wasn't hard to remain silent on the subject.

Celia was so excited to have someone to talk to that Geraldine didn't need to say much. Celia launched into a detailed account of her most recent visit to the hospital, and her sessions with the midwife, as though nothing else mattered.

'I'm not boring you, am I?' she asked at one point, with a rare flash of insight.

Geraldine reassured her she was keen to hear every detail about the pregnancy.

'It's not something I'm ever likely to experience myself, so this is the next best thing,' she added.

Celia accepted that readily enough. Having completed her account of the progress of her pregnancy, which all sounded fine, she turned to the topic of the nursery. She insisted on taking Geraldine upstairs to view the wallpaper, the small wardrobe, changing table, cot and nursing chair.

'We had to get everything new,' Celia explained. 'We never thought this was going to happen again – I mean, I'm forty-three and we've been trying ever since Chloe was a toddler and she's nearly a teenager now. So we threw out all the old stuff from when Chloe was born years ago. I had nothing!' She laughed. 'I mean, literally nothing!'

Just a husband, a daughter, a baby on the way, and a five-bedroomed house, Geraldine thought. She struggled not to feel a twinge of bitterness. She couldn't help comparing Celia's circumstances with her own solitary life, and Helena's dysfunctional existence.

'So you just had to go out and buy everything new,' she smiled. 'Poor you!'

They both laughed. Geraldine duly praised the rabbits and teddy bears on the wallpaper, the dainty white furniture, and a brightly coloured mat on the carpet. Turning to follow Celia out of the room, she noticed a baby listening device. A thrill of adrenaline ran through her, like an electric current.

'What's that?' she asked.

'It's a listening device.'

'Yes, yes,' Geraldine interrupted impatiently. 'I know what it is.'

'But you just asked...'

'Sorry, Celia, but I've got to go. I've just remembered something I need to do.'

'But you've only just got here,' Celia protested. 'Chloe'll be home in an hour, and she'll want to see you.'

'I'm sorry, but I really can't stop. This can't wait.'

Leaving Celia bemused at the top of the stairs, Geraldine ran out of the house. Putting her foot down, she was back home in record time and leafing through the documents. She couldn't find what she was looking for. She tried her own record book, but there was nothing there to help her. Wracking her brains, she picked up her phone. This time, Emma didn't sound as welcoming as before.

'Can't it wait until tomorrow?' she asked. 'We're about to go out.'

'No, it can't wait. Please, Emma, I only need to talk to her for a second. I wouldn't ask if it wasn't important.'

'As long as you're not going to get her into trouble.'

'I won't, I promise.'

Sam sounded bothered. 'Listen, I spoke to Chris like you asked me to, and he's giving nothing away. He wouldn't say a word. I'll try to contact Louise's husband tomorrow if I can, but it's not easy. I do have other work...'

'Never mind all that now,' Geraldine interrupted her impatiently. 'Do you remember when we went to the garage? Or rather, when we got back? A sergeant stopped me in the corridor the following day. He was using the car we'd taken to the garage and he said he'd found a listening device someone had dropped under the driver's seat. You need to find out who that sergeant was, and what he did with the device he found.'

Sam sounded irate. 'Geraldine, I've no idea what you're talking about. I'm going out.'

'If that device was switched on before we drove out of the

garage, someone might have overheard us talking in the car about Louise arriving at Euston on the seven fifteen train.'

'Yes, we did talk about it, I remember,' Sam interrupted, suddenly excited. 'We talked about it in the car. But would a device like that have a large enough range to transmit our conversation?'

'If we were talking about it before we left the garage forecourt, then I don't see why not. We can look into that once you've tracked down that device.'

'I'm on it.'

Without another word, Sam rang off. She had clearly grasped the significance of Geraldine's suggestion. It might be a false trail, but it was possible Daniel had discovered the time of Louise's train from Geraldine herself. It was a depressing thought. But if it was true, they must at least make sure he was caught. They were too late to save Louise. It wasn't too late to catch her killer.

63

FIRST THING THE NEXT morning, Sam went to see Adam to tell him what Geraldine had suggested. He was tied up in a meeting with the borough commander all day. There was nothing else for it but to proceed discreetly with her investigation on her own. It didn't take long to establish who had used the car after she and Geraldine had driven to the garage. She knew the sergeant concerned by sight and set off to find him. He was surprised when she approached him about it, but he remembered finding something he had believed was a baby listening device under the driver's seat.

'I tried to adjust the seat and it wouldn't go back. So I took a look, and there it was. I took it to your DI, but she didn't want it. She said she'd never seen it before.' He lowered his voice. 'I hear she's been suspended. Shame. She was all right, that DI. I don't suppose there's any chance she'll be back?'

'I'm not at liberty to discuss it,' Sam snapped and he lowered his eyes with a shrug. 'Now, what happened to that listening device?'

'I asked if she wanted it and she said she didn't,' he replied, suddenly defensive. 'It's not like I didn't tell anyone.'

'That's OK, we didn't need it then, but now we do need it. Listen,' she went on, less aggressively, 'we think it might help us with our investigation, so can you tell me what you did with it?'

He frowned. 'Honestly, I can't remember. I asked around at the time, but no one claimed it. After that, I suppose it went into lost property. You can try there anyway. I can't think what else I would've done with it.'

Sam thanked him and hurried away to check the lost property. The listening device was there, along with a selection of watches and other small items. Placing it carefully in an evidence bag, Sam sent it straight off to be checked for fingerprints. She marked the request 'urgent'. Then she returned to her desk, trying to suppress the wild hope that her efforts might help get Geraldine reinstated. The thought that she might be permanently removed from her post was too dreadful to contemplate. Geraldine was by far the most dedicated and effective colleague Sam had ever worked with, and besides that, they had developed a genuine friendship. Sam was not sure how she would control her feelings if Geraldine was kicked off the force, just for trying to help her sister.

'It's not fair,' she had complained to Adam. 'I thought the whole point of our work was to help people. How can you condemn her when she was only trying to save her sister's life? Anyway, aren't we allowed to be human in this job?'

Sam knew she was probably blotting her own record by speaking to the detective chief inspector so bluntly, but she didn't care. Geraldine deserved better treatment than he had given her.

Adam had glared coldly at her. 'I'm sure Geraldine would be the first to admit that she can't continue under the present circumstances.'

'I don't know what you mean. You know perfectly well she's the best DI in London...'

Adam had merely shaken his head. 'If you have nothing further to say, then I suggest you return to your work. We still have a murder case to solve. Unless you can provide evidence that Chris killed Louise Marshall? No? I thought not. Now, get back to work and we'll both forget about your outburst just now. If your DI is in serious trouble, she has only herself to blame. Believe me, no one could be more disappointed than I am about what she did, but there's no way she can carry on here after the way she behaved. She appreciates that as much as I do. You'd do well to think of your own position before you open your mouth like that again.'

The only way Sam could show her support for Geraldine was by helping her disgraced colleague to solve the case. If they succeeded, Adam would have to acknowledge that he needed Geraldine to keep working. He might agree to overlook her one mistake in a long and illustrious career. The thought of Geraldine's troubles spurred Sam on. Her next task was to re-examine all recent purchases of chisels. They had already searched for evidence that Chris had bought one recently, without any success. It was a massive undertaking, and she set a team of constables to work on it. Her justification for the man-hours spent on it was that she wanted to check for evidence that Chris could have bought the murder weapon. But along with Chris's credit card details, she had discreetly instructed them to look for a purchase made on Daniel's credit card. If Adam found out, she would have to talk her way out of it. In the meantime, the search went on.

At lunch time, she nipped out of the police station and called Geraldine.

'Hi, it's me. Emma's lent me her phone.'

'Thank you. And thank her. So, any news?'

When Sam brought her up to date with the latest activity, Geraldine's gratitude moved Sam. More than ever she determined to assist Geraldine to solve the case. After lunch, she received a message that a partial oily fingerprint had been recovered from the listening device. There was no match for it on the system. Somehow she had to obtain Daniel's fingerprint, but she had to get hold of it without arousing his suspicion. If Geraldine was right, and he was guilty, he was hardly going to welcome any interference from Sam. He might even complain about her if he suspected she was onto him, in which case there was a risk Adam would realise she was working with Geraldine. If he decided to take Sam off the case as well, she would never be able to help her friend. One of them, at least, had to be working on the inside.

Mid-afternoon she called Geraldine to keep her posted. Geraldine agreed with Sam's thinking and suggested she try and find the original copy of Daniel's statement. If any of the prints on that matched the partial print on the listening device, they would have enough evidence to bring him in for questioning. Examination of the CCTV and the records at the garage might also help.

'If we can prove the dates on the documentation when Chris's van was in for repairs were tampered with, that would really help too,' Geraldine suggested. 'But before we can get a search warrant, and seize all their records, we need evidence of his guilt. It's down to you, Sam.'

'If it's there, I'll find it,' Sam promised.

Never before had she been so aware of the weight of responsibility that attached to her work. Used to following instructions and working as part of a team, she was uneasy knowing the success of the investigation rested on her shoulders.

'If all else fails, you'll have to go to Adam,' Geraldine added.

Sam didn't say that she had already been to see him, and he hadn't been interested in her suggestions, or sympathetic towards Geraldine.

64

SAM PHONED THE FINGERPRINT team and pressed them to hurry. She was almost bursting with impatience when they finally called her. The result was worth waiting for. There was a clear print on the statement Daniel Saunders had sent them that matched the partial one found on the baby listening device. He had handled both.

'Are you sure?' Sam asked.

'I'm sure it appears to be a match.'

'But it's only a partial print on the device.'

'There's enough there for us to use.'

'Is it enough to hold up in court?'

The fingerprint expert laughed at her anxiety. 'It's as positive as fingerprint evidence can be, as positive as if we'd had a complete print in both places. You know fingerprint evidence isn't infallible, but there must have been a reason you sent us these two prints and asked us to match them. This wasn't a random selection. So you can certainly use this probable match as supporting evidence. We do appear to have a match. And I suspect the chances of that happening by complete coincidence with two sets of prints you've pulled together for other reasons are highly unlikely.'

They hadn't yet found any evidence that Daniel had recently bought a chisel, but that was hardly surprising. He could have bought it with cash, or borrowed or stolen it. The chisel might have been in his possession for years. He might even have found it in Chris's shed. Looking for proof that he had bought the murder weapon was likely to take a very long time, and might never yield a result. Armed with evidence that Daniel had motives for killing both Jamie and Louise, and that he had known where to find them both, Sam decided it was time to make a move. But before she could effect an arrest, she needed to speak to Adam. She went to wait for him outside his office. If necessary, she would stand there all night. At half past four he returned. He didn't look pleased to see her.

At first he tried to dismiss her, telling her he had to deal with paperwork arising from the meeting he had just attended.

Sam took a deep breath. 'This is important, and it can't wait.'

'It's not about Geraldine, is it?'

'No. It's about arresting the man who murdered Louise Marshall.'

'What?'

'I know who did it, and I have evidence to back up what I'm saying. But I need your permission to go and arrest him, and we need a warrant to search his home and place of work I think.'

Adam raised his eyebrows. 'I see. Well, you'd better come in and talk to me.'

It was nearly half past five by the time Sam arrived, and the garage was about to close. As she drove into the forecourt, accompanied by a male sergeant and two more patrol cars, the lights in the office were switched off, leaving the building in darkness. The doors to the workshop were still open, and the interior was lit up. A couple of men in oily blue overalls were working on a car. One of them looked up as a third mechanic put down the spanner he was holding. At the same time, a girl emerged from the office and trotted over to the gate. A female constable stopped her.

'I'm afraid the office has just shut,' the girl said.

Sam and her companion climbed out of their vehicle. One of the patrol cars turned and blocked the exit, while officers from the other one guarded the pedestrian access. The two mechanics continued working on the engine they were fixing.

The third one strode out of the workshop, wiping his hands on an oily rag.

'What's going on, Tracy?' he shouted.

The girl from the office called back. 'I've no idea. The police are here,' she added unnecessarily.

Sam approached the mechanic who had left the workshop. 'Daniel Saunders?'

He turned and scowled, recognising her. 'You were here before, weren't you? What is it this time? Does your car need fixing?' He sneered at her, while his eyes darted around, assessing the situation.

All at once he barged past her and sprinted for the exit. Sam leapt towards him and seized his arm, twisting it up behind his back.

'I may be smaller than you,' she panted, 'but I trained in ninjutsu for over twelve years.'

'What the fuck?'

'It's a form of Japanese martial art...'

'I don't give a fuck about your martial arts, you bitch. What the fuck are you doing here?'

Sam smiled as she snapped handcuffs on his wrists and formally arrested him for the murders of Jamie Cordwell and Louise Marshall.

Daniel refused the offer of a lawyer. He sat, red-faced with anger, watching Sam and Adam across the table.

'We've got enough proof to nail you,' Adam told him, after the charges had been formally read out for the tape. 'And now, we're going to search your office for evidence you altered the dates on your paperwork relating to Chris Cordwell's van, and we're going to search your house...'

'No!' Daniel shouted with sudden passion. 'You've got no right to set foot in my home!'

Adam nodded at a constable standing by the door who slipped out of the room.

Daniel's shoulders slumped. He spoke softly, but with

conviction. 'He took my daughter. He deserved what he got.'

'Is that your daughter who's in New York?' Sam asked. 'Bethany, isn't it?'

'What the fuck are you talking about?' Daniel shouted, violently angry again. 'That bastard took her and he killed her. I saw him, didn't I? But would anyone listen to me? So when I saw his van in my garage, I knew what I had to do. I would've got away with it too if your lot hadn't come snooping around.'

'You can ask your ex-wife if you don't believe me,' Sam said. 'Bethany's in New York. She went there to get away from you.'

Speaking as slowly and clearly as she could, to make sure he understood, she related what Veronica had told Geraldine. With a roar of fury, Daniel leapt to his feet. A constable stepped forward to restrain him.

'It's lies!' he yelled, 'all damn lies! My daughter needs me. I'm going to find her and bring her home.' He broke off, shaking.

Sam glanced at Adam who nodded at her. She placed her phone on the table on speakerphone. Daniel stared at it, his eyes bulging.

A voice spoke from the phone. 'Yes, this is Veronica James, Bethany's stepmother. I've signed a statement to confirm that Bethany's in New York. She went there to get away from her father, and I helped her to go. It was the best thing for her. The best for both of them. I explained it all to Inspector Steel when she came to see me.'

'Steel?' Adam pounced on the name.

Sam kept her eyes averted.

'But, don't worry, Daniel,' the disembodied voice continued, 'Bethany's fine. And she'll be back in touch with you before too long, I'm sure. She just needs some space.'

Sam looked at Daniel who was sitting, shoulders slumped, tears streaming down his face. He shook his head, too overcome to speak. He just kept mumbling his daughter's name. It was not clear whether he was weeping with relief that his daughter was alive, or grief at having lost her.

'I don't think he's crying for the two women he killed,' she muttered.

As Adam was preparing to pause the interview, there was a knock on the door and a constable looked in.

'Is it important?' Adam asked. 'Only we're just finishing off here. Can't it wait?'

'It's just that we've heard from the team searching his house,' he said, 'and there's a woman in a clown's mask…'

'A woman in a clown's mask?' Adam repeated, with a frown. 'Well, bring her in. She could be a witness.'

The constable shook his head. 'I'm afraid not. She's been beaten to death.'

65

GERALDINE WAS RELIEVED WHEN the rehabilitation clinic called her.

'Helena's back, and she'd like to see you.'

Hoping her sister wouldn't have done another runner by the time she arrived, Geraldine drove straight there. Helena was sitting in an armchair in a small reception room, waiting for her. Without make-up, and dressed in jeans and a T-shirt, she looked more like Geraldine than ever, apart from her twitching. She stood up when Geraldine entered, looking even more jittery than when she had thought her pusher was after her, and more frightened.

'I want to do this,' she said in a rush, before Geraldine could speak. 'I been thinking. This is my chance, innit? The only chance a loser like me's ever going to get. I'm going to give it a try.'

Geraldine was stunned to feel tears welling up in her eyes. She shook her head.

'I don't cry,' she muttered, attempting to grin.

'Ha! Me neither,' Helena replied, tears coursing down her gaunt cheeks.

Their eyes met in fleeting mutual understanding, before the gulf in their experience separated them again, and they were once more struggling to communicate.

'The thing is,' Geraldine hesitated.

If she confessed that she was out of a job, and no longer in a position to pay the clinic, Helena might change her mind. But since she was no longer working for the Met, she could rent her flat and move out of London. She was free to go anywhere. Staring into her sister's terrified eyes, she reached her decision.

'You know I'll support you,' she said.

'I know what you done. You went and got yourself nicked.' Helena gave a wonky smile. 'You risked your job for me. For me! No one ever done nothing like that for me before. No one ever gave a toss about me...'

'Milly loved you.'

'So now you know everything about mum? You said you never even spoke to her.'

'The letter she wrote to me was about you. You're the only reason she wanted to see me when she realised she was dying. I can show you her letter if you don't believe me.'

'You said you threw it away.'

'Well, I didn't. Listen, you knew her for forty years. That letter was the only thing I ever had from her. It's pathetic, I know, but I didn't want to share it with anyone. But the point is, she wrote to me to beg me to take care of you. That's why she left me half her savings. She knew money alone couldn't save you, because you'd only blow it on your habit. She was desperate to do anything she could to help you. And once she was gone, she wanted me to take care of you.'

Helena shook her head and turned away to stare out of the window.

'I'm not promising anything,' Geraldine went on. 'You're the only one who can sort your life out. But I want to do whatever I can to help you.'

Helena's answer came out in a whisper. 'Why the fuck would you do that?'

Geraldine shrugged. 'Because we're sisters, I suppose.'

Helena turned round and stared at Geraldine for a long time. 'We're more than sisters,' she said at last. 'And I'm going to do this, for you. I want to be a proper twin sister to you one day.'

Although she was wary of trusting anything Helena said, Geraldine felt a surge of happiness. If their relationship never developed any further, at least they had shared this moment.

'We're closer than sisters,' she agreed. 'We're identical twins.'

'I never even knew I had a twin before. I mean, it's fucking weird. How do we do it?'

'We'll have to work it out as we go along. And now, I'm sorry, but I have to go.'

'Work?'

Geraldine nodded. Hesitating to embrace, they settled on pecking each other on the cheek. It was a start, Geraldine thought, as she felt the touch of Helena's dry lips on her skin. In itself trivial, it felt like a significant moment in her life. She left, promising to return soon. She didn't voice her doubts aloud, but she hoped Helena would still be there the next time she visited the clinic.

It was true that she was going to work, but it would be for the last time. Adam had allowed her to return to the station to inform Chris that he was being released.

'You thought he was innocent all along,' Adam had told her over the phone. 'If it hadn't been for you, the wrong man might have been sent down.'

'You would have uncovered the truth sooner or later.'

Adam hadn't answered. They had both known she was being generous.

Her satisfaction at being there at the conclusion of the investigation was tempered by her sadness on seeing Chris. Sitting on his bunk, he gazed listlessly up at her when she told him he was free to go.

'We've tracked down the man who killed both Jamie and Louise,' she told him. 'It's the man who accused you of kidnapping his daughter.'

Chris shrugged. He showed no sign of interest in anything she had to say.

'Come on, Chris, on your feet,' she said at last, when he made no move to leave. 'You can go home.'

'Home?' he repeated slowly as though the word was unfamiliar to him.

She left him sitting, dejected, in the cell, with the door open. It was going to take him a long time to move on from the trauma he had experienced, but one day he might start a new life, without his wife, free of the horrific accusation of having murdered the two women he had loved. And perhaps one day Helena would be able to start a new life for herself, a life free of drugs. At least Geraldine had given them both a chance. The thought made her feel a burst of optimism. Even Celia had a completely new life growing inside her.

Surrounded by so many opportunities for growth and change, Geraldine wondered whether she should also begin to think about moving on with her life. She didn't want her career to end. She loved her job. But the change she had to confront was easier than the challenges facing Chris and Helena. She pushed her shoulders back, lifted her head high, and went to Adam's office.

'You appreciate you can't stay here,' he told her straight away.

He looked so sad, she felt guilty for having let him down.

'I'm so sorry,' she muttered. 'I don't know what I was thinking of. And I'm really grateful to you for rescuing me, and keeping this all so quiet.'

'But there are limits.'

'Yes, yes, I know my career is over. I'll go quietly.'

She could hardly believe she was hearing herself say the words.

He nodded and she had the impression he was relieved. 'I understand you were concerned about your sister, but we of all people can't allow our personal problems to affect our work. We have to be, and we have to be seen to be, working within the law, and whichever way you look at it, handing five thousand pounds over to a known drug dealer in a private transaction...'

'Hardly appears lawful,' Geraldine interrupted. 'I know, I know.'

'Is really rather stupid, I was going to say,' he replied, with a wry smile.

'Especially if you get caught,' she added.

'So, the question is, where do we go from here?'

Geraldine held her breath, but he didn't say anything else.

'What I did was indefensible,' she ventured.

'Oh, I don't think so, under the circumstances. Who can judge you for being ruled by your emotions in such highly charged and stressful circumstances? Discovering a twin sister, as you meet and lose your birth mother, is hardly a normal situation. Who can say they wouldn't temporarily lose their grip on their sanity if they were in the same situation? Oh, I'm not saying you were temporarily insane,' he added quickly, seeing her expression, 'just that I don't really think anyone else has a right to condemn you for doing what you did.'

'That's very generous of you.'

'It's not generous to speak honestly. What's happened to your sister now?'

'She's gone back into rehab.'

'Do you think she'll see it through?'

Geraldine shrugged. 'God knows. But at least she's going to try.'

Adam sighed. 'That's all any of us can do.' He paused. 'So, what's next for you? Are you really intending to walk away from detective work altogether? Only...' he hesitated. 'This is delicate, Geraldine, and what I'm about to tell you must stay strictly between us. The thing is, I've been speaking to a colleague up in York who thinks there may be a place for you there, if you were to request a transfer. They're setting up a new major incident unit there, and are looking for experienced officers. It seems someone there put in a good word for you. We'd have to do this very quietly, with no mention of the real reason for you leaving the Met.' He paused again. 'So it's up to you if you want to move out of London. And it would mean stepping down from your present rank.'

'To DS?'

'Yes.'

Geraldine grinned. 'For a moment I thought I was being offered a post as a constable.'

'Nothing's been offered yet, you understand. This would have to come from you as a formal request to step down from your post here and move away.'

'Yes, I understand. Would that look odd?'

'No, not really. It's not that uncommon. People have all sorts of reasons for wanting to reduce the stress of their work. Being an inspector doesn't suit everyone. Of course, you were an ideal candidate for higher office, if things had worked out differently...' He left the thought unfinished. 'So, what do you think?'

Geraldine smiled. 'It doesn't matter where I am. What matters is that we get the job done.'

'I'll be sorry to lose you,' he said, with genuine regret. 'I hope it works out for you, Geraldine. You deserve...' he sighed. 'Well, you deserve better.'

'It'll be fine,' she assured him, and was pleased to see him smile.

Although she wasn't sure why she felt the need to reassure him, she was convinced that she was right to be optimistic.

I hope you enjoyed reading this book in my Geraldine Steel series. Readers are the key to the writing process, so I'm thrilled that you've joined me on my writing journey.

You might not want to meet some of my characters on a dark night – I know I wouldn't! – but hopefully you want to read about Geraldine's other investigations. Her work is always her priority because she cares deeply about justice, but she also has her own life. Many readers care about what happens to her. I hope you join them, and become a fan of Geraldine Steel, and her colleague Ian Peterson.

You can read about more of Geraldine's murder investigations in *Cut Short, Road Closed, Dead End, Death Bed, Stop Dead, Fatal Act, Killer Plan,* and *Murder Ring.*

You can follow Ian Peterson's investigations in *Cold Sacrifice, Blood Axe,* and *Race to Death.*

If you follow me on Facebook or Twitter, you'll know that I love to hear from readers. I always respond to comments from fans, and hope you will follow me on @LeighRussell and www.facebook.com/leigh.russell.50 or drop me an email via my website www.leighrussell.co.uk.

That way you can be sure to get news of the latest offers on my books. You might also like to sign up for my newsletter on www.leighrussell.co.uk/news to make sure you're one of the first to know when a new book and is coming out. We'll be running competitions, and I'll also notify you of any events where I'll be appearing.

Finally, if you enjoyed this story, I'd be really grateful if you would post a brief review on Amazon or Goodreads. A few sentences to say you enjoyed the book would be wonderful. And of course it would be brilliant if you would consider recommending my books to anyone who is a fan of crime fiction.

I hope to meet you at a literary festival or a book signing soon! Thank you again for choosing to read my book.

With very best wishes

Leigh

About Us

In addition to No Exit Press, Oldcastle Books has a number of
other imprints, including Kamera Books, Creative Essentials,
Pulp! The Classics, Pocket Essentials and High Stakes Publishing
> oldcastlebooks.co.uk

For more information about Crime Books go to > crimetime.co.uk

Check out the kamera film salon for independent, arthouse and
world cinema > kamera.co.uk

For more information, media enquiries and review copies please
contact marketing > marketing@oldcastlebooks.co.uk